Chapter One

Jennet stared in dismay at Paradise Lane. It bore no resemblance to anything heavenly. The grubby terrace was situated across the road from the towering walls of the mill, which blocked out any light that might otherwise have reached its windows. Number ten was in the middle of the row and although number eight was locked up and quiet, the wailing of several babies coming from number twelve almost undid her resolve to accept this move with good grace. She'd struggled to hold back her tears as the cart had left their cottage at Pleck Gate, where the air had been clean and they'd had a garden to grow their own vegetables, and where she'd made jam from the fruit that grew wild on the hills. She'd dreaded what would await her in the mill town of Blackburn and it looked as bad, if not worse, than she'd imagined. The November day was grey and dismal and every spot of rain that fell brought down filth from the smoky sky. It clung to her shawl and the bags that Titus was lifting down from the cart, and there was even soot on little Peggy's face as she held on to Jennet, thumb in mouth, watching what was going on.

Titus fumbled in his pocket for the key. He put it in the door, turned it and then lifted the sneck to reveal their new home. The door was stiff and had to be shoved open to reveal a small parlour with a stone-flagged floor and whitewashed walls that had grown grubby and were now a faded shade of grey. To one side was the cast-iron range, in dire need of cleaning and blackleading. There were cold ashes left in the grate. Jennet was greeted by the smell of damp and when she ran a finger along the windowsill it came away covered in grime. She glanced at the door that opened into the back kitchen and hardly dared to go and look.

Neither of them had wanted to come. They'd struggled on for as long as they could, but in the end it had become impossible for them to make a living in the countryside. Jennet hadn't been able to spin enough cotton to provide Titus with thread. When they were first married his

2

THE
COTTON
Spinner

Libby Ashworth

arrow books

3 5 7 9 10 8 6 4 2

Arrow Books
20 Vauxhall Bridge Road
London SW1V 2SA

Arrow Books is part of the Penguin Random House group
of companies whose addresses can be found at
global.penguinrandomhouse.com.

First published in Great Britain by Arrow Books in 2020

www.penguin.co.uk

A CIP catalogue record for this book is available from
the British Library

ISBN 9781787463578

Typeset in 11.5/15.7 pt Palatino
by Integra Software Services Pvt. Ltd, Pondicherry

Printed a   f S.p.A.

ted
ness,
ok is
ncil®

FSC
www.fsc.org

To Jennet and Titus, my great, great, great, great grandparents. Without you this book would not have been possible.

Acknowledgements

Thanks to Cassandra Di Bello, my editor at Arrow, who gave me the chance to become a saga writer and who has been so brilliant at helping me close all the plot holes in my storyline. Thanks also to all the rest of the team – my copy editor, cover designer and everyone who has worked so hard to bring my story to publication.

Thanks to my agent, Felicity Trew, and to Caroline Sheldon and everyone at the Caroline Sheldon Literary Agency for all their support, and to Felicity for travelling from London to Preston to tell me that she loved my work.

Thanks to Blackburn Library, especially for their Cotton Town website, which is an amazing source for anyone who wants to study the history of Blackburn. And also to the Tuesday Reading Group for all their interest and support as they've followed the journey of this book.

Thanks to all my online friends, both readers and writers, who always offer support and encouragement. I may not have met you all in person, but I know you're always there to share the ups and downs of turning an idea into a novel. I hope you all enjoy the result.

mother had been alive and his sister had lived with them too. Three spinners could provide a weaver with ample warp and weft, but when there was only her, and she had Peggy to care for as well, she hadn't been able to keep up with the demand.

Then the price of the woven cloth had fallen.

'Six shillings,' the chapman had said the last time he'd come.

'Don't talk daft, man,' Titus had told him. 'There's a full cut there, and look at the workmanship. Tha'll not find a flaw in it.'

The chapman had shaken his head. 'Six shillings,' he'd repeated. 'It's the goin' rate.'

'But he's worked on that piece for nearly a fortnight,' Jennet had argued.

'It's supply and demand, Mrs Eastwood,' the chapman told her. 'The new mills can weave much faster so the price of cloth has plummeted. The mill owners are selling direct to manufacturers and I'm barely making any profit as it is.' He'd put the money down on the corner of the scrubbed table. 'Take it or leave it. I'm only buying from thee as a favour. It's not really worth my while coming out all this way for fifteen yards.'

Jennet had been sure that the cloth was worth more, but six shillings was better than nothing.

'Take it then, and be damned to thee,' said Titus as his fingers had closed around the coins.

'I'm sorry,' said the chapman as he gathered up the cloth and turned to leave.

'Hang on!' Titus had called after him. 'What about the cotton? That must be included as well?'

The chapman had paused in the doorway, his eyes downcast. 'I have none,' he said. 'Tha'll have to get it from the mill.'

Titus had walked into Blackburn to buy the cotton himself, but no one would sell him any. Although there were bales of the stuff piled high in the warehouses, it was all destined for the mills and in the end he'd come home with ready-spun bobbins.

'It'll not be as good as what's spun by hand,' Titus had complained. 'How can a machine make better thread? It's nonsense. I bet I'll be wasting hours at a time havin' to mend it.'

Jennet hadn't replied. She'd unwound an arm's length of the thread and tugged hard. It was strong. It would hold fast on the loom.

At first the bobbins had made things easier for Jennet, but when the putters-out grew greedier and started demanding more and more cloth for fewer and fewer shillings, Titus was forced to work for long hours to make enough money. As the long summer days began to fade and it was dark earlier in the evenings, he'd worked on by candlelight or rushlight, whichever they could afford, until he found it impossible to see his threads.

The last time he'd walked into town with his cloth, Jennet had grown anxious long before she heard his tread coming back up the path. And when he'd come in his hands were empty.

'Where are the bobbins?' she'd asked as he took off his cap.

'There are none,' he'd said. 'I've been every-where, but they've all gone to t' new weavin' mill. Putter-out told me he's shuttin' up shop next week. If I want work I'm to see Mr Hargreaves at the Dandy Mill and ask if he'll put me on.' Titus had come to sit down opposite her. 'It's what I swore I'd never do,' he'd muttered as he poked at the fire, 'but I've no choice. And we'll have to move from here. Mill hours are long and I can't be traipsin' into town and back every day. We'll have to get a cottage in Blackburn.'

'We'll make it nice,' promised Titus as he carried in her precious spinning wheel and set it down on the dirty floor. Jennet nodded, trying not to cry again, but it seemed impossible that she could ever be happy in this place.

She went through to the kitchen. There was a stone sink with a crack that spread like a spider's leg across the surface. Webs crowded the window and there was a puddle in the corner where it had rained in. The single cupboard sagged from the wall. Outside was a small flagged yard. There was no garden and she doubted that anything would grow here anyway.

With Peggy still in her arms, she climbed the narrow twisting stairs and came to a small landing with a step up to each of the two bedrooms. They were as dismal and unkempt as the rest of the house.

'Is this the best tha could get?' she asked Titus in a quiet, trembling voice when she heard him coming up the stairs, wrestling with the mattress from their bed in the tight space.

'It was all I could get,' he told her. 'Now that more and more folk are looking to move into town, property's scarce and it's only because I'm starting in t' mill that I got this.' He propped the mattress against the wall where it folded over on itself, mirroring Jennet's mood.

'I'll get some whitewash. When it's cleaned up and we get our stuff in, it'll be all right,' he said, but she could see by his face that the cottage was worse than he'd expected. 'I need to get the rest of the things and pay off the carter, or he'll be asking for more.' He clumped down the bare wooden steps and Jennet heard him talking to the man, until their voices were drowned out by the wailing of a hooter that startled Peggy and made her cry. Glancing through the dirty window Jennet saw doors all down the street open. Men with their caps pulled down and women with their shawls over their heads, some pulling children by the hand, began to run towards the mill to resume their work after the dinner break.

Jennet jogged her daughter in her arms to soothe her. 'It's all right. Tha'll get used to it,' she said, realising this was the noise that would rule their lives from now on.

Jennet slept badly the first night in her new home. She was woken continually by the sound of footsteps on the cobbles below and she longed for the peaceful nights she was used to, with only the early-morning birdsong to rouse her. A sudden rapping on the bedroom window made her heart race and Peggy began to wail again.

'What's that?' she asked Titus, clutching his arm in fear.

'Knocker-up,' he replied. 'I'm up!' he shouted and Jennet heard the footsteps move on. 'I paid him to call. Don't want to be late for my work.'

Jennet pushed aside the sheets and blankets, which already felt damp, and shoved her feet into her clogs before going across to the window and lifting back the curtain they'd pinned up the night before. A man with a long pole was making his way down the street knocking on each window and waiting until he heard a reply from inside that the occupant was awake. She could barely see the wall of the mill through the clinging fog that had settled in the street and she shivered as she reached for her shawl and picked up the child.

Titus was getting dressed so she took Peggy downstairs into the parlour and put her in the little chair with its tray that her mother had given her. She poured a cup of blue milk from the covered jug on the slopstone and put it in front of her daughter. Since her recent miscarriage, her own milk had dried up and Peggy had had to be weaned, which was an extra burden on their meagre earnings.

She wondered whether it had been the shock of Titus saying that they had to move that had caused it. The night he'd come home without bobbins her back had ached so much that all she'd wanted to do was get to her bed and lie down to help ease the pain.

'I'll just go to the privy,' she'd said, taking the lantern from the shelf near the door and lighting the candle in it with a spill from the fire. The night had been cold and as she walked down the familiar path to the small brick building that they shared with their neighbours, she'd felt a little wet and remembered that it had been the same before Peggy had been born. She'd put the lantern down in the privy and sat on the wooden seat with a sigh of relief, but her bladder wasn't that full and she'd been filled with a foreboding that something wasn't quite right. She'd touched herself and held her fingers to the light. Sure enough they were red with blood.

She'd hurried back to the cottage, clutching her stomach. Every step had sent a jolt of pain through her and by the time she reached the door she'd begun to cry.

'What's to do?' asked Titus.

'Baby,' she'd cried, clinging to his arm. 'I'm losing t' baby. I'm bleeding.'

She'd gasped as another pain shot through her. Titus had stood and stared at her, not knowing what to do. 'Run and get my mam!' she'd said. 'It's bad.'

She'd heard his footsteps running down the path. He would run fast, she'd thought. He wouldn't be long. But by the time her mother had come it was over. She'd taken the remains away in a chamber pot. It had been a boy. Titus had taken him to the churchyard to be buried.

Chapter Two

Jennet filled the kettle and poked at the banked-up fire to see if it would catch. She was relieved to see a flicker of flame and before long the water in the kettle began to sing as she spooned oatmeal into bowls for breakfast.

Since they'd moved in she'd spent every day scrubbing the cottage. The range glowed. The floor was clean enough to eat your dinner off and she'd put down the rag rug over the cold flags. The windows were spotless, although how long they would stay that way with all the smoke and soot in the air, she didn't know, but calico curtains with a cheerful print hung across them and a thicker curtain was hung behind the front door to keep out the draught. The smell of dampness had lessened now that the fire had warmed through the stone walls and although Jennet was still unhappy, it was beginning to feel a little more like home.

Titus blew on the porridge that she'd laced with plenty of treacle to give him enough energy to get through the morning and he ate quickly whilst stirring sugar into his tea. As soon as he'd drained his cup, he reached for his cap and jacket. 'See thee later!' he said as he bent to kiss Peggy's head; then he wrenched open the door as the mill hooter started up. Outside there was the sound of running and through the window Jennet could see the workers hurrying to be on time, shawls and jackets flapping where they had been hastily pulled on.

She tried to spoon more porridge into Peggy's mouth, but the child turned her face away. She was still pining for home, thought Jennet as she took the cups and bowls to wash up in the back kitchen. The constant crying of children that echoed through the wall from the next house was unsettling Peggy. It unsettled Jennet too, and she couldn't bear to think about those poor little mites being left there all day.

After she'd tidied up, Jennet wrapped Peggy in her shawl and balanced her on one hip to go to the market. Her daughter wriggled and cried to get down, but she was still unsteady on her feet and far too small to be on the ground in the busy market place. Jennet picked up her purse and basket with her free hand and struggled to close and lock the door behind her. It was a task she was unused to. They'd never locked their door before, but Titus had insisted that she must remember here. There were thieves about and they had money from the sale of the handloom hidden in the house that they could ill afford to lose, he warned, making her anxious.

There was no room for the handloom here. Their neighbour Jack in Pleck Gate had bought it, saying that he was going to start his nephew on as a silk weaver. He'd been scathing about their decision to move into Blackburn.

'There's bound to be trouble,' Jack had warned them. 'Don't forget what happened Westhoughton way, when they burned that factory to the ground. It'll come to Blackburn too, mark my words. And them as relies on the mills for work'll soon be sorry that they gave up their own looms. Better to stop here and wait it out.'

'Don't think I'm doing it willingly,' Titus had told him. 'Circumstances have forced my hand. I'm not happy about it, but there it is.'

Jack had shaken his head, but he'd paid them well for the loom and the money was hidden beneath the mattress in their bedroom. An emergency pot for a rainy day, Titus called it. It gave Jennet a sense of security and the thought of having it stolen terrified her so she leaned on the door and checked the handle twice before she walked away.

There weren't many people on the street. Most of the women, as well as the men who lived on Paradise Lane, worked in the mill and their older children worked with them. Jennet crossed the bridge over the river Blakewater and made her way towards the cobbled market place where the metal frames and canvas roofs of the stalls were lined up around the market cross and the bell was being rung for the start of business. She was hoping that there might be some bread. But it seemed that not all the women of the town were at work and a crowd of them thronged around the baker's stall, pushing and shoving, swearing at one another as they tried to get near. Some were moving away empty-handed, muttering at the price, and when Jennet managed to get close enough she heard the stall-holder telling his customers that it was one and sixpence a loaf and not a penny less.

'It were only one and fourpence last week, and that were too much,' protested one.

'Take it or leave it, missus. There's other folk as have brass even if tha hasn't.'

14

Jennet gripped her purse tightly. She'd brought two shillings, thinking it would be plenty, but she needed potatoes and oatmeal too, as well as some more candles and milk from the milk-house. One loaf of the wheat bread would take more than half of that and only feed them for one meal. She turned away. No matter how tempting those loaves looked, ordinary folk couldn't afford such luxury, and looking at the pinched faces of the desperately thin women and children around her, she realised that many people could barely afford to eat at all.

She bought a small sack of oatmeal and put it in her basket. There was a stall with fresh eggs, but the price was too high. She regretted getting rid of the little flock of hens she'd kept at Pleck Gate, but the tiny yard behind their new house was barely big enough for the dolly tub, never mind hens. It would have cost more to feed them than they were worth. Once again, Jack and his wife had benefitted by adding them to their own flock.

There were potatoes, but they looked either bad or green so she decided not to bother, and the vegetables were far too expensive and nowhere near as nice as the produce they used to grow in their own garden. She just bought a few candles and collected a jug of milk. Peggy was heavy on her hip and had grown fractious, so she crossed the square, threading through the groups of folk who were chatting, and recrossed the bridge to go home and make the dinner.

As she walked, she saw more people – unemployed men – hanging about on street corners and outside the public houses. They looked cold, with barely enough clothing to cover them, never mind keep them warm. The looks on the men's faces frightened her and she hurried on her way, only stopping at her own front door to put down the basket and fumble in her purse for the key.

'Settling in all right?' Jennet looked up to see a woman at the door of number eight.

'Aye. Thanks. There's a lot to do, but we're getting there.'

The woman nodded. She was older than Jennet, and her hair was greying around the temples already. She looked thin and coughed as she spoke. 'Husband working in t' mill?' she asked.

'Aye.' Jennet shifted the heavy child to her other hip. 'He's been taken on as a weaver.'

'Is tha looking for work an' all?'

'I was thinking of doing some spinning at home, once I've got everything straight.'

'Well, if tha wants to leave the child, avoid her on t' other side,' she advised with a nod of her

16

head. 'She lost one a while ago. There's another woman on Clayton Street who's better. Tell her Lizzie sent thee if tha makes enquiries.'

'Thanks. I will,' said Jennet, although she had no intention of leaving Peggy with anyone. If it wasn't possible for her to make some money from hand spinning then she might take in some sewing. Whatever she did it would have to be work where she could mind her own child. But she needed to find something, she thought. It seemed unfair to let Titus shoulder all the burden and the days were long and lonely when he was at the mill. She missed having him around to talk to. Even when he'd been busy weaving they'd been able to chat as she sat at her spinning wheel, rocking Peggy's cradle with one foot as she worked.

'If tha wants owt, just knock. Not that we have much, but we try to be neighbourly,' Lizzie told her. Jennet thanked her again and kicked open the door, lifted the basket on to the table and settled Peggy into her little chair where she promptly fell asleep. Lizzie seemed nice enough, and friendly, she thought. It would be nice to make a friend. It would help to stop her feeling so alone in this strange place.

'Did tha get to market?' asked Titus when he came in.

'Aye, but there weren't much worth botherin' with. They had bread, but it were one and sixpence a loaf.'

'Lord preserve us! Who do they think can afford them prices?'

'I don't know,' said Jennet. 'They didn't seem to be selling much, though I saw plenty of folk who looked hungry.'

Titus sighed as the hooter went for him to return to work. He looked tired, thought Jennet. The working days were long, with no opportunity to spend an hour or two out in the fresh air as he used to do. She knew that being forced to work at the beck and call of an overlooker made him resentful, and that she ought to be grateful he was willing to do it to make enough money to feed them, but she couldn't help comparing their situation with what they used to have and it made her feel angry. They'd been happy once, but she couldn't imagine ever feeling happy here.

'What's it like?' she'd asked him when he'd come back for dinner on his first day at the mill.

'Noisy,' he'd told her, 'and hot.'

'Hot?' She hadn't expected that.

'Aye,' he'd said, 'from the engine. It starts up with such a hissing and a banging, then all the ropes and pulleys begin to turn and woe betide anyone who's not ready. Looms seem to work on their own, but they all have to be watched.'

'What dost tha have to watch for?' she'd asked.

'If the cotton breaks, I've to rush to mend it afore the cloth gets spoiled. Then the bobbins need changing. I feel like my head's spinning with so many different things and they've only started me on two looms so far.'

After Titus went back to work, Jennet saw that Peggy had hardly eaten anything and looked a little peaky, so she settled her into the crib for a nap. It was too small for her and her feet hung over the end, but it would suffice for now, she thought, as she rocked her until she fell asleep. She went into the back kitchen intending to scrub the sink, but there wasn't much water left. For a moment she was tempted to dash out and fill a bucket from the Blakewater. She'd seen other people do it, but she didn't trust the river water. She'd seen drunken men pissing into it from the bridge. She would wait until Peggy woke and then walk up to the Hallows Spring for a fresh bucket.

She decided to set up her spinning wheel. The smooth, familiar wood felt good under her hands, affording her some comfort. She had the last of the raw cotton that she'd brought with her from Pleck Gate, and when that was done she would go to the mill to see if they would pay her for the thread.

As she sat spinning, Jennet became aware of Peggy whimpering to herself. When she went to lift her up to hush her, she saw that her cheeks looked very pink. She was sweating and her dark curls were plastered to her head in a damp mass. Jennet put a hand to the child's forehead. She was burning hot.

Jennet's first thought was to go for her mother, but she was so far away now that it seemed impossible. It would take her over an hour to walk up to Ramsgreave where her parents lived, even if she hurried. Besides, she was reluctant to take Peggy out in the cold when she seemed so poorly. She wondered what time it was and how long it would be before Titus came home. It was always gloomy in the street outside and she found it more difficult to judge the passing of the day here than when they had lived in the countryside.

Peggy began to cry again, a quiet, wailing sound that frightened Jennet. She held her daughter's head against her shoulder, walking up and down the small parlour, jogging and shushing her to try to get her back to sleep. But Peggy wouldn't be consoled and began to wriggle and thrash so much that in the end Jennet was forced to put her back in the crib where she lay sobbing and gasping.

Jennet went into the back kitchen and wrung out a cloth in a basin to bathe the child's face. She took the cloth into the parlour and pressed it against Peggy's forehead, but her crying grew more insistent and Jennet glanced at the wall that divided her from the neighbour she'd spoken to earlier. She hoped that she wasn't disturbing her. She knew from the noise that came from the other side how the sound carried through the walls.

'Shush, shush,' she soothed, picking her daughter up again and sitting down on the chair to rest her against her breast. 'Shush, Peggy,' she urged, becoming more anxious and desperate. She'd never felt so alone. When Peggy had been unwell in the past her mother had always been close by to help her out and Jennet hadn't realised before how much confidence and support that had given her. She'd been so busy with the move that she hadn't given a thought to what she would do if she or Peggy fell ill in the new house. She pulled the child's head closer to her with the palm of her hand and kissed the wet curls, feeling the heat with her lips and crying tears of her own.

It was a moment before she realised that someone was tapping on her door. It was pushed open a fraction.

'Hello!' called a voice and she turned to see Lizzie peeping in. 'Is everything all right? I could hear the child was very fretful.'

'She's feverish,' explained Jennet. 'I'm sorry if she disturbed thee.'

'Don't talk daft,' said Lizzie, coming in and closing the door behind her. 'I've not come to complain.' She came across and rested the back of her hand on Peggy's forehead. 'She's burnin' up,' she confirmed. 'I see tha's tried coolin' 'er.' She nodded towards the damp cloth. 'Perhaps it's just teethin',' she said, although Jennet could see by her face that she thought it was more serious.

'What can I do?' she asked, glad that there was someone to turn to. 'My husband won't be home for a while yet and I don't know where to get help.'

'There's a doctor at the Dispensary,' Lizzie told her. 'It isn't far. Just on the corner of King Street. They don't ask for much money,' she added when Jennet looked doubtful. 'It's for anyone who's in need. Take the child there.'

Jennet had never considered going to a doctor. It might be the best thing to do though, she thought as she gazed down at Peggy's distressed face. The thought of anything happening to her daughter terrified her.

'Doctor'll have a powder to give her that'll bring down her temperature,' urged Lizzie. 'Go now.'

'But my husband will be coming home for his tea soon. He'll wonder where I've gone.'

'I'll look out for 'im,' promised Lizzie, 'and tell 'im what's happened. Won't kill 'im if he has to get 'is own tea.'

Jennet wasn't sure that Titus would have any idea how to make himself a meal, but her main concern was Peggy, so she got her shawl and wrapped herself and the child up before she went out, remembering to lock the door behind her.

'Go left down Prince's Street to the end, then turn right. It's on the corner. Number fifty-eight.' Lizzie pointed the way and Jennet hurried along the cobbles with Peggy sobbing in her ear. She approached the red-brick building within a few minutes. The main door stood open and she went in, wiping her feet on the mat, and pushed open the vestibule door. A bell sounded and an assortment of people, seated on benches down two sides of the room, looked up and then shuffled along to make room for her to sit down.

'Looks like a long wait, love,' said the woman next to her. 'Poorly child?' she asked, peering at Peggy. 'She'll be teething. Just needs a cooling powder.'

'Aye. I hope so,' said Jennet, trying to settle Peggy more comfortably in her lap. She was just whimpering now rather than crying out loud and Jennet was glad. Everyone else was quiet and she hated to cause a disruption.

A small window was opened in the wall at the end of the room and a woman poked her head out. 'Who's next?' she asked.

An elderly man at the head of the queue stumbled to his feet and went through the dark wooden door to see the doctor. Everyone moved up and Jennet found herself with slightly more room to sit.

Peggy had fallen back asleep by the time it was Jennet's turn and she'd waited so long that she was beginning to wish she hadn't come. She was sure that Titus would be home by now and perhaps Peggy was only teething. At last she was called and the woman asked her if her husband was in work and said that it was sixpence for the employed to see the doctor. Jennet gave her the silver coin she'd taken from the stash under the mattress and then carried the child through the wooden door.

Dr Scaife was sitting at a large desk in a chair that spun around. He turned towards her as she came in.

'Sit down,' he said, pointing to the bentwood chair that was placed adjacent to him. 'Is it the child?' he asked.

'Aye. She's been crying all afternoon and she's very hot. I was worried about her, but she's gone to sleep now,' apologised Jennet, hoping that the doctor wouldn't be angry with her for wasting his time.

'Well, let's have a look at her,' he said. He sounded kind and smiled at her reassuringly.

Jennet unfolded the shawl from around Peggy and the doctor leaned towards her, reaching to pull an oil lamp closer so that he could see better. He frowned as he looked down and then reached out to feel her neck.

'She is feverish and her glands are swollen,' he said. 'Let me listen to her chest.' He reached for his instrument and Jennet gasped as she saw the bright scarlet rash that covered her daughter's body when she unlaced the little cotton bodice. The doctor saw it too, and his silence frightened her.

'What's wrong with her?' she asked, hearing her voice trembling.

'It looks like scarlatina,' said the doctor.

The word sent panic through Jennet. She'd heard of the disease and knew how serious it was.

'Will she die?' she whispered, her fear growing when the doctor didn't answer straight away.

'I have to be honest with you, your daughter is very poorly. I'll do what I can to treat her, but you will have to take great care.' He stood up and went across to a chest with myriad labelled drawers and a brass scale on the top. He opened several of the little drawers and weighed out the powders that were kept in there before tipping the mixture into a paper bag and handing it to her. 'Add a teaspoonful to her milk twice a day,' he instructed. 'It will make her sick, but that's good because it will take the badness out of her system. See how she goes overnight. If she's no better in the morning, or if the rash seems worse, then you must bring her back and I'll try bleeding her. Other than that, keep her cool, bathe her skin with tepid water and watch her carefully.' Jennet nodded, trying to remember all his instructions as she fumbled with Peggy's clothes and wrapped her in the shawl. She thanked the doctor and stepped out into the street.

It was dark and she didn't see Titus, didn't even realise it was him until he said her name a second time.

'Jennet!'

'What's tha doing here?' she asked, puzzled to see him waiting for her.

'Tha'd locked up, and I hadn't taken my key,' he explained. 'What did yon doctor say?'

Jennet told him as Titus took Peggy in his arms to carry her home.

Back in the house he laid her in the cot and unfastened her clothing to see the rash. 'I've seen it once before,' he said. 'My little brother.' His face was grim and Jennet didn't need to ask. She knew that her husband had had a brother who'd died young. He rarely spoke of him and she hadn't known what had killed him before now.

'I'll do the powder,' she said. 'The doctor seemed a good man. Let's hope his medicine works.'

She filled a cup with milk, warmed it a little with water from the kettle, and carefully measured a teaspoonful of the powder, stirring it well. 'Give her to me,' she said, sitting on the chair and holding out her arms for her daughter. Titus lifted the child and settled her carefully on to his wife's lap. Jennet put the cup to Peggy's lips but she wouldn't swallow and some of the mixture spilt. 'It won't do her any good if she won't take it,' Jennet said, filled with anxiety as the child began to cry again.

At last they managed to coax her to drink and Jennet nursed her close until she was suddenly and violently sick.

'Doctor said that might happen,' said Jennet as Titus brought a cloth to wipe the child then sponge down Jennet's skirt. 'We're short of water,' she said, suddenly remembering the empty buckets in the back kitchen.

'I'll get some first thing,' promised Titus, glancing through the window at the pitch-blackness outside. 'I'm not sure I can find my way in the dark.'

Jennet looked up at him and saw that he was exhausted. 'Go to bed,' she said. 'I'll sit up with her.'

'Call me if she worsens.'

He put the bars across the front and back doors and lit another candle to take up the narrow stairs. Jennet heard him moving about for a while, the boards above her creaking, until silence fell. Peggy slept fitfully through the night and Jennet dozed a little in the chair. She kept a rushlight burning and added some coal to the fire from time to time. She didn't want the child to overheat, but she was also afraid of her becoming chilled. Her cheeks seemed just as pink, although she seemed paler around the mouth, and Jennet hoped that was a good sign. Peggy mumbled and muttered in her sleep as if she was having bad dreams and she was sick again, but she did manage to swallow a little more milk and seemed comforted by it.

Titus came creeping down the stairs before the knocker-up rapped at their window and long before dawn broke in the narrow street outside.

'How is she?' he whispered, looking at Peggy asleep in the little cot.

'She's still very hot and there's no sign of the rash going down.'

'I'll go to the well before I have to go to work,' he said as he sipped at the tea Jennet had made. 'Will tha take her back to the doctor?'

'I think I will,' she said. 'Just to be sure.'

After the workers had gone inside the mill, Jennet wrapped Peggy up and stepped out on to the damp and chilly street. She walked briskly to the Dispensary and was pleased to find that she was first in the queue.

Dr Scaife examined her and said that he was pleased with her progress.

'She made it through the night and she doesn't seem quite so hot,' he said. 'But I'll bleed her a little to take the redness away.'

He asked Jennet to bare the child's arm and hold it over a metal pot whilst he made a small incision. Jennet watched the blood drip from Peggy's arm and begin to fill the vessel. She grew visibly paler and at last the doctor pronounced that he was satisfied, bound up her arm and sent them home with the instruction to return if she worsened.

Back in Paradise Lane, Jennet settled the child into the crib once more, and was just beginning to make the oatcakes for dinner when there was a gentle tapping on the front window. She went to the parlour and was pleased to see Lizzie peering in. Jennet opened the door to her and waved her inside with a finger on her lips.

'She's sleeping,' she said. 'But I think she's a bit better. Thanks for tellin' me about the doctor.'

'Aye, he's a nice man is Dr Scaife. Folk round here have reason to be grateful to 'im. I'll not keep thee but I wanted to see how the little one was. Knock if tha needs owt,' she said as she left, and Jennet promised that she would, glad to have made a friend.

Chapter Three

Over the days that followed, Peggy slowly got better and at Christmas Jennet decided to take her to church to thank God for her survival. On Christmas Eve, she brought the basin from the back kitchen and put it in front of the fire. She filled it to ankle deep with water from the bucket and then added boiling water from the kettle to warm it. After bathing her daughter, she gave herself a thorough wash down, shivering as she hurried to get dried and dressed in clean flannel underwear in front of the fire.

On Christmas morning she was up early and after she'd made the breakfast she put on her best skirt and jacket, and boots rather than her everyday clogs. She pinned up her hair and got her bonnet from its box and brushed it before putting it on. She still had to wrap her shawl around herself to keep out the cold, but she felt presentable as she left the house and walked up to St John's, carrying Peggy in the new clothes she'd sewn for her. The bells were already ringing and she hurried, terrified of being late.

It was the first time she'd been in the church, although she'd passed it many times. When she and Titus had been married they'd gone to the parish church, but that was being taken down now because it had become too ramshackle to be safe and the mill owners wanted to build something new that would reflect their status. In fact, the whole town seemed to be turning into a building site as more mills and fancy houses went up, along with rows and rows of terraces to house the influx of workers.

The smell of the evergreens that adorned the church met her as she crept in through the high doors to the murmur of muted conversation and the organ playing carols. From her pew at the back, she could see most of the congregation and she was able to take a good look at the gentry in their Sunday best. There was Mrs Whittaker, the vicar's wife, and the Sudells, who were mill owners. Mrs Sudell looked lovely in her dark fur mantle and her bonnet of sky blue. How she would love to dress like that, thought Jennet.

Peggy enjoyed the singing, although she was restless during the prayers and the interminable sermon from Father Whittaker, and Jennet struggled to keep her quiet. But she was relieved that the child was well enough to misbehave and when the collection was taken she eased the thruppenny bit from the palm of her glove and placed it on the plate, which was filled with mostly low-value coins except for the silver glinting below that had been added by the wealthier families at the front. When the last carol had been sung, they were given the blessing and Jennet picked Peggy up, telling her what a good girl she'd been, and began to make her way to the door where the vicar was greeting people. It took a while to get out. Even though the gentry sat at the front, folk allowed them to leave first and then they spent a while blocking the doorway, chatting, whilst a crowd built up behind them. At last she got out into the weak sunshine. There would be no snow this Christmas, she thought, and she was glad because the spell of unseasonal warmth meant that they hadn't had to raid their savings to buy extra coal. The price of that had increased too, along with almost everything else that they needed to buy. They were beginning to struggle to make ends meet and Jennet had been unable to sell her bobbins. Once she'd finished spinning, she'd taken them to the mill and shown them to the overlooker.

'They're no use to me,' he'd said. 'We have spinning mules here that spin dozens of bobbins. Dost tha want to see 'em?' he'd asked.

He'd ushered Jennet through a door to a huge room where the mules were lined up in rows. Each one was worked by a man who pulled the frame towards him as the strands of cotton were stretched and twisted on to bobbins. Then he pushed it back to begin the process again. Jennet watched in fascination. It was hard, physical work, but it was producing more thread than she could have spun in weeks.

'There's no need for hand spinning any more,' the overlooker had shouted over the noise of the clanking machinery. 'And this isn't women's work. I could find thee summat in t' weavin' shed,' he'd offered. Jennet had declined. She was determined not to leave Peggy with a minder.

Titus was looking out for her as she turned into Paradise Lane on her way home from church. Mr Sudell had provided an ox and it was to be roasted in the market square that afternoon. Crowds were already making their way there and Titus was anxious that they shouldn't miss out. After locking their door they walked towards the sound of the celebrations, Peggy riding high on her father's shoulders and laughing. The aroma of roasting meat was pervading the town and, as the mills

34

were closed, the streets were thronged with people jostling towards the food. Jennet kept a tight hold on Titus's arm, not wanting to be parted from him in the seething mass. She'd never seen so many people all in one place. There was a lot of shouting and raucous laughter and she saw that many of the inhabitants were spilling out from the public houses, having spent their morning there rather than in church. There was such a crush that she thought they would be disappointed and receive nothing, but Titus elbowed his way through and she followed, clinging to the back of his jacket and glancing up anxiously at her daughter who was looking around and laughing as if she were riding the waves of a ferocious sea.

At last she saw the ox, turning on a spit above a fire pit that had been built for the occasion. There were men there, trying to keep some sort of order and handing out slices of meat that they'd cut with their huge knives. Jennet thought that it was probably only the knives and the searing heat of the fire that was keeping the crowd from rushing forwards and taking the whole ox. There was some arguing and harsh words, but others queued patiently and expressed their gratitude for the chance to eat. It would have been a hungry Christmas for many without this generosity. Even though Titus was in work, they couldn't have afforded more than a bit of scrag end to make a pie for their Christmas dinner, and Jennet's mouth was watering by the time her portion of the feast was thrust, hot, into her hand, wrapped in paper. They pushed their way back through the crush and managed to find a seat on a low wall where they shared out the meat, breaking off small pieces for Peggy, who kept holding out her hand and shouting 'Peg!' as she demanded more. Afterwards, Titus bought two flagons of ale from the Dun Horse and they drank them in the street before making their way home as darkness closed in early. The ox was just bones now and the crowd was thinning as people carried their tired children away, wishing each other a Merry Christmas. Peggy was asleep in her father's arms by the time they got home. Jennet lit a candle and Titus attended to the fire whilst she tucked Peggy into the little bed that Titus had made for her. Then they stood warming their hands in front of the growing blaze before taking off their outer clothes and settling into the chairs on either side of the hearth.

'Put the kettle on, Jennet,' said Titus as he poked at the fire again. It had been a good Christmas, she thought as she fetched the water. It was almost like old times, being able to plan their time as they saw fit rather than being beholden to the knocker-up and the factory hooter, but it would be short-lived. The next day, Titus would be back at the mill.

When Titus returned to work after the holiday he sensed an air of gloom throughout the mill.

'What's up?' he asked George, Lizzie's husband, as he collected his bobbins.

'There's talk of folk being laid off,' George told him.

'Laid off?' He stared at his neighbour in surprise, wondering if he was serious. 'I thought Mr Eccles were doing well with all this.' He gestured towards the looms where the lengths of Blackburn Check were spilling into heaps on the floor.

'Doing too well,' said George. 'We're weaving more than there's call for. It's piled up in the warehouse and he can't sell it.'

Worry took hold of Titus as he resumed his work, threading up for a new length of cloth amidst the rhythmic clatter of the looms and throbbing of the steam engine at the other side of the shed. What if he lost his job? What if Jack had been right when he'd said he would regret selling his own loom? Would it be possible to buy it back from him and go home to Pleck Gate if the work here dried up? He didn't know if their cottage was still available, but he hadn't heard that it had been rented out. Everyone was moving into town. And if Jack wouldn't sell him back his own loom he could buy another. There were plenty for sale, and going for a song now that more and more people were working in the mills. But how would he get cotton or bobbins? And how would he sell the cloth? He'd be back in the same bind that he thought he'd escaped from.

At last the warp was threaded and he put in the shuttle and set the loom going, watching for a moment to make sure it was weaving properly before going to check the others. Then, above the racket, he heard the hooter sound for dinner time and suddenly everything powered down and fell silent, and the big engine hissed as it came to rest. He pulled on his jacket and cap and hurried across the street. It had turned cold and there were a few flakes of snow in the air.

He pushed open the front door, even more swollen and awkward with the dampness, and went to the meagre fire to rub his hands together whilst Jennet came through from the kitchen with the dinner.

'What's to do?' she asked as she came across to get the kettle.

'Nowt. Just idle talk from him next door about folk being laid off, but I'm sure it's nonsense,' he said as he pulled out the chair and sat down to eat. 'Why would yon mill owners be flaunting their wealth if times were hard?'

'They do seem to have plenty,' said Jennet.

'Aye, and they'd have nowt if it weren't for the likes of me labouring in their mill all day long.'

It wasn't long before the hooter sounded again and Titus pushed his plate aside and stood up to go back. 'I'll see thee later, love.' He kissed Jennet's cheek and gave her a squeeze. She looked tired, he thought. The town air didn't agree with her. Damn these men and their factories, he thought. They had the money to build their mansions up on the hill where the smoke didn't reach, but the workers and their families were stuck down here in the grit and grime.

He hurried back to his looms as the big engine began to turn, slowly at first, and then reaching full speed, driving the ropes and pulleys that stretched out above him. After checking that there were no broken threads, Titus set his looms in motion. There were five more days to work before it was Sunday again and he would get another day off. He counted the days each week until the one he could call his own, although he often felt at a loss when it came, not knowing what to do with himself now that the house was white-washed and he had no patch to tend. In the better weather they'd sometimes walk all the way up to Ramsgreave to see Jennet's family and get some fresh air, but as he'd come back to work he'd seen that the snow was beginning to settle and it would probably be too deep to walk anywhere by the time Sunday came.

The gloom gathered as the snow fell outside and the oil lamps were lit early. They smoked and Titus found himself rubbing at his eyes as he worked, struggling to see the threads. His back ached. He longed to sit down, but there were hours to go before the end of the day. He hoped that Jennet had saved some of the potatoes they'd managed to get. He fancied a bit of potato pie for his tea tonight. He finished piecing a broken thread on one of the looms and turned to find Mr Hargreaves watching him.

'Tha can leave 'em when them lengths are done,' he said. 'Don't thread 'em up again.'

'What dost tha mean? Just a minute!' Titus called as the man walked away. 'Why've I not to thread 'em up again?'

Hargreaves turned. He looked uncomfortable. 'I'm sorry,' he said. 'Tha's a good worker, but Mr Eccles says we're to rest some looms until the warehouse is cleared. There's no space for owt more.'

'So what am I supposed to do?' asked Titus.

Hargreaves shrugged his shoulders. 'I'll give thee a knock when we need thee again,' he promised. 'Tha can stay in the house for the time being as long as tha can pay the rent.'

Titus stared after the man as he retreated to his little office and closed the door after him as if he were afraid. So he should be, thought Titus. This was the man who'd promised him such a bright future in the mill if he worked long and hard, and now he was saying that he didn't want him any more.

Angry, he left his looms unattended and marched to the office where he flung open the door without so much as a perfunctory rap. 'What about wages?' he demanded.

'I'll pay thee what tha's owed.'

'Then I'll take it now and be on my way!'

'Tha'll get it at the end of the day.'

The two men stared at one another for a long moment. Titus was so angry he wanted to walk out then and there and slam the door behind him, but good sense prevailed. He needed his wages and if he walked out now he would have worked for free all day. Without a word, he returned to his looms and although he was furious, he found himself examining the cloth and checking that all was well; his pride wouldn't allow him to leave it with any flaws.

At last the looms powered down and he found that he wasn't the only worker queuing outside the office door for a last wage packet. How was he going to tell Jennet? He hoped that she wouldn't be too upset. He'd thought that they had made the right decision to come here, but now it had all gone wrong.

Jennet could see that something was amiss as soon as Titus came in. His shoulders were slumped with more than tiredness and he couldn't even summon a smile at her announcement that there was potato pie for tea.

'What's to do?' she asked, wondering if he'd been in a row at the mill. She knew that he found it hard to take orders and she dreaded the day when he lost his temper and spoke his mind.

'I've been laid off,' he said, sitting down by the range and staring at the fire she'd poked into a blaze to welcome him home.

'Why?' She hoped he hadn't said or done something stupid.

'There's so much cloth in the warehouse it can't be sold, so they're restin' some looms. It's last in, first out,' he explained, twisting his cap in his hands. 'I think we might have made a mistake coming here,' he said.

Jennet sat down at the table and stared at him. It wasn't like him to admit that he was wrong about anything and the sorrow on his face shocked her.

'Don't say that,' she said, trying to comfort him. 'We'd have been no better off where we were. Tha's not to blame.'

'No,' he agreed and she saw the anger flash in his eyes. 'It's these mill owners that's to blame. What did they think would happen? It's not natural to be using them machines to weave all that cloth, and then not be able to sell it! Things were fine as they were, with folk doing their bit on their own looms. We've been made fools of, Jennet. They've worked us from dawn to dusk and made their fortunes, and then they think handing out a bit of roast meat on Christmas is enough when they can see that folk are struggling to survive. I don't know how we'll manage ...'

'We still have some of the loom money,' she reminded him. 'We're better off than a lot,' she added, thinking of the pinched faces of the women she saw on the market and the men hanging around the town centre pubs with nothing to do, using their last coppers to console themselves with beer.

'It'll not last long if we've to use it for food and rent,' he said. 'I was hoping to keep a bit put by for our Peggy.'

'And is there no hope of them setting thee on again?' she asked.

'Hargreaves promised to give me a knock when there's work, but he couldn't say how long it might be and when I looked in the warehouse I could see as it were piled to the roof. It's a lot of cloth to sell,' he said, 'and folk can only wear so much at once. It's a mess,' he went on as he stood up to hang his cap behind the door. 'It's a ruddy mess!'

Jennet dished out the pie and carried the plates to the table. It was supposed to be a special treat, but they ate in silence. She'd fed Peggy earlier and the little lass was asleep upstairs in her bed in the corner of their room, blissfully unaware that hard times were ahead. Outside the snow covered the cobbles, deadening the sound of any footsteps. It was quiet on both sides too. The babies had been taken home and, for once, Lizzie didn't seem to be coughing.

'I'll try to get some work,' she said after a while. 'It'll tide us over if I can bring a wage in, even if it's only part time.'

'What about our Peggy?'

'Tha'll have to mind her, if tha's at home.'

Titus pulled his face. 'That's not a man's job,' he said. 'I'll not be shamed by looking after childer whilst my wife goes out to work.'

'Then what?' she asked. 'What else can we do?'

'I'll think o' summat,' he promised. 'Don't fret. I'll go round t' other mills tomorrow and see if they're takin' on.'

Jennet wandered in and out of the stalls on the Saturday market. There were only a few traders who came now and what they had was meagre and priced well above what most people could afford. She fingered the few coins that were all that was left of the loom money and wondered what to buy. They needed oatmeal, of course. It could be made up with water so that any milk she managed to get could be given to Peggy. She was terrified of her falling ill again and even if she went hungry herself she would make sure that the child was fed as well as possible. She'd seemed listless since her illness. Once the red rash had faded it left her face ghostly pale and she still hadn't recovered the healthy complexion she'd had when they lived at Pleck Gate.

The men behind the stalls were quiet. There was no calling out in competition to other traders now, and there were few customers. The market place would have been almost deserted if there hadn't been the queue for the handout of soup, which grew longer and longer every day. The drifting aroma intensified her hunger. It smelled so good. She wished that she could take some home for their dinner, but it would be wrong to ask for help whilst they still had money. Besides, Titus was opposed to it. He hated the idea of charity.

For months she'd stretched the money they had hidden under the mattress, but that morning she'd put the last few coins into her purse to come shopping, hoping that she could buy enough for another week and still have something left over for a bucket of coal. They hadn't had a scrag end since Titus had been put out of work and they did without sugar in their tea. There were neither eggs nor treacle and even though she was heartily sick of oatmeal or oatcakes for breakfast, dinner and tea, it was all there was and she ate them hungrily enough when the time came and wished for more.

It was weeks, too, since they'd had candles. They'd managed with home-made rushlights for a while, but they needed fat, and now she and Titus sat by the light of the fire until their ration of coal was done, then crept up the stairs, feeling their way as they went, and huddling under the blanket until morning came. At least the days were getting longer, she thought, and before long it ought to be warmer, although the spring had been perishing with flurries of snow right into April.

She parted with half of her money for a small sack of oatmeal and carried it home. She would come back on Monday, she thought. Although there would be no market, there might be some cheap potatoes for sale, provided by Mr Sudell, although the last time she'd bought some, she'd cut them open to find that they were black and bad right through and she'd wept copiously as she was forced to throw them away.

At home, Titus was huddled over two small pieces of coal in the grate with Peggy on his knee. He was singing to her – a song about a poor cotton weaver. Peggy was laughing, not because she understood the words, but because Titus made it sound funny. It was good to hear her laugh, thought Jennet. There had been too little laughter recently.

'I got some oatmeal,' she said, putting it on the table, 'but there was hardly a thing on the stalls. Everyone seemed to be queuing for soup. It smelled good.'

'Any tatties?'

'No, not today. I'll try again on Monday. I think I've enough left, but when they're gone we've nothing.' She showed him what was in her purse. 'We'll have to ask for relief,' she told him. 'Other people are and it's no use starving because of stubborn pride.' He frowned, the song forgotten. 'It's not as if those who are well off are short of a few bob,' she reminded him. 'They've made their money from the spinnin' and weavin' so it's only right they should help us when they can't offer work.'

'Aye, I hear thee,' he said. 'But I never thought the day'd come when I'd have to ask for charity to feed my family.'

Jennet took off her shawl, even though it was chilly in the house. She couldn't work with it on and she needed to get the dinner ready. She called to Titus from the back kitchen because she didn't want to see his face. 'I'll go to church tomorrow and try to speak to Mrs Whittaker,' she said. 'I'll ask if we can have some help from the Ladies' Charity, for Peggy's sake.'

Titus didn't reply, but his silence was good enough for Jennet. She would go and ask and take Peggy with her.

Jennet took a pew at the back of St John's and hoped that she could slip out at the end of the service and approach Mrs Whittaker. The idea gave her butterflies. She wasn't used to approaching the gentry, but neither she nor Titus could write a letter so she was left with no choice but to speak up.

She could see Mrs Whittaker sitting alone in her pew on the front row. She was tall and the

48

cream-coloured ribbons on her spring bonnet glowed as a shaft of sunlight lit them from a south-facing window. The vicar and his wife had only recently married and they had no children yet, but Jennet could detect a swell beneath Mrs Whittaker's green velvet coat as she came down the aisle after the service had ended.

Jennet got out ahead of most of the congregation. She bypassed the vicar, who was greeting his friends outside the door, and looked for his wife. Mrs Whittaker was talking with Mr Hornby, a local mill owner, and his wife. Jennet stood a way off, with Peggy restless in her arms, until she saw the Hornbys move away.

'Excuse me, Mrs Whittaker,' she said, her heart pounding with fear. 'May I speak to you?'

The lady turned and looked from Jennet to Peggy and back again. Her eyes were a warm brown and she smiled encouragingly.

'I wanted to ask about getting some relief, to feed the child. She's been ill with the scarlatina, and the soup smelled right good in the market place yesterday.' She stumbled over her words in confusion, afraid that she might be ignored or, worse, told to go away.

'What are you called?' asked Mrs Whittaker as she reached into the reticule that hung from her arm and took out a little notebook and pencil.

'Jennet Eastwood. We live on Paradise Lane. Number ten. My husband Titus was working at Dandy Mill, but he's been laid off. He wants to work,' she added, in case the vicar's wife thought that they were lazy. 'I've looked for work too, but there's nothing.'

'Have you just the one child?'

'Yes. This is Peggy. She was very ill and she needs some nourishment.'

Mrs Whittaker smiled at the child. 'I'll see what I can do,' she promised, 'but there are so many people in need and we rely on donations, so sometimes we can't do as much as we might wish.'

'Thank you,' said Jennet, turning away, hoping that the effort she'd made hadn't all been for nothing. She knew that there were families with six or more children to feed and they would be the ones who got help first. She hoped that Mrs Whittaker hadn't thought she was asking too much when she only had one, but Peggy was so precious and it broke her heart not to be able to give her what she desperately needed.

The next morning there was a knock at their door. Jennet looked at Titus. It couldn't be Lizzie because she would have called out and come in. Whoever it was waited for the door to be opened for them.

Jennet handed Peggy to Titus and went across, glancing around the room to see if it looked tidy.

She always did her best to keep it nice, but she was aware that it was sparsely furnished and their things looked old and shabby. She lifted the latch and pulled hard to get the swollen door open. Mrs Whittaker was standing outside, looking out of place in her fine coat and bonnet.

'May I come in?' she asked.

'Yes. Yes. Please.' Jennet stood back to allow her to enter. She saw Titus frown and then stand up, with Peggy still in his arms.

'How do,' he greeted her with a hint of suspicion in his voice.

She smelled of lavender, thought Jennet as Mrs Whittaker passed her. It reminded her of the garden at Pleck Gate. 'This is Mrs Whittaker,' she told Titus.

'Aye.'

'I see your wife at morning service,' said Mrs Whittaker.

'Aye. She likes the singing.'

'You don't attend?'

'No. I've never been much of a churchgoer. I'm baptised, tha knows, but I don't go regular.'

'I see,' said Mrs Whittaker and Jennet hoped that it wouldn't count against them when the decision was made whether or not they were deserving of help. 'How long have you lived here?' she asked, looking around.

'Since last November,' said Titus. 'We lived at Pleck Gate afore that and I had my own loom. We moved here on the promise of steady work, but now there is none and I'm left with no way to feed my family.'

'It's not an uncommon story, Mr Eastwood. There are many more like you in this town, and beyond. We're doing what we can, but as I said to your wife, we rely on donations and people only have so much to give.'

'Aye. They needs their money for their fancy mansions and new churches,' said Titus. Jennet frowned at him. It wouldn't help them to alienate this woman. They needed her to be on their side.

Mrs Whittaker didn't reply and it was hard to tell from her expression what she was thinking. She took out her little notebook and sat down at their scrubbed table.

'How long have you been out of work?' she asked. 'Have you any savings? Any family who could help?' She went on with her long list of questions, writing things down, until she seemed satisfied. 'You keep a clean house, Mrs Eastwood,' she said. 'You have ample clothing and blankets for the bed. I've seen people in much worse circumstances.'

'I know. I'm sorry if we've wasted your time, but it's not for me or Titus, it's for Peggy.'

'I'll see what I can do,' she said. 'There's a committee meeting of the Ladies' Charity this afternoon and I'll put your name forward, but to some extent it depends on who else has applied and whether their need is greater than yours.'

'I understand,' said Jennet. 'Thank you for coming,' she added as she moved to open the door for their visitor to leave.

'Don't think I'm not sympathetic,' Mrs Whittaker said to Titus. 'I understand your anger, but it's a complex situation that we find ourselves in and it takes time for things to work themselves out. It may seem that those who own the mills don't care, but I can assure you that they do. They're doing their best.' Titus didn't answer and Mrs Whittaker went to the door. 'I'll do what I can,' she said again to Jennet as she stepped out into the street.

As Mrs Whittaker walked away, Jennet saw Lizzie peeping out of her window. She was at the door before the vicar's wife had turned the street corner.

'What did she want?' she asked.

'She came to see if we could have summat for our Peggy, with her being poorly,' said Jennet.

'Don't get thy hopes up,' said Lizzie. 'Gentry don't seem to want to help decent folk. It all goes to them as have husbands who swill it away down the pub.'

'If tha's no childer, or only the one, then tha's no chance,' confirmed George, coming to the door behind her. 'That's what I was told. And tha has to swear as tha has no savings. Though I'd swear, even if I had some. They owe us. How much dost tha think that fancy new church they're buildin' is costing? That's money that could've gone to feeding folk. Prayin'll not fill bellies.'

'Tha's right, George,' said Titus, joining Jennet in the doorway with Peggy in his arms. 'We've all been made fools of with this talk of mills and machinery. There's them that's made a fortune from it, and they don't mind that they've bled us workers dry and then left us to starve.'

'But Mrs Whittaker did come to see us. She promised that she'd try to help,' said Jennet.

'Nowt'll come of it,' Titus told her. 'Didst tha see how she looked at me when I said I wasn't a churchgoing man? She'll give us nowt, Jennet.'

'It's time the voice of the workin' man was heard in this country,' said George, 'but that'll not happen until we get a vote.'

'Tha's right about that,' said Titus.

'There's to be a Reform meeting up on the moor later. One of the speakers is a local man. I were thinking of goin'. Why doesn't tha come an' all?'

'I might,' said Titus. 'Summat needs to be done.'

'Tha's not to get mixed up with them trouble-makers,' Jennet told him when they'd come inside and shut the door. 'No good will come of it.'

'Well, I'm fed up to the back teeth of sittin' here, huddled over one lump of coal and nowt to do all day long,' complained Titus. 'I've a mind to go and hear what's being said.'

'Titus, don't go,' she begged him. 'Tha knows that them troublemakers at Shadsworth were brought up before the magistrate last week and sent up to Lancaster for the Assizes. What would I do if summat like that happened to thee? What if tha got transported?'

'Tha's talking daft now,' he replied. 'I'm going to a meeting to hear what's being said about Reform. That's all. I'm not going to do owt that'll land me in prison.'

Chapter Four

Titus waited at the door for George to come out. His neighbour kissed Lizzie on the cheek and bid her not wait up for him if he was late, and then they set off together towards the moorland that rose outside the town boundary to the south. It was a fine afternoon and as they walked they were joined by other men, with determined looks, all walking purposefully in the same direction.

'I hear as General Ludd 'imself'll be speakin' up,' said one.

'I doubt it,' replied George. 'This meeting's to be about Reform, not about Luddites. Breaking looms isn't the answer to our troubles.'

'What makes tha say that?' asked Titus as they walked on. 'It seems to me that if things went back to the way they were then we'd all have work again.'

'It's not so much the power looms that presents the problem as the lack of trade,' explained George. 'If mill owners could sell their cloth they'd be happy to pay us wages to weave more.'

'So how can Reform change that?'

'It would give a voice to the working man,' explained George, 'which would see the end of such bad legislation as the Corn Laws. Whilst yon government keeps the price of wheat so high, folk have no money to spare for anything other than bread. If bread were cheaper, they'd buy other stuff – like calicos for their clothing – and then there'd be more work for the likes of us. So what needs to be done is to persuade yon government to get rid of them Corn Laws. That's what this meeting is to be about – that and a demand for the vote.'

'So tha's not up for loom breaking?' asked Titus.

'No. It's not a solution. Machines are here to stay and tha might as well spit into t' wind as try to stop progress.'

A large crowd had already gathered by the time they arrived and there was much pushing and jostling as men tried to get near to hear the speakers. A few women had come out too, Titus noticed, but the gathering was mostly men, and what a wretched crowd they looked. Many wore clothes that were hanging in tatters and some had no clogs or boots for their feet, but went barefoot in the cold and wet. And some, he noticed, had armed themselves with thick sticks and bludgeons. He hoped that the meeting wouldn't turn violent and he thought of asking George if they shouldn't go back in case trouble broke out, but George's face was lit with determination, and glancing back at the men following them up the hill, Titus doubted that he would be able to get back through the throng anyway, so he allowed himself to be swept forwards.

At the front, near an upturned barrel that had been brought for the speakers to stand on, the crowd had begun to sing and as the newcomers arrived they picked up the song until it resounded in deep melodic voices across the damp moorland.

The first speaker was helped up on to the barrel and waved his hands palms down at the crowd, to indicate that they should be quiet and listen. Gradually, silence fell from the front to the back of the crowd. Titus had to strain to hear what was being said as the speaker's words were carried away on the stiff breeze, but the gist of his address was about suffrage and the campaign for the vote. It was a recent idea to Titus. He'd never taken much interest in politics until he came to live in the town. It hadn't mattered to him before. Decisions made by the gentry in London seemed remote and whilst he had work enough to do and the means to feed his family it hadn't seemed to have anything to do with him. But since he'd come into Blackburn and seen the hardship that was being caused by them in London, he'd begun to realise that the Reformers were right.

'The Supreme Being in His infinite bounty has given rights to all men!' shouted the next speaker, who was easier to hear. 'Men are born free and equal. We must preserve the natural rights of men. There must be a radical reform of Parliament by means of suffrage for all male persons of mature age and sound mind!'

Speaker after speaker clambered up on to the barrel and all gave out the same message. There were also calls for the repeal of the Corn Bill so that bread would be affordable again, and an end to the embargoes on trade so that cotton goods could be sold abroad and the industry would be profitable once more.

Each demand was met with louder and louder cheers and Titus noticed that the meeting had been joined by groups of latecomers, who had come up behind them. Although many of them looked half starved, they were not all entirely sober. Jugs were being passed from hand to hand and when someone thrust a vessel at him, he took it and drank from it, out of fear of the recriminations a refusal might bring. He passed it on, wiping his mouth. The drink tasted vile, but it flowed through his veins like fire, warming him and helping him feel at one with the angry men who surged around him.

There was an underlying air of menace as the evening drew on and a bonfire was lit. It was twilight when the main speaker, a local man by the name of Dewhurst, climbed up to address them, and by that time the singing had been replaced with a chant of 'Ludd! Ludd!' Titus began to fear that the rally would erupt into violence before the night was over.

'Them Frenchies had the right idea!' came a shout from the back of the crowd. 'It's time us workers took control and showed them jumped-up gentry they can't treat us like slaves!'

There were murmurs of agreement as Dewhurst called for calm. 'I hear you, brothers!' he told the crowd. 'But it is Reform that's needed. Violence is not the answer.'

His words were met by a subtle booing that grew in volume until he began to look panicked. Someone pulled him down off the barrel and another man leaped up in his place.

'The time for talking's over!' he shouted, shaking a bludgeon in the air. 'It's time to act, and act now. Down with the infernal machines!'

The chanting started up again, with men pounding the air with their sticks and staves. 'Ludd! Ludd!' And then, without any outward signal, the mob took on a life of its own and as one mass began to pour down the hill towards Blackburn, men carrying torches as well as weapons.

Titus had no choice but to join the throng. Even though he tried to let others go ahead of him, he found himself being pushed from the back and he knew that if he lost his footing he would be trampled underfoot by the rabble. He lost sight of George and found himself surrounded by men he didn't know, men who were the worse for drink and intent on causing mayhem. He tried to get away from them so that he could run home and warn Jennet to stay inside and lock the doors, but he was one man against hundreds.

The crowd surged down the hill and into town, heading for the Dandy Mill, some dropping off at the Bay Horse to snatch what refreshment they could. Titus tried to push his way to the front of the mob now, but he was pinned tight by other men's elbows and knees and carried along in any direction the crowd saw fit.

As they approached Paradise Lane, Titus thought he caught a glimpse of Jennet's frightened face at the upstairs window as they passed by. At the factory gates, the crowd came to a halt and amid the shouting there came the sound of heavy thuds as stones were thrown in an attempt to break in. Men with torches tried to kindle a fire at the base of the wooden doors and there was the sound of shattering glass after some men managed to clamber over and begin an assault on the mill's windows.

A cheer rent the air as the doors gave way and the crowd flooded into the yard, carrying Titus along with it. The main door was smashed open and they surged inside. The familiar space looked menacing as the machines cast their huge, dancing shadows in the torchlight. The steady thrum of the engine was missing but it was soon replaced by the rhythmic pounding of hammers as the men attacked the looms and began to break them apart. When the looms lay in pieces, the men turned their attention to the steam engine, breaking apart the drums and pulling the drive shafts from their supports.

Titus pressed his back to one of the stone walls and watched. The men's faces were twisted with effort and anger in the gloom and although he felt guilty at not trying to stop the destruction, he was afraid that they might turn their hammers on him if he tried to stay their hands.

'Dragoons!' shouted someone and there was a sudden rush to get out. 'Come on, man!' someone else yelled in his ear and grasped his sleeve to pull him back out into the yard. As the night air hit him, Titus saw the mounted soldiers. They had their swords drawn although they were mostly holding up their arms to protect themselves from the missiles being hurled at them by the mob. Titus saw the constable heave himself up on to an empty wagon and call for order. He pulled a paper from his coat and began to read the Riot Act.

'Our Sovereign Lord the King chargeth and commandeth all persons, being assembled, immediately to disperse themselves and peaceably depart to their habitations ...'

The mob paid little attention to his words and continued to throw anything àt hand. Titus saw one of the soldiers get hit on the cheek by a stone and another lost control of his horse as it was hit by a missile. Then there was a deafening explosion followed by moments of muffled silence. The mob froze and then ducked for cover.

'They're firing on us!'

'Run for it!'

'Only blanks.'

'Look out!'

Titus tried to get out of the yard. He was desperate to get across the street and into the house to make sure that Jennet and Peggy were all right, but his way was barred now, not only by the crowd, but by soldiers. Reinforcements had arrived and the dragoons charged into the mill yard, scattering the mob as men desperately tried to avoid being trampled by the horses. The crowd began to thin as men spilled out into Paradise Lane and ran back towards Darwen Street. Titus stayed put, clinging to the shelter of the mill wall and hoping that if the soldiers gave chase, it might clear the way for him to get home. He was just considering that it might be safe to make his move when he felt his shirt tugged tight around the collar, almost choking him. He thrashed out at his assailant and felt a stunning blow as something hit the back of his head. He staggered to his knees, the cobbles looming up as he fell, disorientated. All he wanted was to get home. He began to crawl, aware of warm blood running down the back of his neck, and his only thought was that Jennet would be angry with him for spoiling his only decent white shirt. A heavy boot crashed down on his hand sending pain throbbing through him. Then he was hauled to his feet. He turned to thank whoever had helped him up, but saw that it was one of the constable's runners, truncheon in hand.

'Come quiet, or I'll have to strike thee again!' he threatened.

'I've done nowt wrong,' said Titus as he tried to pull away. 'Let me go. I work here. I only live across the street!'

'Shut yer mouth!' spat the man. 'Tha can tell it to the magistrate.' He pushed Titus roughly towards the mill gate.

'I only live there.' Titus glanced at his own front door and up at the bedroom window where he saw the curtain move. 'Jennet!' he called.

'This way!' said the man, grabbing his arm and forcing it up his back until Titus thought his shoulder would tear from the agony. He was marched away, not able to look back. Dizzy with pain and reeling from the blow to his head, he stumbled along as noise and chaos reigned around him. As they turned into Darwen Street, he heard the Manchester coach coming in fast. The mob was hurling stones at it and the coachman was urging the horses on to get himself and his passengers away. Titus felt himself pulled back out of its path, but another man was not so lucky and his shrieks pierced the night. Titus caught a glimpse of the man lying in the roadway. His head looked broken and he was twitching as a circle formed around him to watch him die.

Titus was pushed roughly towards the Old Bull. The pub was thronged with men and women with tankards in their hands and for a moment he hoped someone might get him a drink. But he was steered around the back towards the steep steps down to the cellar and pushed inside with several others, the door slamming behind them. Left in pitch-blackness, Titus sat down on the damp stones. He tentatively reached around the back of his head and his fingers came away sticky. He was bleeding, but he had no idea how badly. He pulled off his stock from around his neck and bound his head with it, hoping it would be enough to stem the flow. Outside, the noise of the riot rose and fell above them, but in the cellar no one spoke. Titus rested his forehead against the rough wall and wondered how many hours there were until daylight when he could explain his innocence to the magistrate and go home to get cleaned up properly.

Jennet had waited for Titus to come home, growing more anxious and restless as the hours had passed. At last, she'd gathered Peggy in her arms and gone next door.

'Only me!' she'd called after knocking on Lizzie's door and going in. Lizzie had been sitting with some knitting on her lap. Jennet thought she looked poorly.

'Is tha not so good?'

'It's just a cough,' she'd replied. 'Everyone coughs in this town.'

'I thought they'd have been back by now,' said Jennet, perching on the edge of the other chair as

Peggy reached out her hands to grab at the knitting wool.

'These things go on and on,' observed Lizzie. 'I wouldn't worry. Get to bed. They'll be back soon enough.'

'Aye. I suppose you're right. Peggy's tired out,' she said as the child began to cry. 'I'll go and put her down. Take care,' she added as she went out of the door.

After she'd settled Peggy, Jennet hung up her dress and put on her cotton nightgown before climbing into bed. It was chilly and she snuggled down under the blankets, missing Titus beside her. She hoped that he was all right and hadn't done anything silly. Still, it was quiet enough outside. There was no sign of trouble. Perhaps George had taken him for a drink before they came home.

She must have dozed a little because she didn't think she'd been asleep when she heard the chanting in the distance. The sound was menacing. As it drew nearer she slid out of bed and pulled back the curtain slightly to peep out. She couldn't see anything, but it sounded as if it was coming closer. Then the mob surged around the corner and into Paradise Lane. The gaslights were still burning outside the mill gate and she could see that some of the men were armed with what looked

67

like home-made pikes. Others carried hammers and handfuls of stones that they began to throw at the mill windows. She jumped at the sound of breaking glass and drew back, afraid that a stone might be thrown in her direction. In her bed, Peggy turned restlessly, and Jennet hoped that the noise wouldn't waken her. She prayed that Titus was safe somewhere and hadn't got mixed up in this. He should never have gone to that meeting. He'd assured her it would be peaceful, but now her worst fears had been realised.

She hoped that the mob wouldn't turn on the houses. There was no reason for them to, but she feared that the men, fired up with their righteous anger, might be capable of anything. She crept carefully down the stairs to lock and bar the front door. She would have to get up again and open it for Titus when he came.

'Please God, let him have the sense to wait until this has died down before he tries to get home,' she said as she went back upstairs. She wanted him home. She was terrified on her own with Peggy, but she could see that getting down Paradise Lane at the moment would be impossible.

She heard hooves on the cobbles and watched as the dragoons galloped past, scattering men left and right as they charged into the mill yard. She jumped as the shots rang out and then ducked down, instinctively shielding her head. Peggy began to wail and she picked her up, soothing and rocking her. 'It'll be all right. It'll be all right.' She sat down on the floor with her daughter in her arms, singing to her as the riot went on outside. After what seemed like hours, she heard the dragoons leave and gradually silence fell. Peggy nodded off and Jennet tucked her back into bed before going to peep from behind the curtain again. Most of the rioters had gone, leaving the mill gates hanging. She saw a constable with a truncheon marching one of them away. The man seemed to be bleeding from his head and for a moment she thought it was Titus, but it couldn't be, she reassured herself. He would never have gone into the mill to break machinery. He would soon be home now that the mob had gone on its way.

She watched for him, and listened for his familiar footsteps approaching the door. He didn't come. The street remained deserted, and the fire that had been lit in the mill yard burned itself out. Jennet shivered and got a blanket from the bed to wrap around herself as she knelt at the window, resting her forehead on the cold glass as she waited. The gas lamps went out and silence fell. She must have slept like that for a while because she was wakened by the sound of someone approaching. He was here. For a moment she was overwhelmed with relief as she struggled to her feet to go down and let him in, but then she saw that it was George.

She hurried down the stairs in the pitch-blackness. She knew she mustn't fall, but she wanted to catch George before he went inside, to ask him about Titus. Her neighbour must have had the same thought. She heard a gentle tapping just before she reached the door. She pulled back the bolt, turned the key and opened it a crack.

'Is Titus home?'

'No. I was hoping tha'd know where he was,' said Jennet.

'We got separated,' George told her. 'I've been looking for him, but he's nowhere to be found.'

A chill ran through Jennet. Was he hurt somewhere? Fallen into the river? Arrested?

'Tha doesn't think he got mixed up with the breakers?'

'No, not Titus. Go back to bed,' advised George. 'I'm sure he'll be home soon.'

She went to bed, but lay awake until daylight cast a stripe across the wooden floor through the gap in the curtains. It was quiet outside, like a Sunday. No knocker-up. No mill engine. No hooter.

Peggy was still asleep and Jennet risked dashing down the yard to the privy before having a quick wash in cold water in the back kitchen. She would

70

have to go to the well if Titus wasn't home soon. She lit a fire and put the kettle on, and then went up to get Peggy. Her daughter was awake and laughing as she grasped at the dust motes floating above her. Jennet wished she could feel the same.

'Upsadaisy,' she said as she lifted the child. She took her down to change her nappy and wash her, putting the soiled cloth to soak. Moments later there was a knock at the door and someone pushed the handle.

'Titus!' She ran across to open it, but it was George again.

'Not come?' he asked. He looked concerned.

'No. I thought it were him. Where can he be?' she asked, glancing up and down the street.

'I've heard talk,' said George. She saw that he was carrying a milk jug and must have been up to the milk-house. 'They're sayin' that the constables rounded up all manner of folk last night. I'm worried Titus might have been caught up in it after all.'

Jennet stared at him. 'No,' she said, but she knew in her heart that it would account for why he hadn't come home. 'What have they done with them?'

'Locked in the cellar at the Old Bull. Then being taken to Preston to appear before the magistrate.'

'But they'll let him go, if he's done nowt wrong.'

'Course they will, love. But I thought I'd better forewarn thee, just in case.'

Quickly, she made some porridge and fed Peggy, before hurrying into the town centre. The broken glass crunched under her feet and the air smelled strongly of burning.

A crowd had gathered outside the Old Bull. She hoisted Peggy further up her shoulder and stood on tiptoe as there was a commotion near the door and the prisoners were brought out to the accompaniment of cheering from the crowd. People kept getting in her way, but then she saw Titus. She was horrified. There was dried blood, from a wound on his head, all down his shoulder and across his shirt. He looked dazed and filthy. He needed a doctor not a magistrate.

'Titus!' she called, but he didn't hear her. His head was hanging down and he looked unaware of what was going on.

A flat wagon with wooden seats down each side was waiting and she could do nothing but stare as the men were pushed aboard and it rolled away down the street. She stood and watched it go, unsure what to do. Peggy was crying, but she scarcely heard her. She'd never felt so helpless or afraid in her whole life.

Chapter Five

Without knowing what she was doing, Jennet began to walk and as it approached dinner time she recognised her parents' cottage at Ramsgreave. She hurried to the door and went in without pausing to knock or call out. Her mother and her sister Hannah were busy preparing food and her father was sitting at his loom. They looked up in surprise.

'Hello, our Jennet!' said her father. 'What's to do?'

'Titus was arrested. He's been taken to Preston for trial.'

Her parents stared at her, speechless.

'Is tha sure?' asked her father after a moment.

'Of course I'm sure. I was there. I saw him taken!'

Peggy was crying again and Jennet's mother took the child and shushed her. 'Sit thee down,' she said to Jennet. 'I'll make a cup of tea.' She handed Peggy to Hannah.

'What happened?' asked her father, getting down from his loom.

'There was rioting,' said Jennet.

'But surely Titus weren't involved?'

'He went to the Reformers' meeting. He must have got mixed up in it somehow. He never came home and they were burnin' the mill and smashin' everything. I were on my own with Peggy and it were terrifying. Then, this morning, George from next door came to say they'd arrested folk and I were hopin' as Titus wasn't one of them, but when I went to town I saw him being pushed on to the wagon and taken away.'

She'd begun to sob and her mother knelt beside her and pulled her into her arms. 'It'll be all right,' she said. 'He'll explain himself and they'll let him go. It's just a misunderstanding.'

'He were hurt too,' Jennet cried. 'His shirt were all covered in blood and his head were broken.'

'Nah then, stop tha cryin',' said her father. 'It'll not help.'

Jennet wiped her nose on her sleeve and took the hot, sweet tea from her mother. 'What'll I do?' she asked. Her father glanced at her mother and she gave a slight shrug. Jennet had been hoping that they might offer some solution, but it seemed they were as perplexed as she was.

'Is there anyone who'll speak up for him? Who was he with?' asked her father.

'George.' Jennet suddenly saw a glimmer of hope. 'He went with George. Dost tha think he'll swear as Titus weren't involved?'

'Tha'll have to ask him, lass. What say tha has a sup o' dinner with us and then I'll walk back into town with thee and we'll see this George?'

'But it means takin' thee away from tha work.' She glanced at the half-woven length of calico and felt guilty.

'I'm stuck for bobbins,' he said. 'Besides, I'll not let thee go home alone when tha's so upset.'

Jennet was grateful. She felt better now that she could see a way of doing something practical. She sat up at the table and ate some stew. When she'd eaten she felt better, more like herself. It would be all right, she thought. Surely George would give a character for his friend and Titus would be allowed home.

After dinner she walked back to Paradise Lane, with her father carrying Peggy on his shoulders. It was quiet around town when they eventually got back, as if the trouble of the previous night had never occurred. The broken glass had been swept away and the mill gates were repaired and locked shut.

With her father beside her, Jennet tapped at her neighbour's door and pushed it open. 'Hello!' she called.

'Come in!'

'Is George here?'

'He's gone for water. He would've brought a bucket for thee an' all, if tha'd been here.'

'I went home,' she explained. 'This is my father. He's walked me back.' She paused and looked at Lizzie's pale face and rheumy eyes. 'They took Titus to Preston,' she told her.

'Aye. I heard. I'm right sorry.'

'I was hopin' George might put in a good word for him. Tell them as Titus weren't involved in it.'

'I'm sure he will.' Lizzie began to cough again and held a soiled rag to her mouth.

'I'll take Peggy next door,' said her father with a frown. 'We don't want her catching owt else.'

'I'm sorry,' said Jennet when he'd gone. 'I know that sounded rude.'

'He's right though,' said Lizzie. 'I think I'm proper poorly, and I wouldn't want little Peg to be taken badly again.'

The door opened behind them and George came in with the buckets. 'All right, Jennet?' he said.

'They've taken Titus to Preston,' she told him. 'He'll be up afore the magistrate.'

'Aye. I heard. It's a rum do.'

76

'It must have been a mistake,' said Jennet. 'Will tha speak for him? Say that he was with thee?'

'I'll speak for him, aye,' he said. 'But I lost sight of him after the meeting, so I can't swear to what he did or didn't do. But I'll speak up as he's an honest man and was set against the breaking.'

Jennet would have preferred him to say that he'd been with Titus and that he was witness to him taking no part in the violence, but she had to accept that George could only tell the truth as he knew it. He wasn't a close friend, after all, and it was generous of him to agree at all, seeing that he would have to travel to Preston to give witness. 'I'm grateful,' she said.

'It's the least I can do,' he said. 'I feel a bit guilty, seeing that it were me as persuaded him to go to the meetin'. If there's owt I can do, just ask. Dost tha need any water fetching?'

Jennet shook her head. 'My father's come so he can mind Peggy whilst I go,' she said. 'Look to Lizzie,' she added, glancing at the woman sitting silently by the fire. 'She's not good.'

'I know,' he agreed with a frown. 'We're going to the Dispensary in a bit to get some more medicine for that cough. It's gone on long enough.'

Jennet left them and went back to her own house where her father had put more coal on the fire and had a great blaze going. She hadn't the heart to tell him that he'd used all she had.

'It's chilly in here, and damp,' he said. 'Tha doesn't want our Peggy gettin' poorly again.'

'I know,' she said, 'but we've nowt left now that Titus isn't bringing a wage in.'

'I thought tha had some put by, from the loom?'

'It's all been spent,' she told him. 'I've had to ask for relief, but I'm not sure I'll get it now.'

'They'll not refuse, surely? Not when tha's got a young child?'

Jennet shook her head. 'I don't think they'll help anyone who's been arrested.'

'What will tha do if he's found guilty?'

'Don't talk like that.'

'It needs to be said, Jennet. There's a chance he might be found guilty and tha needs to face that possibility and think on what tha's going to do.' He paused, but didn't offer any resolution to the problem. Jennet thought that he would like to ask her to come home to Ramsgreave, but she knew that her parents were struggling too and had no spare money to keep her and Peggy.

'We'll see,' she said. 'If George speaks up for him, it might be all right.'

'He's agreed then?'

'Aye, he has. And it's generous of him.'

*

78

Titus caught a glimpse of Jennet with Peggy in her arms as the cart lurched away, escorted by a detachment of hussars. He wanted to wave to let her know he'd seen her, but his hands were chained and it was taking him all his strength not to fall over into the dirty straw where he would be kicked by other men's clogs. He could scarcely believe what was happening. He'd expected to be brought before a magistrate in the Assembly Rooms, not sent off to prison without any chance of explaining himself. But there was nowt he could do. He just had to keep himself together until he got the fair hearing he deserved and was allowed to go free.

The journey to Preston seemed to take hours. The jolting of the wagon sent stabs of pain throbbing through the wound in his head and with every passing mile he worried more and more. How would Jennet cope without him? How would he get back when they realised their mistake and let him go? He supposed he would have to walk. He had no money for the coach.

Thankfully the day was dry, or he would have been soaked to the skin. The sun even shone a little as they rumbled over the bridge into Preston where the gates of the House of Correction opened for them and they were drawn inside. The horses stood, breathing deeply with the exertion. Steam rose from their haunches as the iron gates clanged shut and the flap at the back of the wagon was let down with a bang.

'Get down! Stand in a line! Don't speak!'

Titus staggered down and stood with the other prisoners. They were in an outer ward between the main entrance and a huge, high wall that surrounded the main buildings. The turnkey came out of his lodge with a bunch of keys rattling in his hands and unlocked a small door. They were marched through and the door locked behind them. Inside, hidden from the street, was a small garden. Early flowers grew there and the apple trees were smothered in blossom. It reminded Titus of his patch at Pleck Gate. Beyond the garden stood a house, built to look like an old castle, and from it stretched two wings of low buildings.

The turnkey read them a long list of rules and regulations that meant little to Titus and then they were marched inside and down a long corridor with doors on one side. As each man was put into a cell, the door was banged shut behind him and the others moved on in slow procession. When Titus came to the head of the queue he walked meekly into his cell and heard the door slam and the key turn. He looked about him. The walls were very white and everything was iron or stone. He'd expected a dank cellar but the cells were recently built with a window at one side and a fanlight and grating in the door, which gave them a free current of air. It could have been much worse, thought Titus.

Now that his hands were free he raised a hand to his wounded head and flinched as he touched it. It didn't seem to be bleeding now, but it was sore and bruised and probably swollen.

The voices and footsteps in the corridor outside continued for some time. Then everything fell silent and Titus sat down on the small three-legged stool. He was thirsty and hungry and longed to have a good wash and most of all to sleep, but he didn't dare lie down on the bed though it looked clean and comfortable enough with a flock mattress, a pillow and blankets.

After a while he heard movement outside again and the door was opened. A turnkey came in with a bowl of steaming soup. He thrust it into Titus's hands and went out without a word. Titus sipped at the gruel. It was thin but good and he savoured the aroma and the taste, drinking it more quickly as it cooled and even suffering the pain of tipping back his head to drain the dregs. He'd barely finished when the door opened once more and he was told to bring the bowl to wash it in a sink at the end of the corridor. Then he was led away to another room where he saw a bathtub filled with hot water.

'Get scrubbed,' he was told as he was handed a bar of carbolic soap and a small, rough towel. 'Leave thy clothes there.'

He stripped off, putting his filthy clothing on the floor, and stepped into the water. It was a long time since he'd had the luxury of a bath; a wash down in a basin in front of the fire was all he'd managed since they'd moved into Blackburn. He sank his weary and aching body as far down as the shallow water would allow and scrubbed himself all over, doing his best to wash the blood from his head, but making the wound bleed afresh.

'We'll get doctor to take a look at that,' said the turnkey when he was finished and had dried himself. 'Here. Put these on.' There were cotton underpants, a grey shirt, trousers and a waistcoat. When he was dressed he was taken to another room where a young man introduced himself as the doctor and bound the wound on his head. Then he was escorted back to the solitary confinement of his cell.

'When will I come up afore the magistrate?' Titus asked the turnkey as they reached his door. 'I need to explain as I did nowt wrong.'

'Sometime tomorrow,' he replied. 'There's quite a few folk come in today so it'll take time for 'em all to be heard.'

'I did nowt wrong,' Titus repeated.

'Aye. We'll see,' said the man, closing and locking the door.

Jennet had just finished feeding Peggy when there was a knock on her door. She knew it wasn't Lizzie. George had called to say that she'd taken to her bed and would knock on the wall if she needed anything whilst he was out.

She opened the door to find Mrs Whittaker standing on her doorstep.

'May I come in?'

'Aye.' Jennet wrenched the door wider and stood back as the vicar's wife came in. She must have come to say that there was no money for her, she thought.

'I heard your husband was arrested,' said Mrs Whittaker.

'It's a mistake. He's innocent,' Jennet told her.

'Well, that's for the court to decide.'

'George next door has promised to speak up for him, as a character witness. He was with Titus, but they got separated. He'll tell them that Titus was dead set against any loom breaking.'

'That will be helpful. It's a pity that your husband wasn't a regular churchgoer, like you. The vicar could have spoken for him as well.'

'What about the relief?' asked Jennet. 'If not for me, then for Peggy?' She hated to plead, but she wouldn't see her child go hungry and she didn't even dare think of the only other alternative, which was to take her to the workhouse.

'I'll do my best to make sure that you get something,' promised Mrs Whittaker, 'but it will be easier to persuade the other ladies on the committee that you're a deserving case if your husband is found not guilty,' she warned. 'Some of them are the wives of mill owners and they take a very dim view of anyone who was involved in last night's destruction.'

Mrs Whittaker made her way to the door and bid Jennet good morning. Jennet watched until the vicar's wife had turned the corner. Then she took Peggy next door to see if Lizzie wanted anything.

'What did the doctor say?' she asked as Lizzie lay on the bed and coughed into a rag.

'He's given me some different medicine.' She waved a hand at the bottle of brown liquid that stood on the table beside her bed.

'Is that all?'

'He looked at me wi' pity in his eyes. He saw I was going to die.'

'Don't talk daft,' said Jennet, shocked by Lizzie's words. 'Tha'll be up and doin' again in a day or two.'

'Nay.' Lizzie reached out and grasped her hand. 'Look out for George when I'm gone,' she said. 'He's useless on his own, has no idea what's what.

Keep an eye on him. Don't let him go without a clean collar or two.'

'Tha's bein' silly,' said Jennet, squeezing her hand. 'Tha'll get better now tha's seen the doctor. He made Peggy better,' she reminded her.

'Nay, lass,' said Lizzie. 'I'll not kid myself that he can do owt for me. I'm not long for this world. Open yon chest of drawers, will tha? Bottom one.' Jennet knelt and pulled back the oak drawer. 'See that package? It's a fine cotton nightgown. See that they bury me in it.'

'Lizzie, tha's frightenin' me,' she said as she eased back the paper to look at the garment. 'It'll be years and years afore tha needs this.'

'Promise me, Jennet. I've no one else. No sisters. No childer. And George is useless. Promise tha'll see me buried in it.'

'I promise – when the time comes,' she said.

Lizzie relaxed back against the bolster and Jennet shoved the drawer shut again. 'Dost tha want a cup of tea?' she asked.

'Aye. That'd be nice. There's sugar in the larder. Put two in and make one for thyself an' all.'

'Watch Peggy for me then,' said Jennet, settling the child on the floor with a bobbin or two to play with before going down to put the kettle on. It was alarming how quickly Lizzie had worsened. She'd been such a rock when Peggy had been poorly and her own mother too far away to help, and Jennet was afraid that she was going to lose her new-found friend. Although she'd tried to reassure her, she saw what the doctor had seen. Lizzie seemed to be wasting away, growing thinner and paler every day and struggling to get her breath. It was the filth, thought Jennet as she waited for the tea to brew. People had never been poorly like this at Pleck Gate where the air had been fresh. All the smoke and smog in the town, and the dust from the coal and the cotton, and the filthy sewers that ran alongside the streets were bound to make folk ill. She wished that they'd never come here.

She took the tea up the steep steps and handed a cup to her friend. Lizzie's hands were trembling as she raised it to her lips and sipped at the scalding brew.

'Look after George for me,' she said again.

'I will,' promised Jennet in an attempt to soothe her.

'Find him a good woman. A man shouldn't be alone. They're such childer.'

Jennet waited until Lizzie had finished her tea before she washed up and went back to her own house to get Peggy some dinner. She could hear Lizzie coughing every now and again. At least it meant she was still alive.

*

The next day she and George were supposed to be going to Preston for the hearing. Her parents had walked down from Ramsgreave to collect Peggy so Jennet wouldn't have to take her with them. She was grateful, but her mother said that she needed to get some things from the market anyway and it was the least they could do in the circumstances.

Jennet was ready, dressed in her Sunday best, when George came to the door. His face was grave.

'I'm right sorry, Jennet,' he said, 'but I don't think I can leave our Lizzie.'

Jennet's first thoughts were for her friend and she hurried next door and up the stairs. Lizzie was lying in bed. Her breathing was laboured and her chest rattled. Her eyelids fluttered when Jennet said her name, but apart from that she seemed unaware. It was clear that she was very poorly. Jennet couldn't expect George to leave her. She would have liked to have stayed and nursed her herself, but someone had to go and speak for Titus.

'I'm right sorry, Jennet,' said George. 'Tha knows I would have come willingly, but ...'

'No, tha can't leave her like this. Willst tha get the doctor?'

'Aye. He's said he'll come. But I'm not sure there's owt he can do.' Jennet saw George brush aside a tear as he gazed down at his wife. 'I wish it were different,' he said. 'I'm right sorry.'

'It can't be helped,' she said, touching his arm. 'Stay with her.'

'Perhaps thy father'll go with thee?'

'I'm sure he will.'

'Don't go alone.'

'Don't worry about me,' she told him. 'Take care of Lizzie.'

She left him sitting on the edge of the bed and hurried back down the stairs. She closed the door gently behind her and went back next door to tell her parents.

'Of course I'll come,' said her father, 'though it's a pity yon chap won't be there to speak for Titus.'

Her mother said she'd take Peggy back to Ramsgreave when she'd got her shopping, then Jennet and her father set off on the road that led to Preston, Jennet wondering what the day would bring. It had begun badly and she could only hope that it would improve, and that by the time they were walking back Titus would be walking beside her. But at least the morning was fresh and fine, she thought, and it would have felt good to be out in the countryside if she hadn't been so worried. They walked on, keeping to the side of the road to allow the wagons and coaches to go past, and reached Preston at dinner time. Her father had some oatcakes in a bundle that her mother had made and they ate them before going up to the prison where they asked if they could see Titus. They were told no, but they could go to the Sessions House where the prisoners were coming up before the magistrate.

They had to wait outside with the crowd who had come for the hearing. Jennet began to worry that they wouldn't get in at all, but at last the door was opened and they were told they might enter. Jennet took a seat beside her father on a hard bench. It wouldn't be long now, she thought. Soon it would be Titus's turn to come in and he would explain the mistake to the magistrate and then they could go home.

Several men came in before him, all charged with breaking machinery in Blackburn and other surrounding towns. All the men professed their innocence, but the magistrate seemed in no mood to listen. He was insistent that they should be tried by jury and sent them all back to prison to await trial at the Assizes in Lancaster. Jennet grew increasingly concerned.

At last Titus came up. He glanced around the room and met Jennet's eyes, giving her a brief smile before turning his attention to the magistrate. He had been cleaned up. His head was bound and he looked as if he was being treated well. The charges were read out that he had been part of a group of men who had broken into the Dandy Mill and smashed the power looms.

'I took no part in it,' said Titus. 'I live just across the street on Paradise Lane and I was making my way home to my wife and child.'

'Yet you were in the mill yard?'

'I was. I was swept in by the rush of men. I was there against my will.'

The magistrate frowned. 'There's no clear evidence that you weren't involved. I'm sending you to the Assizes for trial. Next!'

'No!' Jennet had called out before she could stop herself. 'He wasn't there. I can speak for him!'

'Remove that woman!' said the magistrate and Jennet felt a rough hand grasp her arm and pull her towards the door. She heard her father shout at the man to let her alone, but within moments they had both been bundled out on to the street and the door slammed behind them.

'What'll happen to him now?' she asked.

'They'll keep him in prison until the next Assizes in August,' said her father.

'But that's over three months. Is there nothing we can do?' she asked. She expected him to have a solution, but he was shaking his head.

'There's nowt we can do except wait and hope that the jury finds him not guilty. Meanwhile, we've no option but to go back without him.'

'But I need to see him!' she protested.

'They'll not let thee into the prison.'

Jennet found herself crying. She'd been so sure that Titus would be free to walk home with them. She couldn't bear the idea of leaving him behind and going back to Paradise Lane alone.

'Come on. Cheer up,' said her father. 'Crying won't bring him out. Tha needs to be brave. Think of little Peggy.'

'I know,' sobbed Jennet, picturing her daughter and thinking that she would forget her father if he was away for months.

'He seemed well treated at least.'

'Aye.' It was some sort of consolation, thought Jennet as they turned their steps for home.

It was late when they got back to Blackburn. The gaslights were burning in Paradise Lane and casting an eerie glow across the quiet street. Her father saw her safely to the door.

'Stay the night,' she urged him. 'Tha's walked far enough for one day.'

'I'd best get back,' he said. 'Thy mam'll be fretting. Come up tomorrow for Peggy. She'll be asleep by now.' He kissed her cheek. 'It'll be all right,' he said. 'He'll be home soon.'

Jennet watched him to the end of the street and when he'd turned the corner she closed and locked the door, and wearily climbed the stairs to bed. It was odd being alone. She'd never slept in a house on her own in her life before. Even next door was quiet. She hoped that Lizzie was a bit better and sleeping peacefully.

It took her a while to get off. She couldn't get warm and although she felt restless she didn't dare move because the sheets were icy except for the small spot where she was lying. The events of the day played over and over in her mind as she searched for solutions that were impossible to find. Towards dawn she must have dropped off, but she was awake again early and got up. She dressed with chattering teeth in the cold and went downstairs. There was no coal to light a fire to boil the kettle for tea and she was worried about how she would warm the house when she brought Peggy home. Perhaps she could get some wood up at Ramsgreave that would keep her going for a while at least.

She could hear George moving about next door, so before she set off to collect Peggy, she tapped on the door and pushed it open, not wanting to call out in case Lizzie was still sleeping.

George was sitting in his chair. The fire had gone out and Jennet saw straight away that something was wrong.

'She's gone,' he told her.

'Gone?' It was a moment before she realised that George meant Lizzie. 'No! Oh, George, I'm so sorry,' she said. He looked a mess. His clothes were rumpled as if he'd slept in them. His eyes were red and he hadn't shaved. 'When?' she asked.

'Yesterday afternoon, around four o'clock. She worsened after tha went. I fetched the priest and I think she were comforted by that. At least I hope she was.'

'I'm sure she was.' Jennet sat down on the edge of Lizzie's chair, remembering the promise that she'd made to her friend. 'Where is she?' she asked.

'Upstairs. I've slept down here,' he said.

'Has she been laid out?'

'Aye. A woman came. From church.'

'She had a gown, in the bottom drawer ...'

'Aye, I know. She's wearin' it.'

'Can I see her?'

'Aye.'

Jennet climbed the gloomy stairs and pushed open the bedroom door. It creaked. Lizzie lay on the bed in the cold morning light, dressed in white, with her hands folded. Except it wasn't Lizzie. Her soul had flown and all that was left was the body that had once held it, thin enough to show every bone. Jennet knelt by the bed to say a prayer. She hadn't realised that her neighbours were Catholics, but she was sure that they all prayed to the same

God. She hoped so anyway, and she hoped, too, He wasn't fed up with all her prayers. She'd had a lot to pray for these past couple of days.

'Hast tha eaten owt?' she asked George when she went back down. He shook his head.

'I never thought,' he told her.

'Get the fire going and I'll make thee summat. Tha needs to keep thy strength up.'

She went into the back kitchen and found some oatmeal to make porridge. She would have loved to help herself to some, but she couldn't bring herself to take what wasn't hers, though when George told her to pour herself a cup of the hot tea she didn't refuse.

'I've to go to Ramsgreave for our Peggy,' she told him. 'Will tha be all right?'

'Aye. Thanks, Jennet. It's been a shock. Even though I knew she were ill, I kept thinkin' she'd rally.'

'I know.' She laid a hand briefly on his shoulder. 'I'll come round when I get back to see if tha wants anything.'

She walked up to Ramsgreave to get her daughter, feeling numb. It was just one bad thing after another and she couldn't help wondering what disaster would strike next. By the time she reached her parents' home she'd convinced herself that more bad news would be waiting for her, but Peggy was laughing and happy. Her daughter reached out to be picked up and Jennet lifted her and kissed her soft little cheek.

'Have summat to eat afore tha goes back,' said her mother. 'I've made a broth.'

It smelled good and Jennet sat down at the table. She told them about Lizzie and they sympathised, but it was what would happen to Titus that they talked of most.

'Tha could come home ...' began her father. Jennet shook her head. She was determined not to be a burden on them.

'There's nothing for me to do here,' she said. 'If I stay in town there's a chance of getting some work. And Mrs Whittaker has promised to try to get me something, for Peggy at least.'

'Well, if tha needs me to mind Peggy, I'll do it gladly,' said her mother.

'I know. I'm grateful,' she said. She didn't want to leave her daughter at Ramsgreave but she knew that if she got work she might have to.

'Will tha go to Lancaster for the trial?' asked her sister.

'Of course I will.'

'How will tha afford it?' asked her father.

'I don't rightly know,' she said. 'Perhaps if I get work I can save enough to pay for the coach.' She wished now that she'd kept back some of Titus's loom money, but she'd never considered any emergency other than feeding themselves.

After they'd eaten, she walked back into Blackburn, carrying a sack with some logs and kindling, and alternating between walking very slowly with Peggy toddling beside her and walking quickly with her on her hip to make up the time. Peggy howled all the time she was being carried and by the time they arrived, Jennet was cross with her.

'Shush!' she told her as she pushed open the reluctant door. 'George next door doesn't want to hear thee skrikin'. He's sad enough.'

She put the child down on the rug and hung up her shawl before lighting the fire. She wondered if she should call on her neighbour. She didn't want to intrude but she'd made a promise to keep an eye on him and she knew he had no one else to make him his tea. She washed her hands, put on an apron and set to making oatcakes. Peggy was quiet now, playing with a little rag doll her grandmother had made for her.

When Jennet was done, she plated up some of the cakes and went to take them to George. 'I thought tha might be glad of summat to eat,' she said, putting them down on the table. He was still sitting beside the hearth and she wondered whether he'd moved at all other than to put more coal on the fire.

'Will tha come to the funeral?' he asked.

Jennet wasn't sure how to reply. She would have liked to see Lizzie buried, but she knew that the service would be at the new Roman Catholic church and she felt afraid of going in there. She'd heard her parents and others talk about it, about the things that were there, crucifixes and such, and it frightened her.

'She would've liked thee to be there. She were glad of thy friendship,' he added.

'Aye. I'll come,' promised Jennet. She would be brave. It couldn't be as bad as people said. She wouldn't tell her parents though.

Lizzie was buried at St Alban's. It rained and the ground was churned to mud as they stood beside the grave. George had paid for a simple coffin, but there was no money for a headstone. There were a few other mourners, other Catholics, but George and Lizzie seemed to have no close friends or family.

After it was over they walked home, feet splashing in the puddles on the cobblestones. Jennet went into George's house and put the kettle on to boil. No one else came back with them and Peggy was at Ramsgreave.

'Take off thy jacket. It's soaked through,' said Jennet. Her own clothing was wet too and she longed to go next door and put on something dry, but she didn't like to leave him on his own. He looked so sad, so lost, as he stood there not knowing what to do next with his saturated cap in his hands. He pulled at the sodden jacket and she helped him, tugging at the sleeves. 'Thy shirt's wet through an' all. Tha's soaked to the skin. Go and put summat dry on and I'll hang these up.'

Jennet put her best bonnet and coat on the peg by the door, hoping that they wouldn't be spoiled. She had no way of replacing them. She hung George's things on the string above the hearth and threw more coal on the fire to help them dry, hoping that she wasn't being too wasteful with it. By the time she'd brewed tea, he'd come back down in a dry shirt with no collar and his work trousers. He was barefoot and his hair stuck up on end where he'd rubbed it vigorously. He looked young and vulnerable. She'd never really looked at him before, thought Jennet as she poured their tea. She'd always assumed he was of a similar age to Lizzie, but now she saw that he was probably much younger and she wondered if Lizzie had been married before. He sat on his chair with his feet on the fender and his tea in his hand. She sat opposite him, her dress steaming as it began to dry.

'I never asked about Titus,' he said. 'I were so full of my own woes that I never thought.'

'He were remanded for the Assizes.'

'Oh, I'm right sorry, Jennet. I would've spoken up for him except ...' His voice trailed away as grief overcame him again.

'It would've made no difference,' she said. 'Yon magistrate wouldn't hear a word from anyone. He just put them all down for the Assizes.'

'When are they?'

'Not 'til August.'

'And he's to stay at Preston meanwhile?' She nodded. 'It's a mess,' he said. 'Will tha manage?'

'I'll have to.'

'Aye. There's stuff as we can't change, no matter how much we wish it.' He sighed. 'Go home and get out of them wet clothes, Jennet. I don't want thee takin' badly an' all.'

'Will tha be all right?' she asked.

'Aye. Don't worry about me.' He tried to give her a smile but it was forced. He looked like a lost boy as he sat there in his shirt; all the joy had gone from the blue eyes that she'd seen twinkle with such mischief when they'd first met.

She took the cups to the back kitchen then put on the wet coat and took her bonnet in her hand. She would stuff it with paper when she got home and hope it would keep its shape.

'I'll call round tomorrow, to see how tha's doing,' she promised.

'I'm grateful. More grateful than I can say,' he whispered as she closed the door behind her and ran the few steps to her own house.

Chapter Six

Titus lay awake on the narrow bed for a long time and watched as the stars moved across the grille in the high window. At last morning came and he heard the rattle of pots and pans in the corridor outside. Someone was knocking on the doors to wake them all up and he could hear keys being turned in the locks. He was sitting on the side of the bed when his door was thrust open and he was handed a bowl of gruel and a lump of bread from a trolley that was squeaking along the stone passage. The bread looked good. He took a bite out of it and savoured the taste. It was a long time since he'd eaten bread. He drank from the bowl and wiped the last of the gruel up with the crust. It was a good meal. Better than he would have had at home.

'Bring your pot,' said the turnkey, nodding to the chamber pot that was provided for him to relieve himself during the night. Titus picked it up and followed a silent procession of prisoners into a walled yard where they were shown how to empty, rinse and stack them. Then they were led into a room filled with forms, set at several feet from each other, and at the side of each form were sacks of raw cotton. The men were allocated a form and told that today they would be cotton picking.

'Dost tha know what to do?' the turnkey asked him.

'Aye,' said Titus as he sat down. He knew that all the seeds had to picked out by hand before the fibres could be carded, ready for spinning. It was women's work really, but he knew what he was about and took a handful to begin. When all the prisoners were seated and working, the turnkey went to a desk at the front from where he could watch them. No speaking or making eye contact with another prisoner was allowed and, as Titus worked, he found himself thinking of Jennet. He was worried about her. How would she manage fetching water and coal with little Peggy to look after as well? He hoped that George might help her out. He and Lizzie were good neighbours. Surely they'd keep an eye on her. And she had her family at Ramsgreave. He'd seen her father with her in the courtroom.

He mulled over the night of the riots. He wished that he'd kept closer to George, who must have got home safely. Perhaps it would have been better if he'd never gone in the first place. But he couldn't blame his neighbour for that. He'd been thinking of going anyway and George's invitation was only the excuse he needed. He felt strongly about the way that working folk were being treated and he was sure that the time for change was nigh. George had talked about going to America to begin a new life, but Titus thought that it was better to stay and try to change things here.

He worked diligently until a bell was rung and they were lined up to be taken for their dinner. The smell was appetising and Titus stood in line hoping that the meal would taste as good as it smelled. When his turn came, he was given a dish into which was spooned a generous portion of boiled beef and potatoes. He returned to his form with the dish and a spoon and ate with relish. It was clear that he wasn't going to go hungry whilst he was here.

After they'd eaten they were lined up again and allowed to walk round and round a closed yard at a distance of several feet from one another. They were still forbidden to speak and the turnkey stood at the centre and watched them for any transgression. Later, they were returned to their cells for supper and given another quart of gruel.

Titus ate and then sat down on the bed, waiting for the light to go out. He'd spoken only a few words all day and looked no one in the eye. He'd never been alone like this in his life before and he would never have imagined how hard it was to go a whole day without holding a conversation with another person. The thoughts and worries that he would have talked about were all bottled up inside him like a keg that was ready to explode. He wondered if he would go mad if he had to keep them all to himself day after day. They were not even allowed to whistle or sing whilst they worked. It had to be done in silence. And when one prisoner had begun to sing in his cell – though granted it was a radical song – the turnkey had banged on the door and bid him cease immediately. On the other hand, he'd been well fed and although the work was tedious, he supposed it could have been worse. Three months, he thought as the gas lamps fizzled out, leaving a pungent smell. Three months to the Assizes and then I'll be able to go home.

Jennet was given tokens for soup and a small allowance of coal. Her rent would be paid by the parish until Titus came to trial. It wasn't really enough to live on. Peggy needed her milk and porridge as well as soup, and, even though the weather was turning a bit warmer, the cottage was still icy cold because the sun never reached any of the windows. Jennet tried to light the fire only in the evenings, but even then one bucket of coal was nowhere near enough to last the week out. She knew that she'd never have managed without George's generosity. He was back working in the mill, helping to clear up the mess left by the rioters, so she went round every day to do a bit of cleaning and cooking for him, and to wash his shirts as she'd promised Lizzie she would. In return he shared his food with her and fetched her water from the well. She worried that she'd be found out, that people would talk, and that Mrs Whittaker would take the relief away, but he told her not to be so soft and to keep her mouth shut.

'Come and have thy tea with me,' he said one day after knocking on her door. 'I've summat to tell thee.'

Jennet picked Peggy up and went next door. George already had the kettle on and was spooning tea into the pot. There was a loaf of bread on the table, some butter, and slices of bacon in a pan ready to go on the hotplate to be fried.

'Where's all this come from?' she asked, sitting down on Lizzie's chair and reaching out to warm her cold hands at the fire as George fried the bacon. It smelled so good.

'I've come into a bit of money,' he said with a shy smile as he spooned generous amounts of sugar into their cups and sliced thick wedges from the loaf.

'How?' She wondered if it was something Lizzie had left to him.

'I've helped Mr Eccles out a bit with the spinning mules,' he said. 'He was unhappy about the way the threads kept breaking. I like tinkering about with the machinery and I solved the problem. He's paid me extra for my trouble. A tidy sum.' He grinned again, looking almost sheepish. 'I never asked for owt,' he said. 'I just enjoyed finding a solution.'

He stabbed the slices of bacon with a fork and put them on to the bread, dripping with fat, and handed a plate to Jennet.

'Peg!' demanded her daughter.

'Aye, there's some for thee an' all!' He laughed. 'She can eat it, can't she?'

'Let me cut it up first.'

Jennet resisted sinking her teeth into her own tea until she'd fed some morsels to Peggy. Then, when the child was happily chewing on a crust, she bit into her own butty. She thought she'd never tasted anything so good.

'I hope tha hasn't spent it all on this,' she said, wiping her mouth and feeling a little guilty.

'Nay, don't fret. There's plenty more.' He paused. 'I've been thinking of going to America,' he said as he poured more tea. 'Lizzie weren't so sure about it, but there's nowt to stop me now I have some cash.'

'America?'

'Aye.'

Jennet stared at him as if he'd suggested flying to the moon. 'But things are lookin' up here,' she said. 'Tha said that the mill'd be starting up again soon.'

'I could do better in America,' he said. 'I have ideas for how engines could be improved and I'd be well paid for 'em. And there's land to be had an' all. Good land for farming. A man could grow rich there.'

He handed her a cup and she took it, his hand warm against hers for a moment. He sat down again and continued to stir his tea.

'It's a long way,' said Jennet, feeling angry with herself for her disappointment. He was only a neighbour. She was someone else's wife, and Titus would be home before long. It was none of her business whether he went or not. But she didn't want him to go.

'Come with me, Jennet,' he said. She wasn't sure if she'd heard right. 'Come with me,' he repeated, looking her straight in the eye.

'I can't.'

'But tha can! I'd pay thy passage. We'd take Peggy.'

'And what about Titus?'

George frowned. 'Tha could leave him.'

'Don't talk daft,' she said. 'He's my husband and he's done nowt wrong. He'll be home as soon as this misunderstanding is sorted out.'

'He went off with them Luddites, the night of the riot,' said George. 'I know as I promised as I'd speak up for him, but I can't be certain that he wasn't involved in the breakin'. I know he said he were set against it, but that doesn't prove owt.' Jennet stared at him. He looked down and put his cup on the hearth. 'I've never been in bother,' he said. 'I'm a hard worker. Tha knows that. I'd look after thee and the child. I'd raise her like she were my own. I promise thee that. Say that tha'll think on it, Jennet,' he pleaded. 'I'd like nothing better than for us to go to the New World together and make a fresh start. It would be a good life.'

Jennet put her cup down and gathered up Peggy. 'I'd best go,' she said.

'Don't fall out with me over this, Jennet.'

No, she thought. There'll be no one to make thy dinner for thee if we fall out, or wash thy clothes. On the other hand she knew she would struggle to manage without him.

'Let's pretend nowt were said,' she told him. 'I'll see thee later.'

Back in her own house she wondered what on earth had possessed him to suggest such a thing. She'd given him no encouragement. At least she didn't think she had. Maybe she'd rested a hand on his shoulder, or touched his arm, or squeezed his hand as she thanked him for the things he'd done. But she'd only meant to show sympathy or gratitude. It hadn't meant owt else. Yet she couldn't deny that she found him attractive. It was hard without Titus, and they were spending a lot of time in each other's company. It was only natural that affection should grow between them.

She must be more careful, she thought as she put Peggy to bed. She mustn't give George the wrong idea. She'd promised Lizzie that she'd look out for him, not that she'd be a wife to him. And as for going off to America, that was out of the question. But she couldn't stop thinking about what he'd said. Was it possible that Titus was guilty of breaking looms? She didn't like to think so, yet she knew how much he hated the industrialisation. How much he wished that the machinery had never been invented and that they were back at Pleck Gate with the handloom and the spinning wheel.

And what if George refused to speak up for him at his trial? What if the judge and jury found him guilty? What then? Breaking machines was a hanging offence. She wished that she could see Titus and ask him to tell her the truth about what had happened that night, but visitors were not allowed, and the next time she would see him would be at his trial in August – if she could get to Lancaster.

'I'm right sorry if I offended thee yesterday,' said George as Jennet was frying the oatcakes for their tea on the hot griddle, flipping them expertly and piling them on to a plate to keep warm. 'Please tell me as we haven't fallen out.'

He looked worried and vulnerable as he sat at the table watching her. He'd had a wash after coming in from the mill and put on one of the clean shirts she'd ironed for him. He was a handsome man, she thought, and kind too. He'd only meant for the best when he'd asked her to go to America with him. She was sure of that.

'It's all forgotten,' she said. 'We'll not speak of it again.'

'If there's owt I can do for thee, tha only has to ask.'

'I know. I'm grateful. I'd miss thee if tha went,' she admitted.

'Tha'd miss me haulin' buckets from yon well.' He smiled to reassure her that he was teasing.

'Don't go, George,' she said. 'Don't go to America. At least not whilst I'm on my own. Wait until Titus comes home. It won't be long.'

'I don't know, Jennet.' He shook his head. 'Every day that passes, I feel like my life's slipping away. I could be making something of myself if I went.'

'I'm bein' selfish,' she said.

'Not thee, Jennet. How can tha say such a thing when tha's doin' so much to look after me? Lizzie would have been so pleased to see the way tha cares for me.'

'She was a good woman. She helped me when our Peggy were poorly and it's only right I return the favour.'

'Is it just a favour?' he asked. She looked into his blue eyes and found it hard to break the gaze. 'Tell me that there's not summat between us?' he said.

'There's nowt but friendship,' she replied.

'Tha's a poor liar,' he said as she put the tea on the table and they began to eat in silence.

'Shall we take Peggy up on the moor this Sunday?' he suggested after a while. 'Fresh air'll help put a bloom in her pretty little cheeks,' he said, winking at the child, who giggled at him.

'I don't know.' Jennet would have liked to go walking with him, but she had doubts. What if people saw them together? What if they talked? Besides, she usually went to see her parents on Sunday afternoons. But he looked so sad at her uncertain reply that she found herself relenting. 'We'll see,' she said. 'If the weather holds.'

She was sweeping her floors the next morning when there was a knock at her door. It was Mrs Whittaker.

'Please, come in,' Jennet said, wondering what she wanted.

'How are you, Mrs Eastwood?'

'I'm managing, thank you, Mrs Whittaker, just about. Although I could do with a few bob to get me to Lancaster for Titus's hearing.'

'That's what I thought,' she said. 'I think I may be able to help.'

'Sit down,' said Jennet, brushing at the bentwood chair with her duster even though it was already spotlessly clean. She watched as Mrs Whittaker straightened her skirt before she sat so as not to crease it too much. How she wished she could afford such a lovely gown. 'How can you help?' Jennet asked, too intrigued to be reticent.

'Well, you know how popular the soup is at dinner time. We could do with more help in the mornings, to prepare the vegetables, and I wondered if you might be interested in the work. You'd be paid, of course.'

'Well, the money would be welcome,' said Jennet. 'But what would I do with our Peggy?'

'Have you no family?' asked Mrs Whittaker.

'My mother lives up at Ramsgreave. It's too far to take her and fetch her back every day. And if I left Peggy with a baby-minder, I'd have to pay so I'd be no better off,' she explained.

Mrs Whittaker frowned. Jennet felt a bit sorry. She'd been so pleased when she came in with her offer and seemed frustrated that Jennet wouldn't take her up on it.

'I see your problem,' said Mrs Whittaker at last, unable to suggest a solution.

'Don't think I'm not grateful, or that I don't want to work,' said Jennet, afraid that her relief might be taken away because she'd refused. 'I'd be glad to do any work that I can do here whilst I can look after Peggy at the same time.'

'I don't know of any home work,' Mrs Whittaker said as she stood up to go. 'But come and see me if you find someone to care for your daughter and I'll make sure there's some employment for you.'

'What did she want?' asked George, having seen Mrs Whittaker leaving as he came back for his dinner. Jennet explained, but he didn't look convinced. 'Yon's a busybody,' he said. 'She'll have come around snooping on thee, checkin' up.'

'I don't think so,' said Jennet as she put the kettle on.

'Likes of her are meddlers,' said George, sitting at the table and lifting Peggy on to his knee. 'Mind what tha says to her.'

Jennet wondered if he suspected that the vicar's wife had heard talk of their friendship, but she said nothing. It really was nobody else's business and all she was doing was keeping her promise to Lizzie. That was all it was, she reminded herself as she set the table.

'If I could earn summat I could maybe put a bit by to get to Titus's hearing,' she said as they ate.

'Hast tha nowt?' asked George. 'Nowt hidden away that tha didn't mention to Mrs Busybody?'

'No. We had money from when Titus sold his loom, but it were all spent ages ago on food and clothes for our Peggy before we asked for the relief.' She watched as George broke up an oatcake and gave morsels to the child to chew. After each one Peggy held out her hand and demanded *more*. Laughing, George indulged her. He would have made a good father, thought Jennet, wondering how long he and Lizzie had been married and if there had ever been any babies. She didn't like to ask.

'Tha should have kept a bit back and said nowt,' he told her. 'They'd never have known.'

'It would have been dishonest.'

'Others do it.'

'I wouldn't want it on my conscience.'

'It would have meant being able to pay for the coach to Lancaster, though.'

'And then they'd have seen I had money and taken the relief away.'

'Aye,' said George. 'Tha can't win. Tha'd be better off in America.'

Jennet began to clear the table without replying. She didn't want to talk about that again.

'I'll pay for us to go to Lancaster,' he said after a moment.

She put the plates down and sat back on the chair, feeling tears well up. 'I'm that grateful,' she said, wiping her face on the cloth she was holding. 'I were plannin' to walk it.'

'Don't talk nonsense,' he said, reaching across to take her hand. 'I've plenty to pay for a couple of outside seats and the coach goes early enough for us to be there in good time.'

'I'll make more tea,' she said, not knowing how else to express her gratitude. It was a huge weight off her mind and her acceptance of the offer seemed to have pleased George, who grinned at her and continued to bounce Peggy on his knee.

'Put four sugars in mine,' he said. 'I have another bag stashed away at home.'

Chapter Seven

Early in the morning, on 23 August, Jennet and George stood in the market place as the sun rose, waiting for the coach. As she heard the shrill note of the guard's key-bugle in the distance, Jennet felt her stomach lurch. She hadn't slept much, but had tossed and turned in her bed for hours, imagining what it was going to be like, riding on the coach, arriving in Lancaster and going to the Crown Court. She glanced up at George. He seemed confident and composed and she would have liked to slip her hand into his for comfort.

She heard the rattle of hooves and the rumble of wheels on the cobbles before the brightly painted coach swerved into sight around the corner. The coachman had four in hand and he cracked his whip as he brought them skidding to a halt from their brisk canter right on the doorstep of the Old Bull. Jennet stepped back and was surprised to find that the other passengers surged past her. One gentlemen pulled open the door and climbed into the interior with its plush blue seats, whilst others began to climb the ladder to the wooden benches on the roof. For a moment she thought that there would be no room and they would be left behind and panic overcame her as she thought of Titus, all alone. She grabbed George's arm.

'We were here first!'

'Don't fret,' he said. He tapped the coachman on the shoulder and said something in his ear. The coachman nodded and grabbed the back of the coat of a man who was halfway up the ladder.

'Oy! Get down! There's folk here who've paid up front as needs to get on first! Then we'll see how many seats are left.' The man shook off his arm, but did as he was bid. 'Up tha goes,' the coachman said to Jennet, offering his hand to assist her.

It seemed very high when she got to the top and the coach kept rocking as people got on. She held tightly to the rail as she stepped over and lowered herself on to the bench. A moment later George was up beside her and she was thankful for his presence, to shield her from the wind and the curious looks of the other passengers.

The coach continued to rock as people climbed aboard, then the doors slammed, the bugle sounded and with a crack of the whip they lurched away, throwing Jennet backwards and making her gasp. She thought she would never catch her breath as they rushed down the street. The wind tugged at her bonnet and she clung on to George's arm, sure that the whole contraption would overturn and they would be flung off and killed.

He squeezed her hand and smiled. 'Just wait until we get out of town, then he'll let them fly.'

The woman who sat opposite to them clutched at her precious bonnet and looked terrified as the coach swayed and bumped over the ruts in the road. She exchanged a nervous smile with Jennet as they were flung up from their seats and down again with a thump that made her wince. They raced towards Preston with the bugle sounding as they passed people on foot, making them leap out of the way to the side of the road. Looking down, Jennet was thankful that she wasn't one of them.

They arrived at the Old Dog and George helped her down the ladder and took her inside the noisy inn to drink tea whilst the horses were changed. Then they were on their way again, galloping through the countryside, which passed in a blur.

Jennet began to relax a little as she became more confident that they were not destined to overturn. The day turned warm as the sun rose higher and whilst they waited at Garstang, George pointed out various landmarks to her – the Longridge Fells and the silver expanse of water in the far distance that he told her was the sea.

'America's over there,' he said.

They arrived in Lancaster in good time and followed the crowd up to the castle. It was a huge building, not like the one that Jennet had once seen at Clitheroe when she and Titus were walking out. It housed the prison too and Jennet gazed up at the pale, high walls wondering if Titus was in there. She was looking forward to seeing him, but afraid of how he might appear after all these weeks locked up.

She and George climbed the stone stairs into the room where the court was held. It was furnished in dark, polished wood and they sat on benches at the back, shifting up again and again as more people squeezed in, until Jennet was crushed so close to George that she could feel the pulsing of his heart. An usher, dressed in black, brought in the men of the jury and they sat on two special benches at the side of the court. Jennet saw that one of them was Mr Sudell. She thought the others were probably mill owners too. Someone called for silence and a man wearing a curly wig came in through a back door, up some steps, and sat down on a chair placed very high up, from where he could look down on everything.

'Judge Mr Justice Park,' whispered George. 'I've heard he's a fair man.'

The first of the accused was brought up from below and the charges against him read out, that he had unlawfully and riotously assembled with other persons unknown, at Blackburn, on 24 April, and broken into certain buildings with intent to break and demolish certain engines and machinery, the property of Mr Bannister Eccles.

The prosecution called John Kay, the constable of Blackburn, who told the court that on the night in question there was a great assemblage of people, many armed with home-made pikes, two with guns, and others with hammers and bludgeons. He said that when he and his runners arrived at the mill, they found the military were already there and being assailed with many stones, and that the mob was breaking the machinery inside the factory.

As each prisoner was brought forward, the constable and his runners took the stand to swear that they had seen them in the mill yard. *I saw*

Richard Entwistle there and he was striking at the power looms. I am sure he is the man. I have known him twelve months.

Some men said, in their own defence, that they were only onlookers and had done no breaking. Most had someone swear to their good character. Then Titus was brought up. It was odd to see him after being parted from him for four months. Jennet thought he looked clean and well fed and, as he glanced around the courtroom, she waved a hand to attract his attention, but he didn't see her and turned towards the judge as the charges against him were read out.

'I took no part in it,' he said. 'I'd been to the Reform meeting on the moor and I was swept along in the crowd. I was trying to make my way home. I live on Paradise Lane, opposite the mill gate, but I couldn't break out from the mass and I was forced into the yard against my will.'

George was called as a witness and had to fight his way down to the stand where he told them that he was Titus's neighbour and believed him to be a man of good character and that he had heard him say that he thought the breaking of the engines was wrong. No one else had agreed to speak for him and even to Jennet the words in his favour seemed flimsy and inadequate.

When all the prisoners had been examined, the judge addressed the men of the jury, telling them that it was not necessary for there to be proof of actual breaking for a man to be found guilty. It was enough that they were present, siding with the mob and encouraging them to do damage.

'That's not fair,' protested Jennet as the jury withdrew from the court and a babble of excited conversation filled the room. 'How can a man be guilty if he didn't do owt?' She stared up at George, who shook his head. The jury were already filing back to their benches and the judge was calling for silence, banging his gavel again and again.

The prisoners were brought back and placed in the prisoners' dock. They crowded in, looking solemn. Titus kept his eyes downcast and Jennet began to cry, wanting to run from the court with her hands over her ears so that there would be no need for her to hear what was to come. She knew that a guilty verdict was a hanging offence and she didn't know if she could bear to hear such a sentence passed on her husband. But the crush was so great that escape was impossible and the assembly fell silent to hear what the verdicts would be.

'Guilty!' pronounced the foreman of the jury in response to each name.

'Titus Eastwood.'

'Guilty!'

'No.' The chamber seemed to recede from Jennet. The polished mahogany benches faded to black and white and the roaring in her ears blocked out any other sound. She felt herself slipping away and desperately tried to keep her gaze focused on Titus, but the blackness over-whelmed her.

'Give her some air! Give her some air!' someone was saying and she wondered who needed air. 'Jennet? Jennet?' She was unsure who was calling her name. What did they want with her? The knocker-up usually tapped on the window. He didn't call her by name. How did he know her name?

Then she realised that she wasn't in bed, but was lying on a hard floor and it was George who was calling.

'She's coming to,' said a voice.

'Fetch a sip o' water.'

'What happened?' she asked as her senses began to return and she found herself in the hallway outside the courtroom.

'Tha fainted away,' said George.

She tried to sit up. She felt very odd. She'd dreamed that Titus had been found guilty. Surely that wasn't right.

'The verdict were too much for thee,' George went on. 'Here, take a sip o' this. Tha'll be all right in a minute.'

The liquid flushed fire through her, hot and cold at the same time. It wasn't water that he'd given her. Someone thrust a vial of foul-smelling salts under her nose and she roused herself enough to be helped to a bench.

'The only good thing is that Judge Park has called for leniency,' George was saying.

'They're not going to hang him, are they?' she asked, seeking reassurance.

'I'm sure they'll be lenient, given the circumstances, considerin' that folk are starving an' all.' George sat down beside her and took her hand. 'Don't tha fret, Jennet. It'll be all right.'

'What'll happen to him?' she asked, wishing that she hadn't fainted in the courtroom. She should have stayed strong to support Titus, to give him a sign that she loved him and was there for him. What would he be thinking now if he'd seen her carried out? She felt guilty that she might have worried him.

'Transportation to Australia'll be the worst outcome.'

'Australia?' She had no idea where it was. Even further than America, she thought. 'But they won't hang him,' she repeated. At least it would be some comfort if they didn't take his life, but if he was transported she knew she would never see him again.

She slumped on the bench and stared at the crowd milling around. She'd allowed herself to believe that Titus would be going home with her. It had been foolish. She realised that now. There were witnesses who'd said he was in the mill yard and although no one had seen him take a hammer to the looms he was guilty by association and that had been enough for the jury. They were determined to make examples of these men, to make sure there was no more trouble.

'When will we know?' she asked.

'Tomorrow probably.'

'But we'll be home by then. How will I find out?'

'Tha's in no state to get on the coach tonight,' George told her. 'I'll get us rooms.'

'Rooms?' she asked. 'You mean at an inn?'

'Aye. I know somewhere. It's not far,' he said. 'Dost tha think tha can walk?'

Jennet nodded. 'It were just the shock,' she told him. 'I'll be all right.'

George took her arm and tucked it through his before he forged a path through the crowd that was surging in through the door for later hearings. Outside, Jennet took some deep breaths to steady herself and then allowed George to help her down the steep cobbled street towards the quay. There was a salty tang to the air and she could hear seabirds circling and crying with raucous, persistent cries. The water was sparkling in the sunshine and the tide was high. In the distance a tall ship was disappearing over the horizon. Was it on its way to America? she wondered. Or to Australia?

George led her past the warehouses to an inn by the name of the Blue Anchor. It seemed respectable enough and she stood quietly by as he asked for accommodation.

'We've just a little 'un under th' eaves as might suit thee and thy wife,' said the landlord. 'Tha's lucky. It's t' last one we have, what with so many folk comin' up for th' Assizes. Dost tha want to see it?'

'I'll take it,' said George, pulling coins from his waistcoat pocket and counting them into the landlord's hand. 'She needs to lie down,' he added, nodding his head towards Jennet. 'Had a bit of a funny turn up at the court.'

'Someone she knew?'

'Relative. Found guilty. He weren't, mind, but tha knows what it's like.'

'Aye,' replied the landlord as if he'd heard it all before. 'Dost tha want dinner an' all?' He continued to hold out his hand and George added another sixpence. 'Tha can take it upstairs if she's feelin' poorly,' he told them as if he was bestowing some great favour.

George followed Jennet up the steep wooden stairs, carefully balancing a jug of ale and two bowls of stew.

'Sit thee down,' he said and she perched on the edge of the mattress. The chamber was small with a low, sloping ceiling and a tiny window. There was just the bed and no room for anything more. She wondered where George was going to sleep. Surely he didn't intend them to share the bed?

She took off her bonnet and shawl and George hung them on the row of pegs on the wall. Then she managed a few mouthfuls of stew, although she was far from hungry and her head still ached.

'Dost tha feel better now?' asked George. 'I'm sorry as I could only get the one room. It weren't my intention, but when the landlord presumed we were man and wife, I thought it best to keep my trap shut in case he refused us. Have a lie down,' he said. 'I'll go and take a walk around and see what I can find out.'

He pulled on his cap and took the pots with him. As she heard him clattering down the steps, Jennet slid the bar across the door. She felt safer with it locked and he would knock when he came back. She took off her best blouse and skirt and hung them up so they wouldn't crease before getting into the bed in her underclothes. She couldn't hold back the tears any longer. She hadn't cried in front of George, but now that she was alone she sobbed until there were no more tears to come. Then she fell into an exhausted but light sleep, waking with a start at each fresh and unfamiliar sound.

It was growing dark before George tapped gently on the door.

'Just a minute!' she called, struggling into her clothes before opening it for him. His breath smelled of beer and he handed her a cup of ale and a platter with oatcakes and cheese. He took off his cap and jacket, then his shoes and his waistcoat, and sank on to the bed with a sigh. Jennet offered him the plate but he shook his head.

'I've had summat downstairs,' he told her.

'What time is it?'

'Almost ten. Hast tha been asleep?'

'I think I must have been,' she said.

'It'll have done thee good.'

He watched her as she picked at the food. He showed no sign of moving and she wondered how to broach the subject of the arrangements for the night, let alone the use of the chamber pot.

'Prisoners are to be brought back into court tomorrow morning to hear their sentences,' he said. 'Dost tha want to be there?'

'Aye. I need to know,' she said. 'Even if it's bad, I need to know.'

'That's what I thought,' he said. 'So I've managed to get us places on a carrier from the Nag's Head at noon. He'll take us as far as Garstang and we'll get a different cart from there. It's all arranged.' He didn't say how many places he'd booked and she didn't ask. She knew that Titus wouldn't be coming home with them.

'I'm that grateful,' she said, putting her plate aside. 'I couldn't have done this without thee. I promise I'll pay thee back when I has the money,' she told him, not wanting him to think that she was willing to take advantage of his generosity.

'Don't trouble thyself, lass.' He put his hand on hers. 'I wouldn't have done it if I hadn't wanted to. I'll take these away,' he said, picking up the plate and cup, 'and give thee a while to ready thyself for bed.'

When he'd gone, she quickly used the chamber pot and then got back into the bed in her under-clothes, putting the bolster down the middle to separate them. When he came back up, George looked at what she'd done but made no comment. He took off his trousers and shirt and got into the other half of the bed. He'd brought a candle up with him and asked if she wanted it blowing out.

'Aye,' she said. 'We should try to get some sleep.'

Moonlight slanted in through the uncurtained window and Jennet could see wisps of cloud floating across the night sky. Even though she was still tired, her mind wouldn't let her rest and she relived the day's events over and over again in her head, wishing for a different outcome.

She could hear George's breathing beside her and knew that he was awake too because every so often he shifted restlessly.

'Jennet?' he whispered after a while. 'If the news is bad tomorrow—'

'Don't talk of it.'

'But if it's bad,' he continued, 'what will tha do?'

'I don't want to think on it.'

'But whatever happens, tha'll need somebody to care for thee. Tha can't manage alone.' She didn't reply. 'Promise me tha'll think again about coming to America with me, Jennet,' he said.

'No!'

'At least think on it,' said George. 'I know tha doesn't want to consider what might happen. I can't blame thee for that. But if they send him off to t' other side of the world tha'll be left alone with little Peggy and nowt to live on other than soup tokens and handouts.'

'I have my family.'

'But they can't afford to feed and clothe thee and the child as well,' he persisted. 'Be realistic, Jennet. Thy father's only a handloom weaver and he must be strugglin' same as everyone else. It wouldn't be fair to expect him to keep thee.' He paused and they lay side by side in the darkness for a while. 'I have plenty, Jennet, with what I were paid,' he said. 'Tha knows that I've grown fond of thee and I want to share my good fortune with thee. Nothing would ever be too good for thee and Peggy. Promise me tha'll at least consider it.'

'But I'm married to Titus.'

'No one need know. Tha could take my name, and Peggy too. We'd be man and wife.'

'Not in the eyes of God. It would be a sin.'

'Promise me tha'll think on it, Jennet,' he pleaded. 'I'd like nothing better than for us to go together and make a fresh start. It would be a good life.'

'I can't promise,' she told him, 'not now, not until I know what's going to happen to him.' She felt the tears well up as she considered what the verdict might be. How could she bear to lose him and to lose him like that – either with a noose

132

around his neck or in the filthy hold of some ship in leg irons for weeks and weeks? He might not even survive the voyage and she would never know what had happened to him. She choked back the sobs.

'Don't cry,' said George. She felt his hand close around hers. 'Don't cry,' he repeated as she felt the bolster pushed aside and he gathered her into his arms. 'Don't be unhappy, Jennet. I can't bear to see thee unhappy,' he whispered, his breath warm on her face as he smoothed back her hair.

Titus was crammed into the dock with all the other prisoners. Judge Park came in and took his chair with a flourish of his robes. He had some papers, which he shuffled and appeared to study as he waited for complete silence in the court. Then he looked up over the top of his spectacles and surveyed the crowd of anxious friends and relatives who filled every inch of the courtroom. Titus had already picked out Jennet. He was thankful to see that she was all right. He'd seen her carried out in what looked like a faint when the verdicts had been returned the day before and he'd been fretting about it ever since. But he could see her now, in her best bonnet, sitting beside their neighbour

George. He was relieved that someone was taking care of her.

After stretching out the taut silence for as long as he dared, Judge Park began to speak.

'There has, God knows,' he said, 'been a great pressure of distress in this county. But it cannot be permitted to individuals to carve out their own relief. You are the most deluded persons,' he told the prisoners, 'for you have been destroying the means by which you were to live, and taking out of the hands of those persons most disposed to serve you the means of doing so. It is of high importance that these things should not be tolerated, and that men guilty of such offences should receive a very severe punishment. The law has affixed to the crime, of which you have been found guilty, the punishment of death.' There was a sharp gasp from the crowd and the judge glared down, waiting for silence. 'It is not my intention, however, to carry that sentence into full effect and I shall recommend it to His Majesty to be pleased to pardon you so far as your lives are concerned. William Sutcliffe,' he began as he addressed each prisoner in turn. 'Guilty of high treason. Sentenced to death by hanging. Commuted to transportation. James Chambers. Guilty of high treason. Sentenced to death by hanging. Commuted to transportation ...'

Titus waited for his own name. It seemed that his life was to be spared, but that he would be sent to the other side of the world as a prisoner, to God only knew what fate. He glanced at Jennet. She looked ashen. How would she cope? What would she do? He was more worried for her than for himself. He would survive, somehow, but Jennet would be punished for something that was not her fault – little Peggy too. How he wished that he'd listened to her when she'd begged him not to go to that meeting. These cruel verdicts made it clear that Reform was long overdue, but would it have been better to leave the fight to other men, for Jennet's sake?

'Titus Eastwood.' He turned to the judge. 'Guilty of riot and loom breaking by association. Sentenced to death by hanging. Commuted to six months in the House of Correction at Preston.'

Titus stared at him, not able to believe what he had heard. He wasn't to be transported after all. Jennet was sobbing. George was trying to put an arm around her to comfort her, but she was shrugging him off. Titus felt a tap on his shoulder and he was led back down the steep stairs to the cells.

'Wait there,' he was told. 'Those of you going back to Preston will be put on the wagon directly.'

He sat down on the bench and found that his legs were shaking. He wanted to cry himself, but he also wanted to laugh. It was ridiculous, he thought, to be so overjoyed at the thought of returning to prison.

The other prisoners were brought down one by one. Everyone looked thankful that their lives had been spared. It had been a long and torturous night for them all as they'd contemplated their fates, and he wondered if Jennet had lain awake as long as he had, and where she'd slept. At least he knew she was safe for the time being and that was a huge weight off his mind.

Jennet cried with relief when she heard that Titus wouldn't be transported after all. She felt George's arm around her shoulders but she pushed him away. She couldn't bear his touch and the relief she felt was tempered by the guilt of what had happened the previous night.

'It'll be all right,' he whispered as the crowd began to surge past them towards the door. She was spared making a reply as he took her arm and guided her through the crush. She wondered if he thought she would still go to America with him.

'We'll get a bite of dinner. There's time before the carrier,' he told her as they went down the street to the Nag's Head where he found her a seat at the end of a table.

'Sit thee down,' he said, glaring at the others who were already sitting there and defying them to object. 'What dost tha fancy to eat?'

'I don't know. Whatever they have.' She wasn't hungry even though she'd been unable to eat any breakfast and hadn't eaten much the previous day, but she knew it was important to try to get something down. She didn't want to be fainting away again. She had to be strong now because it was up to her to care for Peggy until Titus came home and she was determined not to let her child suffer. Her relief quickly turned to anger as she considered the verdict. There had been no evidence against Titus and she was certain now that he'd done nothing wrong and had only been trying to get home to make sure she and Peggy were safe. These mill owners probably had the judge in their pockets. They were determined to make an example of everyone who had been rounded up that night, guilty or not, and there was nothing anyone could do. At least he hadn't been sent to Australia, she thought, trying to see the bright side, but another six months in the prison would do him no good and it wasn't going to be easy for her either.

George came back with two tankards of ale and told her that he'd ordered hotpot. 'It weren't too bad in the end,' he said. 'Six months. He'll be out by next spring.'

'I was so scared when they kept saying transportation,' admitted Jennet. 'I really thought he was going to be sent away.'

'I suppose it means tha won't be coming to America with me,' George said. He looked so sad that she reached out and laid a hand on his arm.

'I can't come, not now,' she said. 'If things had turned out different then I might have done, but tha must see that I can't go away and leave Titus. It wouldn't be fair.'

'Aye, tha's right, I suppose,' he said as the food arrived and was put down in front of them. Neither of them began to eat. Jennet stared at the dish with no appetite. They hadn't spoken about what had happened the night before. Maybe they both thought that if they didn't mention it, it wouldn't matter. But it did matter and the guilt of what she'd done almost overwhelmed her.

'Tuck in then,' urged George as he picked up his own spoon.

'Will tha still go?' she asked him.

'I think I must,' he said. 'There's nowt left for me here now.' She knew that he meant her.

'When?' She wasn't sure whether she wanted it to be sooner or later. She didn't know how she would manage without him if he went straight away, but she was afraid of what might happen if he stayed longer.

'I'll make enquiries about ships when I get back.' He ate in silence for a while. 'Tha can still change thy mind,' he said.

The carrier came to the door and shouted for all those who were going to Garstang. Jennet followed George out and got up on to the benches on the back of the wagon. It had started to rain again and she knew that this time her best bonnet would be completely ruined. It seemed only a small thing compared with everything else that had happened, but she found herself sobbing over it. George held her hand. She knew that he had no idea why she was crying and he didn't know what to say. Some of the other passengers cast sympathetic looks at her. They probably thought her husband was one of those being transported.

They rolled down the bumpy street into the centre of Garstang towards teatime. There were several other wagons pulled up around the market square and George went to speak to one of them as Jennet took shelter in the Royal Oak. She was soaked through and the landlady bid her sit by the roaring fire to dry off whilst she waited.

George came in to say that he'd secured them passage to Preston, but that it would be late when they got there. The last coach would have gone and there were no more carriers to Blackburn until morning.

'I'll walk,' she said, although she already felt so tired that she could barely stir. 'I just want to get home, and I can't ask thee to pay for more beds.' She knew that her reluctance was more to do with not wanting to share a room with him again rather than the money. She already owed him so much that she doubted she could ever repay it, and a few more shillings wouldn't make a difference.

'Well, he'll be going in a few minutes,' said George and, with her wet clothes clinging to her, Jennet boarded another wagon and they set off again over the uneven streets.

'Sure tha doesn't want to rest up 'til morning?' he asked when the carrier had dropped them in the middle of Preston.

'No,' she said. 'It's still light. We may as well get home.'

They walked in silence, Jennet feeling thoroughly miserable and tired. She just concentrated on putting one foot in front of the other as the miles went by. At last they saw the outskirts of the town in the distance and Jennet increased her pace. They would be back soon and she could get into dry things then go to bed. The gaslights were on by the time they trudged around the corner into Paradise Lane. It seemed weeks, not just a day since she'd left it. Wearily she put her key in the door and shoved it open.

'Dost tha want me to come in?' asked George.

'No. Thanks. I'm that pow-fagged I'll just get to bed,' she said, closing the door on him. She pushed the bolt across and stood, alone. There was no coal to light a fire to boil a kettle for tea, and she couldn't be bothered anyway. So she climbed the twisting stairs and stripped off all her clothes. She left them in a pile. She would deal with them in the morning, if they weren't too ruined. And if they were, well, she couldn't replace them so she'd have to go to church in her everyday clothes come Sunday. She climbed into bed and lay down, but when she closed her eyes she couldn't stop thinking about the previous night. She'd never meant it to happen. She didn't think he'd meant it to happen either, but when she'd begun to cry and he'd put his arms round her she'd felt such comfort in his touch that she'd clung to him, thinking that he only meant to reassure her. She couldn't remember when things had changed. She didn't think it was anything she'd done. He'd smoothed her hair back from her face and wiped her tears with his thumbs, and then he'd kissed her. She should have put a stop to it then. She knew that, but she'd needed someone, needed someone so badly. And she'd thought that she was going to lose Titus. Jennet sighed and turned over in the cold, damp bed. The gaslights had gone out and the darkness was all consuming. There wasn't even a hint of moonlight and the wind rattled the ill-fitting frames in the window.

Chapter Eight

A week later, Jennet heard George's door slam. It was barely light, and she wondered what he was doing out on the street this early in the morning. She got up from the bed and went to the window as she heard his footsteps pause at her door. She expected him to knock and, wondering what was wrong, she pulled her shawl around herself and hurried down. There was an envelope pushed partly under the door. She stooped to pick it up and then drew back the bolts and heaved the door open. He wasn't there. She stepped out on to the cold flags in bare feet and looked up and down the street in time to see him turning the corner with a heavy bag in his hand.

'George!' she called after him, not pausing to think that she was waking the whole of Paradise Lane. She saw him hesitate and ran after him, not caring that she wasn't properly dressed. He waited for her, looking uneasy, and she realised that he'd intended to leave without saying goodbye to her.

'I didn't want to wake thee,' he said, shifting his bag from one hand to the other. 'I left a letter.'

'Aye. I got it,' she said, realising that she was still clutching the envelope in her hand. 'Is tha goin'?'

'Aye. Carrier'll be here shortly and I don't want to miss him.'

'Then tha'll get the boat?'

'Aye. Out o' Liverpool. Name o' the *Manchester*. Sails on the early tide tomorrow.'

He settled his cap more firmly on his head and glanced back at his own house one last time. 'Keep an eye on our Lizzie's grave?'

'I will,' she promised.

'Aye. I'll see thee then,' he said.

As she walked home she couldn't hold back the tears, despite the twitching curtains of her neighbours. She knew that she'd come very close to falling in love with him, very close to agreeing to go with him to see what the world was like on the other side of that great expanse of sea. If Titus had been transported, or worse, she and Peggy would have been going with George this morning. But she'd made her choice very clear, and she knew that she would never see him again.

She closed the door, sat down at the table and sobbed. When she'd had a chance to gather herself and wipe her eyes on the corner of her shawl, she remembered the letter in her hand. It was limp and damp and she carefully eased it open. Inside there were two pieces of paper with writing on them. She stared at them for a while with no idea how to decipher what they said. Maybe it was the address of where he was going to in America, in case she changed her mind. She wondered who she could ask to read them for her. She knew that Mrs Whittaker could read, but what if the letter said things that she would rather the vicar's wife didn't know? In the end she put the papers back into the envelope and took it upstairs and hid it inside an old darned stocking in the bottom drawer of the tallboy.

She felt alone and vulnerable when she went to bed that first night after he'd gone. She'd become accustomed to the security of him being on the other side of the wall. Now there was no one she could knock for if she was poorly or frightened.

A new family soon moved in; Joe and Nan Sharples, with their three daughters and son, John.

'We've come to work in t' mill,' Nan told her. 'It's opening again soon. Dost tha live alone?' she'd asked her suspiciously.

145

'I have a little lass,' said Jennet. She was reluctant to say more. She hated to tell anyone that her husband was in prison.

The Sharples family made much more noise than George and Lizzie ever had. It seemed they were given to arguments behind closed doors. Jennet missed George. She struggled without him to help her. She had to go to the well herself, taking Peggy along with her, which meant she could only fill one bucket at a time. She found herself rationing the water to make it last so that she wouldn't have to go twice in a day. She had to ration the coal too. And as summer gave way to the late September chill, she began to dread the coming winter.

Peggy still looked pale. Jennet tried to get her out in the fresh air every day, but there was little to be had and the only time she felt that she could breathe freely was when she walked up to Ramsgreave. At least the effort made her warmer, but it tired her out and she sometimes felt that she was growing old.

Her family was finding it harder too. Although her father could get raw cotton now that the mills weren't taking it all, he found that after it was spun and woven, the value of the cloth was so low that he could hardly make any money. In the end he gave up weaving to tend his plot, leaving her mother and Hannah with nothing to spin for.

They were all sitting idle when she arrived at the door one afternoon. At least it was warm, she thought as she put Peggy on the rug in front of the log fire. Her mother filled the kettle and put it on to boil.

'She looks peaky,' she said, watching her grand-daughter.

Jennet looked at the pale, quiet child and knew that her mother was right. Peggy had begun to cough in the night, like Lizzie had done, and she was terrified that her daughter would become ill again.

'Tha could come home,' her mother said. She said it every time Jennet walked up, and every time Jennet was tempted to agree. She thought that the air would be better for Peggy out here and the child would be able to run outside and play in the garden, but they would be an added burden on her parents.

'Is Peggy gettin' enough to eat?'

'She has the soup every day. And I'm managing a bit of milk and porridge for her, but they don't give me much – though I wouldn't get anything if I moved back here. Besides, I've heard talk as things are going to get better, and I need to keep the house on for when Titus comes home.'

'Will tha stay for a bit of tea?'

'Is there enough?'

'Aye. We can always manage summat. Hens are still laying and there's some fresh greens from the garden.'

Jennet was grateful. Fresh food had become impossible for her to buy in town, but she worried about how her parents would manage when the weather worsened and whether they'd grown enough to keep them going through the winter.

One morning, Jennet heard unfamiliar noises in the street and went to the window to see what was happening. A big wagon, drawn by four heavy horses, had pulled up outside. There was something big and long, covered by a tarpaulin, loaded on the back of it and the carters were trying to manoeuvre the horses in the narrow lane to get in through the mill gates.

Joe, from next door, had come out to watch too. 'New power looms,' he said. 'We'll be startin' work soon.'

The street seemed to have come to life again. Instead of cowering in their homes, her neighbours came to their doors to watch what was happening. There was a buzz of excited conversation as people talked of work, thinking of wages that would enable them to buy food once again instead of having to live off handouts.

Soon, the mill gates stood open and the quiet that Jennet had grown used to was replaced by the thumping of the steam engine. They must be powering up the new looms, she thought, glancing out of the window and seeing the plume of thick grey smoke rising from the chimney.

A while later there was a knock on her door. No one pushed it open and called out so she went to answer it. Mr Hargreaves, the overlooker from the mill, was standing outside.

'Mornin'!' He greeted her with a smile, holding her gaze for a moment longer than was comfortable before he glanced back towards the mill. 'We're takin' workers on again,' he said.

'Titus isn't here.' She was sure that he knew that and wondered why he'd come.

'I were thinking of thee,' he said, still smiling. 'I know tha has nowt comin' in except from charity. I thought tha might be glad of work. I'll put a good word in for thee if tha wants a job.' He kept smiling at her, and seemed puzzled that she didn't agree straight away.

'I'm grateful,' she told him, 'but I've got Peggy.' She glanced round at the little lass sitting on the rug. The smoke from the mill chimney was creeping in through the open door and she was coughing again.

'Woman next door's a minder,' he said with a jerk of his thumb.

'Aye.' Jennet glanced towards her neighbour's door. She didn't tell Hargreaves that she heard the woman shouting at the children as well as slaps and the intense crying that followed until it all went eerily silent and she worried about what had happened. There was no way she would leave Peggy with that woman, but work was a better option than going hungry. She'd heard that the ladies in the town were growing concerned that their charity funds were running low and that they wouldn't be able to afford to hand out relief for much longer. If the bit of money she was getting stopped, she would have nothing to live on at all; the thought terrified her. Besides, she was beginning to hate standing in that soup queue every dinner time. It felt shaming and she was sure that people were talking about her and pointing her out as someone whose husband was in prison for loom breaking. Many blamed the breakers as much as the mill owners for the loss of their jobs and Jennet hated the enmity.

'I'll see if I can sort summat out,' she said, wondering if her mother would take Peggy, at least until Titus came home. She didn't want to leave her daughter at Ramsgreave – it would break her heart to be parted from her – but it was better than leaving her with a minder, and better than allowing her to go hungry.

'Come and see me then,' said Hargreaves. Jennet thought that he winked at her as he turned to go, but told herself not to be so silly. She must have imagined it, she thought as she closed the door.

'Dost tha want to go and see Grandma this afternoon?' she asked Peggy and watched as the child's face lit up.

'Peg. Ganma!'

She would be happy enough, Jennet told herself. She would be all right. There was no other choice and she must make the best of it.

'Tha knows I'll have her,' said her mother. 'I've nowt else to do now I'm not spinning and it might do her good. That town air doesn't agree with her.'

'What dost tha think about our Hannah coming to live with thee if there's work goin' in the mill?' said her father.

Jennet looked across the table at her sister.

'There's nowt for me here,' said the girl. 'If I can get work in Blackburn I'd be better off there.'

Jennet saw the pleading look in her sister's eyes and realised that this meant a lot to her. 'Blackburn's not as wonderful as tha might think,' she warned her, but she could see that Hannah was straining to get away and spread her wings a little.

'I'd help around the house,' she wheedled.

'All right. But just until Titus comes home,' she agreed. It wasn't what she would have wished for, but she and Hannah had always rubbed along all right, and with two wages coming in they'd be able to help out their parents as well.

Jennet kissed Peggy and told her that she would be back soon. Her daughter was playing with her doll and happily waved and called *Bye-bye* as Jennet left with tears in her eyes. She couldn't blame the child. Peggy was used to staying at Ramsgreave for a night or two and she didn't understand that this time her stay would be for much longer. It should have been easier to leave her when she was happy rather than if she'd been clinging to her neck and sobbing, but it wasn't and Jennet was quiet as she and Hannah walked back to Paradise Lane in the twilight.

That night they slept in the same bed and her sister's presence was familiar and reassuring. She woke twice in the night, sure that she could hear Peggy crying, but then remembered that her daughter wasn't there before turning over and trying to get back to sleep.

She was woken by the knocker-up rapping on the neighbour's window and went down to put the kettle on for tea. Today, she and Hannah were going to the mill to ask for work. As soon as they'd eaten, they put their shawls over their heads and shoulders against the rain and hurried across to the mill yard. The hooter was sounding and the familiar thrum of the engine pounded through the air as the machinery fired up. They waited until the rush of workers had clattered in over the cobbles before going to the door to ask for Mr Hargreaves.

'All right, Mrs Eastwood?' he greeted her with a wide smile. She half expected him to wink at her again, but he was staring at Hannah. 'Who's this then?'

'This is my sister, Hannah Chadwick. She's come to live with me. Tha said tha were takin' on,' she prompted him.

'Aye. That's right. Did tha find someone to care for thy little 'un?'

'She's staying with my parents for the time being. I need the work, Mr Hargreaves, what with Titus not being here.'

'Aye,' he agreed. 'I don't suppose tha knows how to work a power loom?'

'No,' admitted Jennet. 'But I can spin. We can both spin. We grew up spinning.'

'Aye, but not on the mules,' said Hargreaves. 'I'll tell thee what, though, I need workers in the carding room. Dost tha think tha can do that?'

153

'Of course,' said Jennet. The straightening of the cotton fibres between two wooden paddles ready for spinning was second nature to her. She wouldn't have any trouble doing that, even if it was a menial task.

'Come on then,' he said and they followed him inside and up an iron staircase. He pushed open a door and they walked into a room that was choked with cotton fibre. It floated in the air like a snowstorm. There were four huge machines with great rollers covered in raw cotton. Only one was turning and Jennet watched as the girl she recognised as the youngest daughter of her new neighbours spread the cotton evenly across it. The rollers turned on to teeth and, like a gigantic version of the two paddles she was used to using by hand, it combed the cotton into straight fibres and fed them out the other side in snakelike coils. The girl smiled briefly but never paused in her work, bending for the cotton, spreading it out, and checking that the coils weren't breaking. She was covered from the cap on her head to her bare feet in white fluff and she sneezed and wiped her nose on her sleeve as she worked. Once the coils had filled the tub she rolled it away to replace it with an empty one.

Another door swung open and a man came through. He hoisted the tub on to his shoulders and carried it away.

'Yon's t' spinnin' room,' said Hargreaves as the door swung shut on an even louder cacophony than the carding machine was making. 'I need workers to mind these other machines,' he said, 'or t' spinners'll be running out. Dost tha want t' job?'

'Aye. Yes, please,' said Jennet.

'Hang up thy shawls then, and take off thy clogs. They wear t' floor down,' explained Hargreaves, waving a hand towards the wooden boards. 'Tha should 'ave brought caps and aprons, but tha'll do for now. And roll up thy sleeves. Tha doesn't want 'em catchin' in the machinery. Young Mary here will show thee what to do. Tha needs to be here by six to begin. Tha finishes at seven and tha's half an hour for thy dinner. Sundays free, of course. All right?'

'Aye,' Jennet nodded, glancing at Hannah who was still watching the machine. It would be a very different life from the one they'd known growing up, she thought.

Mary showed them what to do to set the machines running. They frightened Jennet as they clanked into life and the big rollers began to turn, but she tried to stay calm and listen to what had to be done. She needed this job.

'Spread it evenly,' advised Mary. 'Spinners'll come and bawl at thee if threads aren't even.'

Jennet and Hannah toiled all morning and by the time the hooter sounded for dinner and the machines powered down they were both covered in cotton. Jennet's back and legs ached and she felt exhausted. She was hungry and thirsty and desperate to sit down. She slipped on her clogs, gathered her shawl around her and she and Hannah then joined the crowd surging out of the mill yard. She fumbled with the key to her door, thankful that she didn't need to go further, went in and sank with relief on to a chair, wondering how on earth she would ever manage to go back and work another six and a half hours.

Hannah sat down too and for a moment they didn't speak. Then Hannah poked at the banked-up fire to get a blaze going. Jennet fetched oatcakes and blue milk and they ate in silence, then sat by the hearth with their eyes closed, resting until the hooter summoned them back.

'It isn't what I expected,' said Hannah at last.

'Me neither,' said Jennet, understanding for the first time why Titus had always been so exhausted when he came home.

When Titus had been returned to the House of Correction he was taken to a different wing of cells and given a prison uniform, brightly coloured in red and yellow. He supposed it was to make him stand out in a crowd, should he manage to escape, although how they thought anyone could shin over the high walls was beyond him.

The next morning he was woken and given gruel. Then the turnkey came to let them out and Titus was taken down to an enclosed yard with workshops all around the perimeter. He saw that each one housed a handloom, not unlike the one he used to have in the cottage at Pleck Gate.

'Canst tha weave?' asked the turnkey.

'Been a weaver all my life,' he replied.

'There's weft and warp there,' said the man. 'Tha'll be paid a few pence for each cut, payable when tha leaves.'

Titus fingered the thread. It was good quality. He took off the red and yellow jacket, hung it on a peg, then rolled up his shirt sleeves and set to work threading up the loom. He didn't have to think much about it. The work was so familiar that his hands needed no guidance. It was daft, he thought, that he'd ended up in here because there was no work on the power looms, but now he'd been given handloom work instead. If he'd been able to stay at Pleck Gate and weave he would never have been in this mess, but here he was, provided with food and clothing and a bit of a wage to do what there'd been no call for on the outside. It made no sense. Them in charge seemed to make up their own rules as they went on and working folk were always the last to be considered.

He was sitting on the edge of his bed one evening when there was a gentle tapping on his open door. He lowered the basin of gruel he was drinking from to see who it was. It was unusual for anyone to observe such pleasantries. The man standing there was a stranger to him. He was tall and thin, dressed in a dark grey jacket with black trousers, a white shirt with a pale grey stock, and spectacles, which he kept pushing nervously with one hand. In the other hand he clutched a book. Titus wondered if he was some sort of clergyman, but knew he wasn't the Reverend Clay, who preached at them in the chapel on Sunday mornings.

'Excuse me,' said the man. 'I hope you don't mind me interrupting your tea.'

'What is it?' asked Titus, putting down the bowl on the floor beside him.

'I'm Mr Wright. I've been employed as school-master. I wondered whether you might care to learn to read.' He pushed the glasses up on to the bridge of his nose again.

'How dost tha know I can't read and write already?' asked Titus as he studied him further. He was younger than he'd first thought, even though his dark hair was thinning at his temples. He looked decidedly peaky, thought Titus. If that's what book learning did for a man then he wasn't interested.

'They have records,' explained Mr Wright. 'Of those who signed their name and those who made their mark. I saw that you made your mark, so I presumed ...'

'Aye. Tha presumed right,' said Titus. 'I never had an opportunity for book learnin'. Too late to start now.'

'No. No, it's never too late. I'm sure you could learn,' the man assured him eagerly. Titus gained the impression that he was short of custom, but he seemed genuine enough. Besides, he thought, he could do with some distraction. Every day here was the same monotonous routine. Up, empty chamber pots, wash, breakfast, work, dinner, work, exercise, work, tea, lights out. It never varied, except on a Sunday. They didn't work on Sundays because God would frown on breaking the Sabbath. So it was chapel and the long sermons about mending their ways, then dinner, which was sometimes meat and potatoes, then more walking around the infernal yard. After that they were allowed to do as they liked for a while. He'd seen some others go to the library to read a book or to get pen and paper to write a letter. It would be nice if he could write a letter to Jennet, he thought. Even though she wouldn't be able to read it, she'd know that he was thinking of her.

'All right,' he said at last. 'What do I have to do?'

'Well, if I may come in?'

'Aye. Come in. Make thyself at home.'

'Thank you.' The schoolmaster perched on the stool and opened his book. It was filled with marks and symbols and Titus knew that the decoding of them was reading. He already knew some words, but he didn't admit it. He knew that the words on the wall of the street where they lived said *Paradise Lane*. The gates of the mill had words on them too – *Dandy Mill* – and he knew figures, enough to make sure he was being paid the right money. But the book had too many marks for him to be able to make much sense of it.

'These are the letters of the alphabet,' said the schoolmaster, pushing at the spectacles again.

'Hast tha no other pupils?' asked Titus suspiciously.

'I've only just come. They say they might make a schoolroom in the future, but for the present I'm to visit the ... er ... prisoners in their cells.'

'All right. Go on then.'

'As I was saying: these are the letters of the alphabet. Some are vowels and some are consonants and we're going to learn the vowels first. There are five of them ... a, e, i, o and u.' He sounded them out whilst pointing to the symbols. Titus recognised a couple. There was *a* and *e* and *i* in his street name. Perhaps this wouldn't be as hard as he'd thought.

'How soon will I be able to do it?' he asked, wondering if he could grasp it all before lights out.

'Well, it depends. A few months maybe to get the basics, if you're a quick learner.'

'Months? I thought I'd learn it tonight.'

'Well, there is a lot to learn.'

'Go on then,' said Titus, looking at the book again. It was a challenge, he supposed. He had nowt else to do with his time and the company was welcome.

'Four bob?' asked Jennet, staring at the coins in her hand after the wages were doled out at the end of the week. 'And you've only paid our Hannah three and sixpence.'

'She's under twenty-one. So she's on t' childer's rate,' said Mr Hargreaves. 'Besides tha's only worked four days.'

'But Titus was paid more than twice this.'

'Titus were a weaver. And he were a man. Them's generous wages for women in the carding room,' he told her.

Jennet had expected a similar wage to the one Titus had brought home, but now she calculated that even though both she and Hannah were earning, there would be next to nothing left after they'd paid the rent and bought a bit of food. She slipped the coins into her purse and she and Hannah crossed the street. She felt as if she was walking through treacle, she was that exhausted. All she wanted was her bed. But there was a house to clean, oatcakes to be made, and shopping to be done before the market shut down for the night. At least it was Saturday and tomorrow there would be some respite. Church in the morning. Then they would walk up to Ramsgreave and she would be able to see Peggy. The thought of being able to hold her little girl in her arms and kiss those soft cheeks sustained her as they completed their tasks and eventually barred the door before going up the stairs to bed. Jennet thought that she'd never been so tired in her life.

It was bliss not to be woken by the knocker-up and Jennet lay in bed and listened to Hannah's gentle snoring for a while. It was a long time since she'd had the opportunity for a lie-in. She'd worked that hard all week and, even though she knew there was a lot to be done, she thought she deserved it.

It occurred to her as she lay there that her monthly period was overdue. She tried to reckon in her head the last time it had come. It had been a while, she thought. She'd had so much on her mind and been so busy that the weeks had passed without her giving it any thought. Her breasts were sore though, and that was usually a sign that it was due. She got out of bed and went to check that her rags were ready. They lay washed and folded in a corner of her drawer.

She went to have a good wash down before putting on clean underwear. Her Sunday best had never been the same since she got soaked coming back from Lancaster and the bonnet had been ruined. Even though she'd dried it out and put it carefully away she knew it was too spoiled to wear, and yet she couldn't bring herself to throw it out. She had to put her shawl on her head for church. They wouldn't let her in bareheaded. It was a sin. She had hoped to save a few pennies from her wages to buy a new bonnet, but now anything spare would have to go in her purse to take to her parents. She couldn't expect them to feed Peggy for nothing.

Hannah came yawning down as the tea was brewing. She wore a printed calico skirt and a nice jacket that she'd sewn herself, with a jaunty little bonnet that matched it. Jennet felt a frump as she walked beside her.

It was to be their first service in the new parish church. The stones were a soft yellow, still clean, yet to be sullied by the smoke-filled air, and Jennet thought it looked magnificent, although slightly marred by the unfinished churchyard, which was a sea of mud. And, like an island in its midst, the bell tower of the old church still stood, unusually quiet without the steady peal of its bells, which were being moved to the new building.

Jennet was eager to see inside. She tiptoed in under the wide-arched porch, beneath the high tower, afraid of leaving any trace of mud on the stone floor from her Sunday boots. Inside it looked huge. There was row upon row of wooden pews with coloured cushions and kneelers, and the vast windows let in enough light to make the space seem bright and airy. It all smelled new – of paint and plaster and the candles that were flickering on the altar. And flowers. There were vases of autumn flowers everywhere. She and Hannah took a seat at the back and watched as those with reserved pews swept in past them in their fine clothes. Hannah stared at the gowns of the ladies, whispering in admiration at the styles and colours as the organ played soothing music. It was all so beautiful, thought Jennet, and peaceful. Just what she needed after a week in the mill.

'Where's your little girl this morning? I hope she isn't poorly again?' asked Mrs Whittaker after they'd made their way out at the end of the service.

'She's with my parents at Ramsgreave. I got a job in the mill. My sister too. This is Hannah. She's come to live with me.'

'I'm pleased to meet you,' said the vicar's wife to a flustered Hannah. Jennet nudged her and Hannah made a clumsy curtsey, almost overbalancing; Jennet would have laughed except that she was worried that Mrs Whittaker might think her dishonest for not declaring her wages.

'We only started this week, but I got paid yesterday. So I won't be needing the soup tokens any more,' she told her.

'Don't worry. I'll make a note about it,' said the vicar's wife, fumbling for her pencil and notebook. 'What sort of work are you doing?'

'Carding. They have a huge machine.'

'Good. Well done,' she replied before moving away to speak to someone else.

After dinner, they walked up to Ramsgreave. When they got out of town they began to run, turning their faces to the sun and breathing in the clear air. They were hot and breathless by the time they burst into the cottage and Jennet ran to pick up her startled daughter and kiss her. Peggy began to cry and Jennet's mother took the toddler from her.

'Tha's frightened her with all that noise,' she reprimanded as she jogged the little girl in her arms and Peggy buried her face in her grandmother's shoulder. The happiness of the day plunged into black sorrow as Jennet also began to cry. She'd expected her daughter to rush to her with open arms. 'She'll be all right in a minute,' said her mother. 'Give her time. It's been hard for her.'

Jennet nodded and sat down on a chair at the table, hanging her shawl over the back of it. She had been looking forward to this all week, but it wasn't how she'd imagined it would be. At last, Peggy was soothed and her mother put her into Jennet's lap. Her daughter sucked her thumb and wouldn't look at her or say anything.

'She's cross with thee for leavin' her. She'll come round,' said her mother as she filled the kettle for tea, but it made Jennet wonder whether she was doing the right thing. She'd missed Peggy so much.

They chatted a while, Jennet and Hannah telling their parents about the mill and the carding room and the new church until it was time to go back home.

'Mam'll come back soon,' Jennet told her daughter as she handed her back to her mother. She kissed the child's cheek and Peggy stretched out her arms. 'No. Tha has to stay with Grandma for a while,' she told her. Peggy began to sob again

166

and Jennet wanted to take her home. 'Don't cry,' she pleaded with the child.

'Just go,' said her mother. 'She's tired. I'll put her to bed now. She'll be right as rain in the morning.'

Hannah chattered as they walked back, but Jennet wasn't listening and rarely answered. Her sister didn't seem to notice. Although she'd also been very tired at the end of each day, Hannah appeared to be relishing her new-found independence and she swung her bonnet in her hand as she headed eagerly back to Paradise Lane. Jennet's steps were forced. All she wanted to do was run back and get Peggy. Her daughter's initial rejection had broken her heart and then she'd had it broken all over again when Peggy hadn't wanted her to leave. She couldn't blame the child – it wasn't her fault. She wasn't old enough to understand. She couldn't really blame Titus either, even though a nagging anger had crept up on her – anger at him for getting mixed up in the rioting that night. She'd told him not to go to the Reform meeting. She'd known that no good would come of it, but he'd insisted. She partly blamed George too. Titus might not have gone if it hadn't been for him. And she was angry with George for taking advantage of her that night in Lancaster when she was so upset and only needed his comfort. She was angry with him for going off to America as well. He could have stayed. The mill was up and running again and he could have worked on his inventions here. Mr Eccles had paid him well and would have paid him more, she was certain. In fact, as she trudged home, it seemed to Jennet that she was angry with everyone.

'Do stop harping on, our Hannah!' she snapped at last, irritated by her sister's chatter. 'I'm tired out and it's work again tomorrow.' Hannah didn't reply but fell silent with a sulky look that reminded Jennet of Peggy. They walked into Blackburn in silence and went up to bed without a word, but Jennet lay awake for a long time, annoyed with herself at having fallen out with her sister.

She was woken by the insistent tapping of the knocker-up on the window. It was still dark.

'We're up!' she called as she pushed the blankets aside, knowing that if she hesitated she would fall back asleep and be late. Hannah grumbled, but got out of bed and took a candle down the back yard to use the privy. Jennet put the kettle on to boil and began to make the porridge as she yawned. She was not looking forward to another long day at the carding machine.

The hooter went and she pushed her bare feet into clogs and wrapped the shawl around her. It was a drab day and the mornings were becoming increasingly cold. Footsteps clattered past them as she turned to lock the door. The workers seemed to be mostly women now, although some men were running the power looms and most of the spinning mules. She trooped up the wooden steps listening to Hannah behind her, chatting with Mary from next door. They went into the carding room and slipped off their footwear and hung up their shawls. Mary called a farewell to her father and little brother, John, as they disappeared through the far door. Joe was a spinner and John worked with him as a little piecer, twisting together any threads that snapped.

The machinery clanked into life as the day began and Jennet reached for the cotton to spread on the roller. Daylight was breaking through the high windows and she saw that the sky was clearing. It would be a nice day after all. Not that she would see much of it. It would be dark again by the time they finished.

The work was monotonous, but not in the soothing way that hand spinning was. It was noisy, which left little opportunity for talking, and as she worked Jennet began to wonder what Titus's day was like in the prison. She'd never known anyone who'd been there so she had no idea what it was like, but the vision of him chained to a damp wall with only gruel to eat tormented her. He deserved better than that.

Suddenly her daydream was cut short by a shrill screaming. She, Hannah and Mary stopped, with cotton in their hands, and exchanged glances. The sound was coming from the spinning room and had been joined by shouting. Mr Hargreaves came pounding up the stairs yelling at anyone who would listen to shut down the pulleys. He slammed open the door of the spinning room and the sound increased.

'John!' gasped Mary, leaving her machine to its own devices. Jennet and Hannah also crowded the doorway. Jennet couldn't see what had happened, but one of the mules was powering down and Hargreaves was bellowing for help. John's father was on his knees under the machine and John was still screaming. His hand appeared to be caught in the machinery.

'Oh God,' whispered Hannah as Mary ran to help. 'I think it's taken his fingers off.'

'Tha should 'ave bin more careful!' Joe was shouting at his son, although tears were streaming down his face at the same time. 'Tha should've shifted thy hand faster.'

'It's too late for that now,' said Hargreaves. 'Run to t' Dispensary and see if the doctor's there,' he told Mary. 'This'll need more than a bandage.'

Mary pushed past them, came back from halfway down the stairs for her forgotten clogs, then clattered to the bottom.

'Get back to work!' Hargreaves shouted at Jennet and Hannah and the spinners who had abandoned their mules to come and see what had happened. 'And all tha little piecers, remember to keep thy fingers well away from t' movin' parts or this is what'll 'appen to thee an' all!'

Jennet went back to her work. Her hands were trembling as she reached for more cotton. The child had gone quiet and looked limp as Hargreaves carried him through the carding room to the stairs, followed by his grim-faced father. A huge rag had been wrapped around John's hand, but Jennet saw that blood was already seeping through it. It was no time to be complacent, she told herself, rolling her sleeves further up her arms. She must keep her mind on her work and make sure that the same thing didn't happen to her. She watched the huge roller with a new terror as she spread the cotton.

'Be careful, Hannah!' she shouted as she saw her sister reach across and her sleeve came perilously close to being trapped.

At last, dinner time came and the machinery ground to a halt. The workers were unusually quiet as they went down the stairs and across the yard. The accident had shocked everyone.

On the way out, they passed John's father coming back in through the mill gates.

'How is he?' asked Jennet.

'Doctor's seen him,' he said. 'Our Nan'll tell thee more. I need to go and sort out the machine afore work begins again.'

Jennet told Hannah to get the dinner ready and she went to knock on next door.

'Come in! It's open,' called Nan's voice. Jennet pushed the door and saw John sitting in the chair by the hearth with a big bandage around his hand and his arm in a sling. He looked deathly pale and was rocking a little, trying to comfort himself.

'How is he?' asked Jennet.

'Doctor's patched him up, but he wants us to see another doctor – a surgeon. Two of his fingers are so mangled he thinks they'll have to come off, but he wants this Dr Barlow to have a look first, in case he thinks he can save 'em.' John whimpered as they spoke. 'He lives up on Preston Road,' she said. 'Usually charges, but Dr Scaife's going to ask if he'll do it for nowt.'

'It would be best if he can keep his fingers,' agreed Jennet, wondering what would happen to someone who only had the use of one hand when all the work was so dependent on dexterity. 'What happened? I only heard him screaming.'

'He were careless,' said Nan. 'He were piecing threads and didn't move his hand quick enough. Yon mule trapped his fingers in its workings.'

'It's dangerous work,' said Jennet.

'Aye. Folk need to be careful, but he's a dreamer is our John. He needs to learn to keep his mind on what he's about.' Nan seemed unsympathetic, but Jennet could see that she was badly shaken and upset. 'Tell Hargreaves I won't be back this afternoon, will tha?'

'I'll tell him,' promised Jennet. 'And I hope this Dr Barlow will see John, and that it'll be good news.'

She gave John an encouraging smile, and vowed that she would never, ever allow her Peggy to get a job in the mill. She hadn't nursed her daughter through the scarlatina to have something like this happen to her.

She went back early to give Hargreaves Nan's message. He was in his little room, sitting with his feet up on a hot pipe and eating a potato pie.

'Come in,' he said when he saw her. 'Fancy a bite?' He held out the pie. It smelled good, but Jennet shook her hand. There was something too intimate about the gesture and it troubled her. 'What can I do for thee?' he asked.

'Nan says she's to take John to see the surgeon. She won't be back this afternoon.'

Hargreaves frowned. 'I hope she knows her pay'll be docked, and I'm going to have to find someone else to mind her looms,' he grumbled. He finished the pie, brushed the crumbs from his hands and wiped his mouth. 'Dost tha fancy havin' a go?' he asked her.

'On the power loom?' asked Jennet.

'Aye. Tha knows what's what. And these new looms do it all for themselves. All tha has to do is watch 'em.'

'Well … I'm not sure …'

'Come on,' he said standing up and grasping her hand. 'There's time for me to show thee afore t' others come back.'

Jennet had no choice but to go with him into the weaving shed. She tried to pull her hand free without making too much of a fuss, but he was holding it firmly and it made her feel uncomfortable.

'Now then,' he said as they approached the big loom. 'Tha's familiar with a handloom?'

'Of course,' she said. She'd grown up watching her father work and he'd even taught her how to use the loom once her legs were long enough to reach the treadles. But this machine was nothing like it. It was much bigger and was made from shiny metal rather than wood.

'This 'ere's the newest thing,' said Hargreaves. 'In fact, we should be grateful to them Luddites because these new 'uns are much better than what we had afore. And they're easy enough for a woman to work 'em.' He released her hand but took hold of her arm and drew her nearer to the machine. 'Nowt to be scared of,' he went on. 'It'll not bite thee. Now, tha understands about warp and weft?'

'Aye, of course.'

'And tha's seen folk beamin' up thread?'

'Aye.'

'Well, next time one's empty I'll show thee what to do and tha can have a go thyself. If tha shapes up I might think on giving thee a couple of looms to run to see how tha gets on – as a favour.' He took her arm again, brushing his fingers against her breast in a way she knew wasn't accidental. 'I know tha needs a better wage, so things may work in thy favour if this Nan turns out not to be a reliable worker,' he said. 'Now then.' He turned back to the loom. 'When th' engine starts up and we flick this switch here, them pulleys will set going and bring power to t' loom. These frames'll go up and down and yon shuttle goes back and forth without t' need to touch owt. All tha needs to do is watch out and add new bobbins as each one empties and mend any broken threads. It's that easy.'

Jennet stared at the machine. It didn't look easy. It looked complex, but she was sure that she could master it.

'Weavin' wages is a lot better than cardin' wages,' repeated Hargreaves as he watched her lean over the machine. 'If tha wants to give it a go this afternoon, I'll stay an' help thee.'

The hooter sounded outside and Jennet knew that she must make up her mind quickly. It couldn't be more frightening than the carding machine, she reasoned, and more money would be welcome. But she was unsure about Hargreaves. There was something about the way that he kept staring at her that unnerved her. She didn't like him. But it wouldn't do to get on the wrong side of him either, and she was left with the impression that she didn't actually have much of a choice at all.

'I'll give it a try,' she said.

'Good lass! Hang up thy shawl and when it powers up I'll show thee properly what tha has to do.'

The workers clattered back in and as Hannah passed, Jennet explained that she'd been promoted to Nan's job for the afternoon. All around her she heard the looms start up until the cacophony of noise was deafening. It was far, far worse than it had been upstairs in the carding room. Only the four looms where she was standing remained silent as she waited for Hargreaves to come back.

'Now then!' he shouted as he flicked the switch and the pulleys began to raise and lower the heald frames. 'Watch this!' Jennet stared as the shuttles shot back and forth and the machine began to weave cotton.

'Tha needs to watch it for any flaws,' said Hargreaves. 'If owt's wrong, tha mends the thread, or puts a new bobbin in the shuttle. But be quick about it. We need to keep 'em runnin'. Dost think tha can manage?'

'Aye,' said Jennet. 'I'll give it a go.'

'Good.' He pressed his hand against her lower back as he moved away. She said nothing, but kept her eyes on the cloth, trying to remember everything that she'd been told.

By the time the day was finished Jennet was beginning to feel more confident. The machines were clever, she thought. It would have taken Titus days to weave as much cloth as had been produced in a few hours, and it was good quality too.

'It were like magic,' she told Hannah as they ate their tea. Her ears were still ringing from the noise, but she couldn't stop talking about the power loom. 'Once it's threaded up it does it all by itself!'

'I wouldn't mind having a go. It sounds better than the carding machine,' said Hannah as she picked fluff from her skirt and threw it on to the fire.

'I'll think I'll pop next door and see how John is,' said Jennet. 'If Nan's back tomorrow I'll be back in the carding room myself.'

She left Hannah to clear up and went to tap on the door before putting her head round it. Her neighbours were sitting at their table.

'I won't disturb thee. I just wondered how John was.'

'Come in,' said Nan. 'Shut yon door. Tha's makin' a draught. Cup o' tea?'

Jennet shook her head. 'Just had one,' she said. 'Did Dr Barlow see him?'

'Aye. We didn't even 'ave to go up the hill. He came down to t' Dispensary. Right nice chap he were too. Treated us proper. He examined John's hand and said he'll try to save it. We've to go to his surgery tomorrow mornin' and he'll sew it up and bandage it proper.'

'I saw thee workin' on Nan's loom,' interrupted her husband.

'Aye. Hargreaves persuaded me to have a go. It weren't as hard as I thought.'

'Aye, well, don't get any ideas. Nan'll be back at work soon enough.'

'Stop it, Joe. She's done nowt wrong.'

'I'm not after taking Nan's job,' said Jennet, shocked at the way he was glaring at her.

'Aye, well, just think on,' he said, turning his attention back to his food.

'I'd best go,' she said and hurried to get out of the tense atmosphere. Joe's accusations had hurt her.

'What's up?' asked Hannah when she got back in.

'Him next door's a funny beggar,' she said and explained what had happened.

'Take no notice,' said Hannah. 'Mary says as her father's a moody one. I don't think she likes him much.'

'Does she not?' The idea was a surprise to Jennet. She loved her father. He'd always been kind and caring and she'd never considered that other fathers might not be the same.

Chapter Nine

The turnkey asked Titus if he would teach a young lad to weave.

'If he has a trade, it'll help him when he gets out,' he explained as he stood at the door of the workroom with the scrawny boy beside him. 'His father were a ne'er-do-well, and his father afore him, but if we can teach him, he might stand a chance of making summat of himself.'

'Aye, he can come in,' said Titus, studying the lad. He was bright-eyed and looked capable enough. 'What's tha name?' he asked.

'Samuel.'

'What dost tha know about weaving?'

'Nowt,' said the lad, eyeing the loom with interest.

'So what's thy father's trade?'

'Trade?'

'Aye. What does he do for a living?'

'Nowt. They hanged 'im a couple o' years ago.'

The lad sounded so indifferent that Titus couldn't reply for a moment.

'Was he guilty?' he asked, thinking of his own narrow escape.

'I 'spect so,' said the lad. 'He were always thievin' summat. Only way he could keep us all fed.'

'So tha's got brothers and sisters?'

'Aye. Ten of us still livin'. Some died, but I don't really remember 'em.'

'And what about thy mother?'

'She's in the workhouse, with the youngest two. I've another sister and brother who've been apprenticed at Quarry Bank Mill. I hear as it's lovely down there. As for the rest of 'em, I'm not sure where they are.'

'And what did tha do to end up in here?' asked Titus, wondering how the lad managed to seem so cheerful given his circumstances.

'I were caught pickpocketing.'

'Well, let's see if we can't make a weaver out of thee,' said Titus. 'Come and sit here beside me and I'll show thee what to do.'

Titus had always hoped that one day he might have a son who he could teach his trade to, as his own father had taught him, but he knew in his heart that there would soon be no call for hand-loom weavers. It would all be mill work, and much as he hated the idea of men and women being at a master's beck and call for twelve or thirteen hours a day, he knew that things could never return to the way they'd been. It was progress, or so they said, and no matter how much he argued against it or protested about it, he'd realised that there would be no stopping it. But at least if the lad learned about warp and weft and how to thread up a loom then he would have some skills that he could take with him into the mill. If he knew how to hand weave then he would soon catch on to the power loom and with luck he'd be able to make an honest living.

'The first thing tha needs is warp,' he told Samuel. 'Warp is these threads here that tha has to attach to the loom. I can't show thee how until this piece is finished, so for the moment I'll teach thee about weft. Weft is what's attached to yon shuttle and it goes under and over each strand of warp. And to do that tha has to move this frame with the treadle, like this.' The lad bit his lip in concentration and watched as Titus sent the shuttle backwards and forwards and then pushed up the beater to pack the threads together to make a nice even cloth. 'Think tha can do it?' he asked as he moved aside to let the lad have a go for himself.

'Aye.' Samuel sent the shuttle slamming back and forth whilst working the frames. He did well for a first-timer and Titus was pleased. He wondered if the schoolmaster gained as much pleasure out of teaching him to read. He was getting the hang of that now. He knew nearly all his letters and could make out simple words like *cat* and *dog* in the little book that Mr Wright had lent him.

Next morning, Hargreaves came up to the carding room and called Jennet to follow him down to the weaving shed.

'I need reliable workers,' he grumbled. 'I'll be the one who gets it in the neck if looms is standing idle and Mr Eccles comes by.'

'Nan's had to take John to the surgeon,' explained Jennet, although she was sure that Hargreaves already knew. He didn't reply but led the way to the loom and set it going.

'I just want thee to watch this one for today,' he told her. 'But as soon as tha has the hang of it, tha'll be workin' on two, or even four if tha has aptitude. Don't look so worrit!' he laughed. He dropped an arm around her shoulders and squeezed her. Jennet pulled away. 'If tha can watch 'em all there'll be good money,' he said, rubbing his fingers together. 'I know that tha needs a little lookin' after, what with thy Titus being banged up an' all.' He grinned and Jennet looked away.

She was determined to do nothing that would encourage him – although accepting work on the loom and the increase in pay that went with it was probably encouragement enough.

'I'll leave thee to it, then,' he said. 'I'll not be far away if tha gets into any bother.'

Jennet glanced at the other women who were working in the shed. Those who were running several looms were constantly on the move between them, checking that all was well. They wouldn't be able to spare a moment to help her out and she realised that she was stuck with Hargreaves and his over-familiarity if she needed any advice. She shrugged her shoulders at the thought of his arm around her. She should have said something, she knew, but she needed the work and it might be worse if she put his back up. It was probably just his way and he was only being friendly. At least she hoped so. Her father had warned her that she might have problems now that she was alone.

'Watch out for men comin' sniffin' round,' he'd told her, although he hadn't elaborated on what she should do if it happened.

At dinner time she waited for Hannah to come down the stairs so that they could walk home together, but when her sister appeared she was deep in conversation with Mary and didn't seem to notice that Jennet was waiting. Jennet followed them across the road and went in to get dinner ready.

'Hast tha got any rags? I've forgot to fetch mine,' said Hannah, coming in the back door from the privy.

'Upstairs in the bottom drawer,' Jennet told her sister as she made the tea. Listening to Hannah's footsteps on the creaky boards above her and the sound of her pulling out the drawer and then slamming it shut, Jennet remembered that her own period still hadn't come. Could she be pregnant, she wondered as she sat down and spooned sugar into her tea. She tried to remember the last time she'd had relations with Titus. She was sure it couldn't have been long before the night of the riot. But that was nearly six months ago and if she'd fallen pregnant then she would have been sure by now. She would have been showing. Of course, if she'd fallen pregnant the night she slept with George in Lancaster it was a different matter. She pushed the thought aside. Perhaps it was just all the worry and the unaccustomed work. It would come in a day or two. She was fretting about nothing.

She heard the door open and close next door and voices came through the wall. Nan must be back with John. She wouldn't bother them now, she thought. She'd call after work and see how the child was, although she was reluctant to go at all after the way Joe had spoken to her. Maybe she'd just ask Hannah to ask Mary. She didn't want to cause any trouble.

When she got back to the mill, Hargreaves was examining the cloth on her loom.

'Tha's let a flaw through there,' he told her, pointing it out. 'That'll come out o' thy wages.'

'But I'm still only learning,' she protested.

'Can't be helped,' he said. 'Cloth's worth less wi' flaws. Perhaps tha needs a little more tuition.' He smiled. 'I don't mind stayin' a bit late to teach thee. It'll be nice and quiet when t' others 'ave gone home.'

'Not tonight,' she said. She really didn't want to stay behind in the mill on her own with him.

'What about tomorrow, then?'

'I'll see,' she promised, to pacify him. She didn't want to stay tomorrow either, but it gave her time to come up with some other excuse. Besides, if Nan came back to work she wouldn't even be in the weaving shed.

'Tomorrow it is then. I'll look forward to it.'

She tried to be more careful with her work that afternoon. It was no use being promised more money only to lose it through carelessness. The time passed more quickly than it had in the carding room and she was surprised when the day ended. Avoiding Hargreaves, she got her shawl and hurried home, hungry for her tea and wishing that there was something more tasty than the potato hash she'd left ready to be warmed up.

'Did Mary say how John was?' she asked Hannah.

'She said his hand's all bandaged up and he's to go back next week. Doctor'll know then if his fingers have been saved.'

'Poor lad,' said Jennet. 'I'll not bother them now.'

The next morning, Jennet arrived at the mill to find Hargreaves and Nan shouting at one another as they stood either side of one of the looms.

'It's my job! I'm a weaver!' Nan told him as he stood with his arms folded and shook his head.

'Not any more, tha's not. Tha can work in the carding room, or tha can go home. I need weavers as I can rely on to turn up every day, not just when it takes their fancy.'

'But tha knows why I wasn't here. Tha knows I had to take our John to see Dr Barlow. I sent messages.'

'Aye. And how didst tha think these looms were goin' to run without thee? They might be power looms, but they need watchin', tha knows.'

'I know that. I'm not stupid! But what were I supposed to do? I had to tend to our John and take him to see the surgeon.'

'Well, I'm sorry for t' lad, tha knows, and I 'ave some sympathy,' said Hargreaves, not looking the slightest bit sympathetic. 'But it's my job to keep these looms weavin' and I've set someone else on.'

'Who?' she demanded, and Jennet watched as both Nan and Hargreaves looked in her direction. 'Her? What does she know about weavin'?'

'I'm teachin' 'er.'

'Oh, I don't doubt it. And what's she learned so far? How to suck up to thee for favours?'

'That's not fair,' said Jennet, going across to the loom as Nan glared at her.

'Pleased wi' thyself, is tha, stealin' my job? And all the time comin' round and askin' about our John like tha cared. Checkin' as I wasn't comin' back to work so tha could sweet talk thy way into runnin' my looms, more like. Joe was right about thee!' she shouted, poking a finger towards Jennet's chest. 'Tha's a smarmy little tart, lookin' for a fancy man whilst tha husband's in prison!'

'That's not true,' said Jennet, shocked at the outburst and horrified at the anger and vitriol blazing in the woman's eyes. She'd done nothing wrong. Why was Nan so angry? 'I were only helpin' out whilst tha were away. I don't want to take thy job. I'm happy to go back to the carding room.'

She turned to walk away, but Hargreaves reached out and caught hold of her wrist.

'Not so fast,' he told her. 'Tha'll work where I says. And I says that's on a loom. This 'un 'ere can shut 'er trap and take 'erself upstairs or go 'ome.'

'Then I'll go home. And I'll take my family along with me!' She crossed to the bottom of the stairs. 'Mary!' she bellowed. 'Get thy dad and come down here!'

Jennet waited, her wrist still in Hargreaves' firm embrace, until Joe and Mary came down the steps.

'What's the matter?' asked Joe with a surly glance at her. 'Will she not give it up?'

'It's 'im as won't give it up!' accused Nan, pointing at Hargreaves. 'He's the one as is insisting the little tart takes over my looms, even though she knows nowt, except how to twist a man around 'er little finger. Says I've to do cardin' or go home. Well, I'm goin' home and tha can come an' all. Tha's not workin' in a mill as treats folk like this!'

'Hang on, Nan,' said Joe. 'We can't all just walk out. What will we live on?'

'Well, trust thee not to stick up for me, either!' she blazed at him. 'Fat lot o' good tha is!'

'This is all because o' thee!' Joe rounded on Jennet. 'If tha hadn't taken our Nan's job whilst our John were poorly there'd have been no problem.'

Jennet stared at him. She had no idea what to say. It was so unfair to accuse her of taking someone else's job and she'd already said she was more than willing to go back upstairs, but Hargreaves still had her caught by the wrist.

'Holdin' tha hand an' all,' said Joe with contempt. 'Little slut.' He turned away as if the sight of her hurt his eyes and spoke to Nan. 'Go home,' he told her. 'I'll sort it out.'

The threat in his voice sounded real and a jolt of fear ran through Jennet. She not only had to work in the same mill as this man, but she had to live next door to him as well. She was fairly sure that whilst she was here, Hargreaves would ensure that no harm came to her, but what about after work? What about when there was just her and Hannah?

'Best get back to work if tha wants to keep thy job,' Hargreaves told him.

'Don't think this is the end of it,' Joe said, then cast another disparaging glance towards Jennet. 'Tha'll regret this,' he warned her before he grabbed Mary by the arm and they went back up the steps.

Jennet was trembling and on the verge of tears as Hargreaves led her back to the loom.

'Don't fret,' he told her, squeezing her hand. 'Any trouble and tha must come straight to me. I'll not let 'em bully thee.'

She nodded and wiped her eyes on the heels of her hands. She wanted to go after Nan and plead with her not to be angry, to explain that it wasn't her fault, but she knew that if she didn't do what Hargreaves wanted, he would lay her off and she would never get relief again because no one would believe that it wasn't her own fault that she'd lost the job.

Chapter Ten

'Mary's goin' to watch Mr Green's balloon ascent on Sunday afternoon. She's asked me to go with her,' said Hannah as they ate their tea.

'Mary? From next door?' asked Jennet. 'When did she mention that?' She wondered how much Hannah knew about the row with the neighbours. She'd been in the carding room when it happened, so hadn't witnessed the exchanges and Jennet hadn't burdened her with it at dinner time. It was her own problem and it was up to her to deal with it.

'This afternoon. She were tellin' me about it at work. Why?'

'It's just that there were a bit o' trouble earlier on when Nan found out that Hargreaves had given me work on the looms.'

'I thought tha looked a bit out o' sorts. What happened?' she asked.

Jennet gave her a brief explanation, leaving out the threats that had been made by Joe. She'd calmed down a little since and thought that it was probably all talk in the heat of the moment and that he didn't mean her any real harm. But she was unsure that he would be keen on a friendship developing between Hannah and his daughter.

'Mary says he's a bully at home as well,' Hannah told her, leaving Jennet to wonder when all these exchanges took place. She could barely hear herself think at the mill, never mind carry on a lengthy conversation. 'She doesn't like him.'

'He's still her father and she has to do as he says,' Jennet reminded her, 'so don't be too upset if tha finds she's not as friendly in the future.'

'He can't stop us going to this balloon ascent together.'

Jennet didn't reply. She knew that her sister could be stubborn. Then she asked: 'What about going home?'

'There's no point me coming to live in town if I've to trail home every Sunday afternoon,' complained Hannah. 'Tha can go to see Peggy. Tha doesn't need me.'

'They'll be sorry not to see thee.'

'Well, they saw plenty of me when I were livin' there. And it's only once.'

Jennet continued to eat. It wasn't for her to say what Hannah could and couldn't do. Hannah was her younger sister, but she wasn't really her responsibility. If she wanted to go to this balloon ascent with Mary, it wasn't for her to forbid it. She just hoped that it wouldn't make matters worse.

The next morning Jennet lingered until she heard the neighbours' door slam shut, and it was only when she was sure that Joe and Mary were well ahead of them that she called to Hannah to come on. She was locking the door behind them when she heard her sister calling to Mary to wait for her. Mary stopped and looked round, but her father took hold of her arm and pulled her through the mill gate, muttering. Hannah rushed after them and Jennet would have liked to follow her up the stairs and warn her to be careful, but as soon as she walked into the mill, Hargreaves appeared.

'Good morning, Jennet!' he greeted her. 'Dost tha think tha can manage two looms today?' With a glance towards the stairs, Jennet had no option but to follow him into the weaving shed. 'Shout for me if tha gets in a fix,' said Hargreaves as he watched her take off her shawl and roll up her sleeves. 'I'm never far away.'

Wasn't that the truth of it, thought Jennet as she set the first loom in motion. He seemed to hover around her like a bad smell, touching her arm or squeezing her hand. She was beginning to hate him.

She settled to her work. It needed all her concentration to make sure that both the looms were running without any snags. It kept her busy until dinner time and on the occasions that Hargreaves did come out to check on her work, she ensured that she kept one of the looms between them.

'Tha's done well,' he told her as the machines powered down for the dinner break. 'Tha's a tidy little worker,' he added, reaching to pinch her cheek. She stepped aside to avoid him and slammed a knee into the edge of the loom. Pain seared through her, although she tried not to let it show. She smiled briefly, grabbed her shawl and fled to the door, leaving him grinning after her.

On Sunday morning, Hannah fidgeted beside her all through matins. She had to agree that the vicar's sermons could be lengthy and at times tedious, but it was bad manners to let the boredom show and she elbowed her sister to keep still. At last it finished, the final hymn was sung and they made their way to the door.

Mrs Whittaker called Jennet's name and she paused to speak to her. She could see Hannah out of the corner of her eye and knew that she was

195

willing her to get a move on. Jennet wanted to get away too so that she could grab a bit of dinner and then go and see Peggy. Every minute she spent with her daughter was precious. But she couldn't be rude to the vicar's wife. It was good of her to take an interest.

'Come on!' said Hannah as Mrs Whittaker said goodbye and moved away. 'I've to meet Mary outside the Old Bull at one o'clock and she won't be happy if I'm late.'

'She's not knocking for thee then?'

'No.' Jennet saw a shadow of regret pass over her sister's face. 'She says as her father's forbidden her to have owt to do with me, on account of thee having stolen Nan's job. I told her it were just a misunderstandin'.'

'Well, be careful,' warned Jennet. 'We don't want them making any more trouble for us than they already have.'

Jennet set off from Blackburn after a quick meal. The streets were remarkably quiet and she could tell from the noise in the distance that everyone had gone to watch the balloon. She would have liked to have fetched Peggy to see it too, and when Hannah had suggested it she was tempted. But she was tired. So very tired. And she knew it would take all the energy she could muster to walk to Ramsgreave and back once, never mind twice and then stand up all afternoon, probably with Peggy in her arms as well.

She knew why she was so tired, of course, and it wasn't just her new job at the mill, although that wasn't helping. She'd been like this before, but then she'd had Titus to fuss over her. She remembered how he'd told her to put her feet up and brought the little stool, how he'd made her a cup of tea and put too much sugar in it, and how she'd been so grateful to him for trying that she'd drunk it down without a word of complaint. How she missed him, she thought as she trudged along the path that was wet and muddy from the persistent autumn rain. The leaves were slippery underfoot and she was afraid of falling. How she wished he were beside her to catch her arm if she stumbled, but most of all how she wished the baby were his, because there was no denying that it was George's. She was worried sick about how Titus would react when he came home and found another man's child in her arms.

She wondered if she might lose it, like the last one. She even considered doing it purposely. There was a woman on Barton Street who helped women like her, but every time she thought about going, she found herself covering the growing child with her hand as if to protect it. This was her baby. It was as precious to her as Peggy was, and the boy that had come too soon. She knew that she couldn't wilfully harm it. She must bear it and deal with the consequences.

When she reached Ramsgreave she was glad to sit down at the table whilst her mother made tea. Peggy looked up with a smile when she saw her.

'Ma!' she said and hauled herself to her feet to toddle over and be picked up. Jennet kissed the child and settled her on her lap, brushing her hair back from her face under the little cotton bonnet she was wearing. 'Ma not go away,' said Peggy, looking up at her with serious eyes. It undid Jennet and she began to cry. She couldn't even promise her daughter that much.

'She's happy enough when tha goes,' her mother reassured her. 'She cries for a few minutes but then she settles down.'

Jennet nodded. She knew that she should be grateful to her mother for caring for Peggy, but when the tea came and her daughter lifted her arms to her grandmother she felt so jealous that it was all she could do not to snatch her back and run home with her.

'Hannah not come?' asked her father when he came in from his plot.

'No. Not today. She's stayed in town with a friend to watch the balloon.'

'Balloon, is it?' said her father. 'I bet our Peggy would have liked that.'

'I can't take her and then walk back again. It's too far!' she snapped.

'I were only sayin',' replied her father, looking shocked at her outburst. They'd never been a family given to rowing with one another. Not like next door in Paradise Lane, thought Jennet, as she sipped her tea, confused and upset that she'd spoken out of turn. She'd been so taken aback when Nan and Joe had turned on her in the mill, but it seemed almost normal behaviour for them. The shouting came through the walls with disappointing regularity. They were always bawling at one another about something – no one had been to the well, someone had used all the milk, somebody had let the fire go out. There was always someone who was at fault and Jennet often jumped and stared at the wall, wondering if she should do something when she heard the sounds of things being thrown or smashed. The bangs and screams unsettled her and her imagination ran riot as she thought they must be killing one another. But next morning they all came tripping out on to the street, laughing and calling each other sweet names and saying they hoped they'd have a good day. It was as if they put on a performance when they thought other people were looking.

'What's to do?' asked her mother.

'I'm just tired, that's all. They're long days in the mill and I've been put on the looms.' She knew that she ought to tell her the real reason for her tiredness, but she was still searching for the right way to begin.

'Tha's weavin'?' asked her father, sitting down in his chair by the hearth. 'What? On a power loom?'

'Aye. I'm in charge of two of them now. Tha wants to see the speed they makes cloth,' she told him.

'Aye. But what sort of cloth do they make? Is it good?'

'It has to be. I get my money docked if I let any flaws through.'

'What's that?' asked her mother and they fell silent to listen. Jennet could hear a strange hissing sound like nothing she'd ever heard before. It sounded like some sort of monster and her heart began to race with the fear of it.

Her father went to the door to look out. 'Come and see this!' he told them. 'It's the balloon!'

Jennet picked Peggy up and followed her mother outside where they stood and gazed up into the sky. There it was. It was huge, striped in crimson and gold, and beneath it was what looked like a tiny basket with a man standing in it. Every few seconds he made a tongue of flame shoot up into the balloon, and that was what was causing the noise. They watched as it came closer. It wasn't very high and Jennet worried that it might come crashing down or even collide with the cottages and set them alight. But at last, with much hissing and fire, it began to rise. The man saw them watching and waved.

'Wave back to the man!' she told Peggy, taking her daughter's hand and waving it. 'It's a balloon.'

'B'loon,' repeated Peggy, gazing at it in wonder.

'Where's he going?' asked Jennet.

'He'll go wherever the wind takes him,' her father said as the balloon drifted higher and the noise faded. How wonderful, thought Jennet, to be able to float through the sky and not even know where you would land. How amazing to be that free.

When the balloon was lost from sight they went back inside. The evening was growing chilly now and Jennet realised that it was almost time to go. The opportunity she'd had to tell them about the coming child had passed. She'd tell them next week, she thought as she kissed her daughter, pulled her shawl from the child's clinging hands and hurried out with the sound of Peggy's crying still haunting her.

*

Titus quite liked Sundays in the House of Correction. There was no work to do, although he didn't mind the weaving and it was rewarding to see young Samuel making progress under his instruction. The lad wasn't bad company either. He had lots of tales to tell about the things that he'd done on the streets that both shocked and delighted Titus, who never knew how much was true and how much he invented. Sam had a lively imagination as well as a sense of humour, and Titus was growing fond of him.

'So how did tha get caught?' he'd asked him one morning when he'd been telling tales of the things he'd lifted from gentlemen's pockets.

'Well, it were right bad luck,' claimed Sam. 'I were waiting beside this gent at the coaching stop outside the Sun Inn, and I could see the chain of his fob watch hanging from the pocket of his weskit and it looked a right expensive one an' all. I lifted it without him feeling a thing and I were just turnin' to walk away when he decides that the coach must be late and he reaches into his pocket to look at the time. He finds it empty, sees me and lets out a holler of *Stop! Thief!* I legged it, but it were my bad luck as the constable were just coming around the corner and I runs smack bang into him.' The lad had shaken his head as if he were the one badly done by and it was all Titus could do not to laugh.

He smiled to himself again as he thought about it now, wondering if that morning's sermon from Reverend Clay had had any more impact on Samuel than his own short lecture on the wrongs of taking things that didn't belong to you. The concept seemed to puzzle Sam, who had been brought up to believe that anything was fair game if you could put your hands on it without anyone noticing.

'Them gents has plenty,' he'd protested. 'Why shouldn't I help myself to a bit of it?'

'You look happy this afternoon.'

Titus looked up to see Mr Wright standing in the doorway.

'Aye.' He laughed. 'I were just thinking on summat. Come in,' he said and told the schoolmaster about Samuel. 'He's a grand lad, really, and he has plenty o' brains if he'd use 'em to good effect. I bet he'd take to this reading and writing lark like a duck to water.'

Mr Wright promised that he'd try again to persuade Samuel to sit down with a book and then they went on with their lesson. Titus had progressed from reading simple words to the ones where two letters made a different sound.

'It makes no sense that *s* and *h* put together makes a sound like *sh*,' he observed. 'Why is it?'

'I don't rightly know,' admitted the school-master. 'It just does. I'd never wondered why.'

'Sheep!' announced Titus with pride as he decoded the word. 'Is it sheep?'

'Yes. It's sheep. Well done. I think that's enough for today,' said Mr Wright as he closed the book.

'So, where's tha off to now?' asked Titus. The schoolmaster hesitated; he had a slightly guilty look on his face.

'I'm going to a Reform meeting,' he said.

'Really? I didn't have thee down for a Reformer.'

'Why? Did you think I was gentry?' asked Mr Wright. 'I'm not. My father was a weaver, like you. But he was keen that I should better myself so he made sure I got a place at the free grammar school. It was a revelation to me, learning to read and write. It meant I could pick up pamphlets and books and read what they were all about. That's how I educated myself. Books opened my eyes to what can be achieved with some knowl-edge and I decided that I wanted to spend my time teaching others, because the working man is never going to rise up to the same level as the gentry without an education. But now, I feel it's not enough. I want to do more and that begins with Reform.'

'Aye. Tha's right,' said Titus. 'What tha's saying is what the speakers said at the meeting I went to. They said as every man should have the vote, not just them as are property owners.'

'Was it after this meeting that you were arrested?' asked the schoolmaster.

'Aye. I were swept along in a crowd and got mixed up with some loom breakers.'

'You were unlucky.'

'Aye. But on t' other hand I would never have had this opportunity to do any learnin' if I hadn't come here,' said Titus. 'They do say as every cloud has a silver lining.'

'Well, I'm glad to see you making the best of it,' said Mr Wright. 'And don't let what's happened make you afraid of fighting for Reform. We all need to fight for what's right.'

He bid Titus good evening and hurried away to his meeting. Titus went to the window where, standing on tiptoe, he could just see the roofs of the buildings beyond the prison wall. It was growing dark and the evening star was out, twinkling in a sky that was clearer on a Sunday night than any other. There was a wider world out there than the narrow one in which he'd lived his life until now, he thought. A few years ago he would have said that none of this was owt to do with him. Them as were his betters made decisions in places like London and it didn't seem to be much of his concern. He'd done his work, sold his cloth and tended his patch, and that was enough. He'd never dreamt that he would end up in prison, much less be learning to read and write and talking with learned folk like the schoolmaster about having a vote. But now that he'd seen more and heard more he'd begun to realise that it did concern him, because if the likes of him sat back and did nowt then nothing would change and life would never be fair for the working man.

At first Titus had vowed that when he got let out he would go home, find work and keep his head down. He'd wanted no more trouble. But now he was beginning to change his mind. No, when he was released he would do his best to keep up with his learning. He'd find out more about Reform. He'd let his voice be heard, and be damned to them as though locking him up would keep him quiet.

Chapter Eleven

As the weather grew colder, Jennet found that she had to fasten her skirt higher and higher as her waistline grew. With her blouse pulled over the waistband and her shawl around her, it wasn't obvious that she was pregnant. She hoped that people would think she was growing plumper because she could afford to eat better now that she had work. But she knew that she couldn't hide it for ever. Hannah continued to use rags every month and Jennet knew that it wouldn't be long before it occurred to her sister that she'd never seen hers rinsed out and hung to dry on the rack above the fire.

Nan, next door, had not returned to the mill, but she'd started going out every morning before the rest of the family and Mary had told Hannah that she was a four-loom weaver at King Street Mill. It made Jennet feel guilty. It took her all her time to work two looms and the thought of watching four seemed impossible. She knew that Nan was better at the job than she was, and she understood her anger at being laid off, but there had been little she could do other than put herself out of work and she saw no reason to let herself starve just to keep on good terms with her neighbour.

John's hand was healing nicely, Hannah told her, and, although he'd never be able to do the dextrous work that was required in the spinning room, he might be able to work again soon, fetching and carrying, or changing bobbins.

Hannah continued to be close with Mary, even though they kept their friendship secret. Each went out alone and they met up in town to go to various entertainments. Sometimes Hannah tried to persuade Jennet to go, but she always said no. She was too tired, for one thing, and she enjoyed her evenings alone in the house when she could rest her swollen feet after a long day and do some sewing. She was making little clothes for the new baby, something she couldn't have done whilst Hannah was there, not without confessing her secret.

Jennet was thinking that it was growing late and it was time that Hannah was home when she heard laughter coming down the street. It sounded like Mary and Hannah, which was unusual

burst out laughing again. 'It isn't funny!' she told her.

Hannah shook her head. 'I know. I know. But I can't stop.'

'I'll make some tea,' said Jennet, taking the kettle to fill it up before putting it back on the hob.

Hannah's mirth seemed to be subsiding a little and by the time she'd drunk her tea she was able to tell Jennet about what had happened.

'It's called nitrous oxide,' she said, 'although it's also called laughing gas.'

'I can't imagine why.'

'They told us that it was good for us, that it strengthens and invigorates body and mind and leaves no lassitude or headache. They asked for volunteers to give it a try, and Mary dared me to go up.'

'And did Mary partake as well?'

Hannah shook her head. 'No. She just kept laughing because I was laughing.'

'I'm beginning to think this friendship with Mary is a mistake,' said Jennet as she banked up the fire for the night. 'I don't want her getting thee into trouble.'

'It isn't me that's in trouble,' said Hannah.

'What dost tha mean?'

'Look at thee,' said her sister as Jennet straightened up. 'Tha's expectin' a child. And Titus is in prison.' They stared at one another for a moment. 'I'm right, aren't I?' said Hannah. 'Tha's stitching baby clothes.' She pointed to the sewing that was still lying on Jennet's chair.

'Aye,' replied Jennet. 'But tha's not to say a word to no one.'

'Tha can't keep it secret for ever.'

Jennet knew that Hannah was right. The thought preyed on her mind from the moment she was woken to the moment she crept back to bed at night.

'Who's the father?' asked Hannah. She was serious now.

'George, from next door.'

'The one who went to America?'

'Aye,' she said.

'Did he know?'

'I didn't even know until after he'd gone.'

'And will tha tell him?'

'How can I tell him?' she asked. 'I have to deal with it on my own.'

'What'll Titus say?'

'I don't know … I really don't know.'

The looms powered down at the end of the next day and Jennet had never been more thankful to hear the silence fall. She was tired and the pain from her back had been shooting down her leg all afternoon until all she could think about was sitting down. But the hours had dragged on and on as she'd worked through the fog of her agony, worrying that she wasn't giving the looms her full attention and knowing that it would all be for nothing if Hargreaves docked her pay. She reached for her shawl as the weavers bid one another goodnight and leaned against the wall as she waited for Hannah. The men came down the steps, and the boys. Then the women from the carding room. Mary appeared alone, but hurried past without speaking. Jennet waited and waited until she wondered whether to go and get the kettle on, but then she heard the sound of something falling over upstairs and went to the bottom of the steps to look up.

'Hannah!' she called. There was no answer, but she could hear someone up there. She went up the steps one at a time because of her discomfort. Every step was torture, but she was sure that something wasn't right. Hannah came down every night with Mary. She wondered if they'd had a falling-out and Hannah was avoiding her friend. Jennet thought that she wouldn't be sorry. Last night's incident had convinced her that Mary was a bad influence on her sister.

'Hannah!' she called again as she reached the carding room and looked around. The fluff was gradually settling on to the floor but there was no one there. Where could she be? Then she heard a sharp scream from the spinning room and hurried across to push open the door. 'No!' she shouted.

Hargreaves had her sister backed up against the wall and Jennet could see Hannah's bare white legs where he'd pulled up her skirts. He had one hand clamped across her mouth to stop her calling out again and, above it, Hannah's eyes were wide with terror.

'Let her go!' Jennet shouted at him as she glanced around for something to hit him with. He was a big man and she knew that she had no chance of forcing him away from her sister. 'Let her go!' she screamed again. He stepped back and Jennet was repulsed by the sight of him with his pants half down. 'What's he done? Has he touched thee?' she asked, clutching her sister's arm and pulling her away from him. 'Filthy bastard!' She spat in his face. 'Get home!' she told Hannah. 'I'll deal with him.'

Hargreaves began to laugh as Hannah's footsteps echoed from the stairs. He tucked himself back into his pants with some difficulty and then wiped her spittle from his cheek. 'Jealous?' he asked.

Jennet's hands grasped around for something to defend herself with, but found nothing. 'If tha's touched her …'

'Well, it's not as if it's the first time, is it?'

'What dost tha mean?' asked Jennet, horrified that he'd done this to her sister before and Hannah had never told her.

'Well, we all know what kind of lasses come home the worse for drink late at night,' he said. 'Carding room wages don't buy that amount of gin.'

Jennet stared at him and slowly realised that he must have seen Hannah laughing in the street with Mary the night before.

'She wasn't drunk.'

'Of course she was. And what about thee?' he said. 'I've done thee plenty of favours and I'm a bit tired of thee fobbing me off.' He took a step towards her.

'Stay back.'

'Aw, come on, Jennet. Tha's a grown woman.'

'No!' she told him as he reached for her wrists. The pain in her back and leg intensified as she tried to twist away from his grasp.

'Just stay quiet. I won't be long,' he said as he forced her backwards. She felt his boot on her bare leg as he tripped her and they both fell to the floor. He landed heavily on top of her and she was afraid for her baby.

'No, please,' she begged.

'It's all right, Jennet,' he told her. 'It'll only take a minute. Then tha can go home for thy tea.'

She felt him reach down to his trousers and then he had his knee between her thighs. 'Tha wants to be a weaver, doesn't tha?' he asked as he fumbled at her with one hand, the other tight across her mouth so she couldn't even bite. 'Better money than the cardin' room,' he reminded her as he pushed into her. The pain was searing, she writhed beneath him, but there was no escape. 'That's nice, isn't it?' he asked. 'Tha's a good lass, Jennet. I prefers thee to thy little sister anyhow.'

Jennet stumbled down the stairs. She was too stunned for tears. What had happened seemed unreal and for the moment she was more concerned for Hannah than for herself. She reached the house before she realised she'd left her shawl behind, but she went in and bolted the front door behind her. She'd get it tomorrow.

Hannah was sitting on a chair by the fire. She still had her shawl pulled tightly around her and she was crying.

'Did he touch thee?' asked Jennet. 'Did he ...?'

'No.' She shook her head. 'But if tha hadn't come ...'

'Don't fret.' She bent and put her arms around her sister. 'Don't fret,' she repeated. 'There's no harm done. Let's get the fire going and make us some tea.'

Jennet went down to the privy. She wiped away the stickiness and examined herself as best she could by the light of the candle. She was sore, but she could still feel the baby moving. It seemed distressed but she hoped it would settle down soon. At least it hadn't been Hannah, she reminded herself. At least she'd kept her sister safe.

'Tha's not going back,' she said as they picked at their tea. 'Tha can find a job at a different mill.'

'But what if I can't?'

'Then we'll manage.'

'I'll be all right,' said Hannah. 'I just need to make sure I don't get left alone with him.'

'No!' Jennet told her. 'Tha needs to get work elsewhere.'

'But we can't risk me being without work. Not with thee ...' She glanced at Jennet's belly. 'Tha's not going to be able to work when the baby comes.'

Jennet knew that her sister was right. It was another thing she was trying not to worry about, but the truth was that they wouldn't manage on just the money Hannah was bringing home even if she was in work.

'We'll manage,' she told her, with no idea how.

*

As each day passed Jennet found it harder to keep her secret. She knew that Hargreaves would never realise, but the other women were harder to fool and she'd noticed one or two of them looking at her shrewdly.

One dinner time, as she was on her way back to her looms, Hargreaves called her into his office. She hesitated, not wanting to be alone with him, but since the night when he attacked her he seemed to have lost interest and had moved on to pestering the girl who worked on the loom next to hers.

'Watch him,' she'd warned her. 'Don't get left on your own with him.'

'I know,' she'd said. 'His bloody hands are everywhere, but I daren't say owt. I need this job.'

Jennet felt herself trembling as she approached his room, but the other weavers were coming back in and she purposely left the door open.

His face was surly and he remained seated at his desk, fiddling about with some important-looking papers and a pile of coins. She wondered what was coming, although she couldn't think of anything she might have done to displease him. The cloth she'd cut from the loom that morning had looked flawless to her.

He stared at her for a moment. 'I've heard talk as tha's expectin' a child,' he said.

She felt the blood rise to her cheeks. She wondered whether to deny it, or to ask who'd told him, but she knew it was pointless. She couldn't keep it secret for ever.

'Aye. I'm with child,' she admitted, twisting the wedding ring on her finger.

'I don't suppose tha can pass it off as thy husband's?' It was a serious question and she realised that he was worried it might be his.

'Anyone who can reckon up will know that Titus isn't the father,' she told him.

'I'll not ask who t' father is then,' he said, 'but I'm goin' to have to lay thee off.'

'What? Why?' she asked. 'It isn't stopping me doing my work, is it? I can work for months yet.'

'Tha work's just fine,' he said, 'but I have my reputation to think on. I can't allow folk to go on sayin' as it's mine because I were owed a favour for givin' thee a chance on the power looms. I have the master to answer to, and I'll not risk losing my position.'

Jennet stared at him. She couldn't believe what he was telling her. She needed this job. If she weren't desperate for the money she would have walked out a long time ago.

'It isn't thine,' she told him.

'Well, I've still no option but to lay thee off. I'm sorry, Jennet. Tha's a good little worker, but there's nowt else I can do.' He picked up the stack of coins and reached across the desk to give them to her. 'That's what tha's owed. Go home now.'

Jennet stared at the money and then closed her fingers around it. She would have to make it last, she thought, because she wasn't going to get work in another mill in her condition.

'What's the matter with thee?' asked Hannah when she came in at teatime. She'd got a job as an apprentice weaver at the Brookhouse Mill and although Jennet knew that her sister missed chatting with Mary all day long, she was glad that Hannah wasn't seeing so much of her, especially now.

'I've been laid off.'

'Why?'

'Because someone's been spreading a rumour that I'm having Hargreaves' baby.'

'Who?'

'Probably her next door. She's been biding her time to get her own back, and spreading nasty rumours is just her style. I want thee to promise me that tha'll have nothing more to do with any of them.'

'That means Mary, I suppose? Tha can't stop me being friends with her.'

'I'll not have thee living under my roof if tha carries on being her friend! Not after this!'

'That's not fair! It's not Mary's fault. And tha's no proof it was Nan anyway. It could have been anyone. It's obvious now that tha's havin' a child.'

'Oh, it was her next door, all right,' said Jennet. 'She'll be like the cat that's got the cream, now that I've been put out of work. I bet she's hoping that I have to give up the house.'

'Well, it's not as if tha enjoys living next door to her,' said Hannah.

'That's not the point. If I move out, she'll think she's won and I won't give her that satisfaction.'

'Then don't threaten to turf me out, because if I'm not here to pay the rent I don't know who will!'

Jennet frowned and went off into the back kitchen to slam some pans and bowls about. It was true that they needed Hannah's wage more than ever, but she was still determined that her sister shouldn't be on friendly terms with any of those neighbours. Not now.

'I'm sorry as tha's lost thy job,' said Hannah from the doorway. 'And if it were Nan that spread that gossip then it wasn't a nice thing, but Mary's a different person from her mother and I'll not blame her for things her mother's done. She's my friend and it wouldn't be right.'

'So she means more to thee than thy own sister?'

'Don't ask me to choose sides,' said Hannah. 'I've said what I think, and I'll not fall out with Mary over it. If tha wants me to leave, I will. I don't know where I'll go, but there must be a family who would be glad of a lodger to bring in a little extra.'

'No, don't go,' said Jennet. She turned and faced her sister. 'I don't want thee to go.'

To her credit, Hannah didn't repeat that it was only because of her wages. She just nodded briefly and took the kettle from Jennet and filled it with water.

Next morning, after Hannah had gone to work, Jennet tidied the house and when the sound of the latecomers running to the mill gates had stopped, she reached for her shawl and set off to Ramsgreave. She wanted to bring Peggy home. And she still had to tell her parents about the baby.

'What's wrong?' asked her mother as soon as she saw her. 'Is it Hannah?'

'No. No. Hannah's fine.'

'Then why hast tha come?' asked her father.

'I've come to fetch Peggy,' she said, looking at the child who was playing contentedly. 'I've been laid off.'

'That's bad news, with Christmas coming,' said her mother.

'I thought trade had picked up,' said her father.

'It wasn't that.' She unwrapped her shawl and hung it on a peg before turning back to them with no attempt to hide her swelling belly. 'I'm having another baby,' she said.

Her mother stared at her. 'How long has tha known? Why didn't tha tell me afore? Jennet?'

'It isn't Titus's,' she admitted.

There was silence for a moment as her parents looked at her and then at one another.

'What dost tha mean?' asked her father. 'How can it not be Titus's?'

'Don't be soft,' her mother told him. 'Titus has been gone since April and if it were his child, she'd be about ready to have it by now. But look at her. She's expectin' all right, but not for a while yet. When's it due?'

'In May, I think.'

'And who's the father? Not him at the mill?'

'No! It were George from next door. It happened when he took me to Lancaster.'

'Did he force himself on thee?' asked her father.

'No.' She shook her head. 'No, not really. We had to share a room and I were tired, and upset, and George comforted me ...'

'And took advantage. If I ever get hold of him, he'll rue the day he were born!' Jennet had rarely seen her father angry before and it frightened her.

'He didn't know,' she said. 'He'd already gone when I found out.'

'But that doesn't excuse him for taking advantage of thee when tha were vulnerable and alone. He should be strung up for what he's done!'

Jennet began to cry. 'Sit down,' said her mother. 'I'll make some tea. And tha can sit down too,' she told her husband. 'Tha frightening little Peggy and threatening a man who's long gone isn't going to solve anything.'

'What will Titus say?' he demanded as he sat on the chair by the hearth and lifted Peggy on to his lap to soothe her.

'I don't know,' said Jennet.

'He won't be happy about getting out of prison only to come home and find his wife with another man's child. What if he refuses to bring it up? What will tha do then?'

'Tha's not helping,' her mother told him. 'There's a baby coming and nothing will change that. Besides, we don't know what Titus will say until he comes home and he's told. What will tha tell him?' she asked Jennet, putting a cup of tea on the table beside her.

'The truth, I suppose,' she said. 'I made a mistake and I'm sorry. I'll tell him that and hope that he'll forgive me.'

'Tha's made a right mess of things,' said her mother. 'Does Hannah know?' Jennet nodded and sipped her tea. 'And what about money? Tha can't expect Hannah to pay for everything.'

'I know. I'll try to get another job.'

'Well, that won't be easy.'

'I'm sure Mrs Whittaker'll help me,' she said, although she wasn't sure at all and she dreaded the censure that she was sure she would receive from the vicar's wife when she heard the talk about her pregnancy.

After dinner she made her way back home with Peggy trailing at her side. After leaving her crying so many times on Sunday evenings, she now had to deal with the child wailing because she wanted to stay with her grandparents. After tugging the reluctant child along for a while she lost her patience and dealt her a hefty slap.

'Stop it!' she shouted. 'Tha's comin' home wi' me and I don't want to hear no more of thy skrikin'!' After a moment of stunned silence, Peggy began to cry even louder and Jennet was forced to pick her up and carry her even though her back and legs ached and all she wanted to do was cry herself. She felt so guilty at smacking her daughter that she wondered if she was a fit enough mother to one, never mind two, children. And what would Titus say? It was a question she'd been avoiding, but she knew that the answer would shape all their futures.

Chapter Twelve

The week before Christmas, Jennet took the last of the coins from the top drawer of her chest and counted them. Whilst she was earning she'd tried to put a little bit away each week to buy a new coat for Peggy. She was growing fast and splitting out of the few clothes that she had. But there wasn't enough to buy a coat and food as well, and she needed to keep some back for the rent because they'd be hard pressed to pay that with only Hannah's wage coming in. She took a shilling to go to the market and get some red flannel to sew a couple of warm bodices for Peggy, then dropped the rest of the coins back into the sock, folded it over and put it back in the drawer. The seams on Peggy's coat were quite generous. She'd let it out as much as she could and hope that it would last another winter.

'What are we going to do on Christmas Day?' asked her sister as they ate their tea. 'Mills are closed and with Sunday as well, that's a two-day holiday.'

'I was thinking of taking Peggy to church,' said Jennet. She knew that she would have to speak to Mrs Whittaker about getting relief again, but she was ashamed to have to ask a second time and kept putting it off. She thought that Christmas morning might catch the vicar's wife in an agreeable mood.

'There's to be a hog roast on the market this year. Mary says it'll be a good do.'

Jennet broke up some oatcake and handed it to Peggy who was sitting up at the table on a cushion that raised her just high enough to peep over the edge. She was getting sick and tired of hearing about what Mary said, and what Mary thought, but she bit her tongue and didn't comment.

'Peggy'll like it,' said Hannah. 'Why don't we ask Mam and Dad to come? We can all go together.'

'If they want to come,' she agreed. At least it meant there would be some meat for them on the day, even if it was a handout.

Jennet woke early on Christmas Day and lay in the quiet of the morning for a while, enjoying the warmth from her sister's body. But shouts of *Ma! Ma!* from her daughter and the need for a trip down the yard prompted her to push back the covers and pull a blanket around her shoulders.

The ground was crisp underfoot and the sky was turning a vivid blue as the sun rose. It looked like it would be a fine day with no snow.

They got their breakfast and then dressed for morning service as the church bells began to ring. Hannah was in her best bonnet. Jennet still had to make do with her shawl over her head, but Peggy's coat didn't look so tight on her now that she'd altered it.

Jennet was worried about bumping into the neighbours, but there was no sign of them until they heard a door slam as they turned the corner into King Street. She glanced back to see Mary running to catch them up. Hannah hugged and kissed her friend and they wished one another 'Merry Christmas', before linking arms and walking on ahead of her and Peggy.

The church was full of greenery and the scent of it filled the place. The organ was playing quietly and they took a pew near the back so that Jennet could take Peggy out if she cried. Hannah and Mary watched the gentry come in, keeping up a whispered commentary on their clothes.

'There's Mrs Sudell,' said Hannah. 'Look at her hat!' Jennet watched as the mill owner's wife strolled up the aisle in her enormous hat, decorated with a huge bow and feathers, her hands warm inside a fur muff that matched the hem of her green coat. It must have cost a small fortune.

Mrs Whittaker came in next wearing a coat of royal blue with cream fur. Her bonnet was smaller as befitted a vicar's wife, but it was exquisite. The woman who helped her care for her child walked behind her, carrying the Whittakers' little girl. The baby was dressed in a pink jacket and matching bonnet and Jennet couldn't help but feel jealous. How she wished she could dress Peggy as well as that.

When all the important people were in their places, it was time to stand for the opening carol 'Hark! Hark! What News the Angels Bring'. Jennet held Peggy up in her arms so that she could see. She loved the singing and tried to join in although she could hardly form the words and most of them were *la!* Thankfully, the vicar didn't preach long, but his theme was Joseph's acceptance of Mary's baby and Jennet, who couldn't claim that her conception had been immaculate, could only hope that Titus would be half as understanding.

But as they came out of church into the bright sunshine, she had a more pressing concern, and as Hannah and Mary went off without her, she hung back to try to speak to Mrs Whittaker.

'Merry Christmas, Mrs Eastwood! I see you have your little girl with you today. Hello, Peggy,' she said as the child grasped at the folds of Jennet's skirts shyly. 'Are you taking her to the roast this afternoon?'

'Yes. We're looking forward to it.'

'And how are you getting on at the mill?'

'I've been laid off,' she said. 'I'm having another baby.'

'That seems harsh. How are you managing?'

'Well, Hannah's working, so we have some income, but not enough to feed us after the rent's paid. I need to ask for relief again.'

Mrs Whittaker frowned and Jennet could see that she was going to refuse. 'What about a job?' she asked. 'There's work at the sewing room on Chapel Street. The Ladies' Charity has bought some rolls of calico to be made into garments for poor women and children. Would you be interested in that?'

'I would,' said Jennet. 'It would be less tiring work than being on my feet all day in the mill, and I could carry on until the baby's born.' She made no excuse about having to look after Peggy this time. The child would have to go back to Ramsgreave.

'When is the baby due?'

231

Hannah hesitated, feeling her face grow hot and red with the shame.

'Not for a few weeks yet,' she said, hoping that Mrs Whittaker wouldn't count the months too carefully.

'Well, come to see me at the vicarage in the New Year,' she said. 'I'll have spoken to the rest of the committee by then and I'll see what I can do for you.'

'I am grateful!'

'Enjoy your Christmas, and take care of this little one,' she said, gently patting Peggy's cheek before turning to speak to more of her parishioners.

When Jennet got home her parents were waiting for her. Her mother had made a new rag doll for Peggy, but she looked at it suspiciously and insisted on carrying her old, chewed doll instead as they walked up to the market square.

The sound of music and laughter floated on the breeze and Jennet followed her father through the crush. The meat was tasty, dripping in fat, and there were hot potatoes too, all doled out for free. They stood and ate their fill whilst listening to the carol singing. As Jennet wiped her hands and Peggy's face with her handkerchief, her brief happiness was spoiled as she remembered the previous year when Titus had been at her side. What sort of Christmas was he having? She wished he was with her and that the baby in her belly was his. They could have been so happy.

'All right, Jennet?' asked her father, glancing down at her.

'Aye, I'm fine,' she said, using the hanky to wipe her eyes and blow her nose.

'He'll soon be home,' said her father. Jennet nodded. It was hard to explain that although she was counting the days, she was dreading his return too.

Even though Titus enjoyed his weaving, and teaching young Sam, the days crawled by. With the coming of the shorter days, their working hours had been cut to save candles and he was left alone in the evenings with nothing to do.

He knew that by Christmas he would have served more than half of his sentence. Come the New Year, he would only have to wait another couple of months and then he would be free to go home. But it seemed a long, long way off. He worried about being away from Jennet and Peggy. The rest he could bear with a good grace, even if it was undeserved, but missing his family was the hardest part of his punishment. He hoped that they were coping without him. He knew that it would be hard for Jennet, caring for Peggy alone, feeding her, clothing her, making sure that there was clean water and milk for her to drink. He knew that her parents would help, but they weren't close by – unless she'd moved back home. He wondered if she had, if she'd given up the house on Paradise Lane, and if so, would there be a place for him went he went back? The worrying thoughts circled in his mind. To silence them, he reached under his mattress for the pamphlet that Mr Wright had given him. It was about Reform and the schoolteacher had told him to keep it hidden from the turnkey lest it cause any trouble. When he got out, thought Titus, when trade picked up and he got another job in the mill, he would buy a copy of *The Truthteller* every week. He would join the fight for the rights of the working man, and he would never give up until the Parliament had been reformed and every man had a vote. He would strive for a fair society and next Christmas things would be different. It would more than make up for this one. He would save up for a goose, and Jennet would roast it in its own fat with potatoes and carrots and peas. And there would be a Christmas pudding. And they would have a feast, sitting around the table, with the fire roaring in the hearth and gifts for everyone.

The thought of it consoled him as darkness fell outside and the drizzle thickened into sleet. Next year would be perfect. There might even be a new baby on the way. He would like that. He missed little Peggy and still felt sad about the baby that had come too soon. His lost son. A new lad in the cradle would make the picture complete, he decided, as he waited for the lights to go out.

Chapter Thirteen

With the coming of the New Year, the weather turned viciously cold. Wrapped in her shawl and holding Peggy by the hand, Jennet walked down King Street and climbed the steps to ring the doorbell of the vicarage, hoping that Mrs Whittaker would remember that she'd asked her to call.

After a few moments she heard steps approaching and the door was opened by a girl wearing a dark dress covered by a white apron.

'I've come to see Mrs Whittaker.'

'Are you expected?'

'Yes,' replied Jennet, trying to sound more confident than she felt.

'Name?'

'Mrs Eastwood,' said Jennet, thinking that the girl could have been more polite. It wasn't as if she'd come to beg, she thought, as the girl told her to wait and left her on the doorstep as the sleet drove sideways against them. She shifted Peggy to her other side to shield her from the worst of it.

Time passed and Jennet wondered if she should simply pick up her daughter, go home and pretend that she'd never come. It was too shaming to be kept standing outside like this.

She was on the verge of leaving when she heard footsteps again and the door opened a little wider this time.

'Mrs Whittaker says please come in.'

Jennet stepped into a hallway that was more than twice the size of her own living room. The walls were a pale peach and hung with paintings. The floor was tiled in black and white squares and she wiped her feet vigorously on the rough coir mat before stepping on to them.

'May I take your shawl and the child's coat and bonnet?'

'Yes. Please. Thank you.' Jennet was flummoxed by the formalities. She knew that the maid was no better than she was, but her attitude was condescending and her face held almost a sneer as she put the shawl over her arm and whisked it towards the hall stand.

'This way.' Jennet followed her down the passageway to a door, which the maid opened. 'Mrs Eastwood, ma'am,' she said as she stood aside.

'Come in!' called Mrs Whittaker as Jennet hesitated before stepping on to the plush, colourful carpet that stretched to the edges of the room, glad that she'd wiped her boots so well and that she hadn't come wearing her clogs. 'Come in,' repeated Mrs Whittaker. 'Kitty, bring some tea. Or would you like some hot chocolate? Yes,' she said without waiting for an answer. 'Bring us some hot chocolate.'

'Yes, ma'am,' said the maid and went out, closing the door behind her.

'Come to the fire,' said Mrs Whittaker. 'It's a dreadful morning out there. You must be frozen.'

Jennet went across to where Mrs Whittaker was sitting in a low chair by the fire. She had a small table beside her where she'd put down her notebook, and she waved towards a matching chair on the other side of the hearth.

'Sit down,' she said. Jennet tugged on Peggy's hand as her daughter stood and stared around at all the things in the room. Jennet would also have liked to take a closer look at the portraits that hung from the picture rail, and the vases and ornaments displayed on the little tables, but instead she brushed imaginary dirt from her skirt and sat down on the soft pink upholstered chair and lifted Peggy on to her knee to prevent her touching anything.

'Hello, Peggy,' said Mrs Whittaker. 'How are you today?'

'She's well,' said Jennet. 'I hope your own little girl is well too?' she ventured.

'Yes, she's very well, thank you. She's upstairs in the nursery. This is my time for getting on with my work,' said Mrs Whittaker, indicating her notebook. 'There's so much to do for the church, and the Ladies' Charity. I hardly have a free moment. But how are you, Mrs Eastwood? Are you managing?'

'Well, just about,' she said, thinking that she might as well be honest. 'As I said, my sister's in work, but I can't expect her to keep us.'

'Of course not,' said Mrs Whittaker. She looked up as the door opened and Kitty came in carrying a silver tray. 'Ah, here's the chocolate. Put it down here on the table, Kitty. I can pour it. Will you ask Nanny to come down? She can take Peggy upstairs for a drink of milk and a biscuit.'

'Ma'am,' said Kitty as she placed the tray down carefully so that it wouldn't overbalance. 'Anything else, ma'am?'

'No, thank you, Kitty. You can go.'

Jennet watched as the girl left the room, her arms tightening around her daughter. She didn't want some stranger taking Peggy away but she was at a loss to know how to refuse.

'Have you ever had chocolate?' asked Mrs Whittaker.

'No.' She turned her attention to the tray. There was a silver pot with a wooden handle on the side and steam was wafting up from the spout. Mrs Whittaker eased herself forwards to sit on the edge of her chair and poured a thick, dark liquid from the pot into two delicate cups. The aroma that rose was delicious, like nothing Jennet had smelled before. She hoped that it tasted as good. This was a luxury she'd heard of, but never thought she would be lucky enough to try.

'Here's Nanny,' said Mrs Whittaker as the door opened again and a woman in a blue gown with a white apron over it came in.

'Hello,' she said to Peggy, holding out her hand and smiling. 'Would you like a biscuit and a look at the toys upstairs?'

'It's all right,' said Jennet. 'Tha can go with the lady. I'll come and fetch thee in a minute or two, when I've talked to Mrs Whittaker.'

She thought that her daughter would cry and refuse to go, but there was something

240

about the woman that Peggy seemed to like and she slid from Jennet's knee, put her little hand in Nanny's and went without a backwards glance.

'She's a good girl,' said Mrs Whittaker, passing one of the cups to Jennet. 'I think she would do well at the school.'

'School?'

'Well, we call it school, but it isn't sitting on benches like the older children do. The Ladies have employed a teacher who will look after the little ones whilst their mothers work in the sewing room. She'll teach them some basics like counting and Bible stories. I think Peggy might enjoy it. She's a bright little girl.'

'Yes.' Jennet wasn't sure what was being offered.

'It would solve your problem with childcare,' said Mrs Whittaker. 'The hours wouldn't be as many as in the mill. Just three days a week. And we could only pay a shilling a day, but dinner is provided and you would be earning the money rather than taking charity.'

'Yes,' said Jennet. 'Thank you!'

'Drink your chocolate before it gets cold,' said Mrs Whittaker. She sipped her own and Jennet raised the delicate cup to her lips and tasted the drink. It was bitter and sweet at the same time and smooth on the tongue.

'Do you like it?'

'I do!'

'I like to take a cup in the mornings,' said Mrs Whittaker after draining hers and putting it back on the tray. She seemed eager to move and although Jennet would have loved to stay sitting by the roaring fire, savouring her drink, she didn't want to outstay her welcome. She finished the chocolate and carefully returned the cup to its fragile saucer.

'Come and see the nursery,' said Mrs Whittaker.

Jennet followed the vicar's wife out of her parlour and up the carpeted stairs. The vicarage was how she had always imagined a palace might be with its luxurious papered walls and thick curtains. Everywhere she looked there were more paintings, tables with ornaments and cabinets filled with all manner of wonderful things. At the top of the stairs Mrs Whittaker led her to a room with a white door. She opened it and Jennet saw that it was filled with children's toys. The floor was wooden and her boots seemed to make an intolerable amount of noise compared to Mrs Whittaker's soft indoor slippers, but she forgot all her anxiety when she saw Peggy, seated on a rocking horse with the widest smile she had ever seen.

'Ma! Gee-gee!' she called when she saw her mother.

'How sweet she looks!' Mrs Whittaker turned with a huge smile of her own. 'I can't wait until Sophia is big enough to ride on it.' She scooped up her own daughter and kissed the baby's blonde head. 'Look! Look at Peggy on the horse.' She smiled at Jennet as if they were friends. 'She's enjoying it. And she hasn't cried at all at being parted from you. I don't think you need have any worries about leaving her at school.'

'Where is this school?' asked Jennet. Surely Mrs Whittaker wasn't planning to have all her workers' children in her own nursery?

'It's on Chapel Street. Number seventeen. The school is in one of the upstairs rooms and the others are sewing rooms. That way the nursing mothers can feed their babies at dinner time. Mrs Haworth, the teacher, is a kindly woman. You know her, don't you, Nanny?'

'I do, ma'am. She's very respectable and she loves children. You need have no concerns,' she told Jennet.

'So, can we expect you at the sewing room?' asked Mrs Whittaker. 'You could come tomorrow if you like?'

'I will. I'm very grateful to you, Mrs Whittaker.' Jennet wasn't sure what else to say. She felt awkward standing in the vicarage nursery. 'I won't take up any more of your time,' she said, tiptoeing across the floor to lift Peggy from the horse.

Peggy bellowed in protest and screamed all the way down the stairs. Jennet wanted to run out into the street, but she was forced to wait until the maid brought their outdoor clothes and then she had to battle her daughter's flailing arms to get her into her coat. Red in the face and not knowing where to look, she pulled her shawl around herself and thanked the maid as she opened the street door for them to leave. The girl didn't reply, but continued to look down at Jennet, who almost slipped and fell on the steps, which were now covered in snow. It frightened her and her first thought was for the baby. She knew that she couldn't bear to lose it now and whenever she remembered that she'd even considered getting rid of it she felt guilty, as if the thought of it had cursed her and the unborn child.

Peggy sobbed all the way home and people stared. Jennet walked as fast as she dared with Peggy kicking on her hip until they turned the corner into Paradise Lane. She unlocked the door and pushed Peggy over the step, thankful to be home.

'Stop it!' she shouted at her daughter once they were inside. 'You've shamed me enough today!'

'Gee-gee! Want gee-gee,' sobbed the child as Jennet poked the fire into a blaze and hung up their wet things to dry.

Next morning, Jennet waited until the last of the mill workers had gone in through the gate before she came out and shut the door. It was still snowing hard and had been all night, and the thick snow on the ground muffled the familiar sounds of the street. It was so deep that it came above Peggy's little boots and she had to pick up her daughter to carry her down to Chapel Street. At least it wasn't that far, she thought as her back ached with the effort, and she would be able to sit down when she got there.

She pulled her shawl around them both and walked head down into the wind-blown flurries. It was slippery underfoot and a couple of times she felt her feet slide from under her, but managed to keep her balance. She must not fall. As well as the danger to her children, a sprained wrist or a broken arm would render her useless.

She knocked at the door of number seventeen and it was opened almost immediately.

'Come in! Don't stand there knockin'!' The matron moved back to make way and Jennet wiped her wet clogs on the mat. Her skirt was sodden almost up to the knees and her teeth were chattering with cold, but the crowded room felt warm, if a little steamy from the damp clothes of the women who sat around a large table in front of the fire. 'I'm Mrs Aspinall,' she told her. 'I take it tha's Mrs Eastwood? Mrs Whittaker said to expect thee.'

'Aye. And I've brought our Peggy.'

'Aye. That's right. She's to go up to the schoolroom. Take off thy wet things and hang 'em in the kitchen. I'll take thee up.'

Jennet followed the woman upstairs. The twisty, narrow steps were the same as her own at home, so Peggy went up first, on her hands and feet like a little dog, eager to discover what adventures there might be. If she was hoping for another rocking horse, she would be disappointed, thought Jennet, as she pulled herself up with the help of the handrail.

At the top, Jennet grasped her daughter's hand and guided her into the front room. There were several other children in there already. A couple of tots about Peggy's age were sitting on a rug in front of the little fireplace where a fire was blazing, and Jennet was pleased to see that a metal guard had been fixed up to keep them from getting too close to the flames. In cots there were three babies, all sleeping soundly, and the room had a peaceful feel to it.

A lady greeted her with a smile. She was sitting on a low chair by the fire, watching the children play, and on the table beside her were a pile of books, some slates and chalk, and some strings of beads. It all looked very organised and homely, and very different from the way the woman next door ran things. She might even be able to bring the new baby here, thought Jennet with growing optimism.

'Gee-gee?' asked Peggy.

'Not here, love, but there are lots of other things to play with, and tha can make some new friends,' said Jennet, hoping that she might be able to do the same.

'I'm Mrs Haworth,' said the teacher. 'This is Peggy?' Jennet nodded. 'Hello, Peggy. Would you like to draw something?' She offered a slate and chalk, which her daughter took eagerly and plonked herself down on the floor to see what it would do. She seemed delighted with the marks she could make and didn't even look up when Jennet told her that she would just be downstairs.

Back in the sewing room, she was provided with some red flannel to make vests for babies and she wielded her needle and thread with quiet efficiency as she listened to the other women chatter. Most had husbands who were out of work. Some had been employed by Mr Hornby on building work, although today they had been tasked with clearing the snow from the fronts of the houses on King Street. When they asked her about her husband, she was ashamed to admit that Titus was in prison.

'He just got caught up in it. He were trying to get home,' she said.

'I've got no sympathy with loom breakers,' announced one woman. 'They should all be transported!'

'Don't talk like that, Lily,' said another woman. 'It's not because of the loom breakers that thy Harry's out of work. There were no work before the riot happened. It must be hard for thee,' she said to Jennet. 'Especially with another baby on the way.'

'Aye, it is,' she agreed, hoping that no one would begin to count the months from the riot and compare the time with the growth of her pregnancy. Eyebrows would be raised and more conclusions would be jumped to if they did, and Jennet desperately wanted to be on good terms with these women.

'When's it due?'

'May,' she said, knowing that it was pointless to pretend otherwise. She could sense the others adding up the months in their heads.

'That Hargreaves at the Dandy Mill is a nasty piece of work,' said a woman whose name was Alice. 'I heard as he sacked thee for being pregnant.'

'Aye, he did,' said Jennet, not surprised that the story had got around.

'My niece were workin' there and had to move on account of him,' said another. 'He's well known for bein' a pest. It weren't fair of him to lay thee off though,' she told Jennet.

'Well, it were hard work being on my feet all day,' she said. 'I don't know how much longer I could have gone on. This is easier.'

'Aye. But not the same money.'

'We're better off than them as has no work at all,' replied Alice, as she fastened off a seam and snipped the thread. 'Even though trade's pickin' up again there's still plenty as can't afford to feed themselves.'

'Except for t' gentry.'

'Aye, but it's t' gentry as is providing work for thee, so mind thy tongue,' warned Alice as the matron came back in from the kitchen.

A baby began to cry upstairs and one woman kept glancing towards the ceiling.

'Mrs Haworth'll see to it. Don't thee be breakin' off from thy work,' said Matron.

At length she declared that it was dinner time. The aroma of potato pie had been drifting in from the kitchen for the past hour or so, and Jennet had been embarrassed by her stomach growling with hunger. She'd allowed Hannah the last of the porridge and given Peggy the oatcakes before they left home. All she'd had was tea, laced with as much sugar as she could spare, and she was anticipating her dinner with pleasure.

The mothers of the babies went upstairs to feed them and Peggy and the other little ones were brought down to sit at the table with them. The sewing was carefully cleared aside so that it wouldn't get spoiled and the women with no children began to bring in bowls and cups and lay the table. Then the big pot was carried in. It was steaming hot and Alice stirred it before spooning out a portion for everyone. She put plenty in Jennet's dish and there was a little plate for her to share some out for Peggy as well.

'Tuck in,' she urged, and for the first time in months Jennet ate until she felt full.

Outside, the snow had stopped falling and what little sky could be glimpsed from the window confirmed that it had brightened and that there might even be a glimmer of sun for an hour or two. The dinner was cleared away and after a cup of tea, the children went back upstairs and the sewing resumed. Jennet enjoyed the work and although she still felt shy, most of the other women seemed pleasant enough and she hoped that they would accept her.

The lamps had to be lit by three in the afternoon and by four o'clock they were told that they could go home. The weather seemed to be worsening again and Jennet was glad when she reached Paradise Lane. It hadn't been too bad, she thought as she began to get the tea ready for Hannah. In fact, she'd actually enjoyed herself.

A thaw set in overnight and by the following morning much of the snow had melted away. In the afternoon Mrs Eccles came to the sewing room and stood, blocking the light from the window, whilst she inspected their work. She never spoke to any of them though, just talked about them with Matron as if they were too stupid to under-stand. Jennet kept her head down but she saw the mill owner's wife glance at her with dislike. She was thankful that Mrs Whittaker had spoken up for her because it was obvious that this woman didn't think she deserved to be here. She knew that she would have to work hard if she wasn't to lose her place.

Chapter Fourteen

Titus was helping Sam to mend a thread on his cloth when the shadow of the turnkey fell across the loom, blocking the low winter sun. He continued with his work as he had both ends of the thread between his fingers and didn't want to lose them. Then, when it was done, he straightened up and turned around.

'Governor wants to see thee,' said the turnkey. His face gave nothing away and Titus began to run events of the past few days through his mind, wondering if he'd done something to cause any displeasure. His guilty conscience immediately provided an image of *The Truthteller* that had been hidden under his mattress. Had his cell been searched whilst he was working? Had the pamphlet been found? Had he ruined all the good work he'd done towards securing his release in a few weeks' time?

The thoughts tumbled around his mind as he followed the turnkey across the inner ward to the governor's house. The sun shone on to the sundial above the central window and indicated that it was around ten in the morning. The turnkey pulled at the bell under the canopy of the front door and they waited. Titus had never been inside the house, although he'd volunteered to do some tidying in the garden on a couple of Sunday afternoons when the weather had turned warmer. He missed working on his patch back at Pleck Gate; the feel of the soil under his fingers and the smell of the earth had done him good. He wished he could have a garden of his own again and wondered if it might be possible to grow something in barrels in the little back yard on Paradise Lane.

A maid came to the door and asked them to wait a moment whilst she told Mr Liddell that they were here. She left the door ajar and Titus glimpsed the black and white tiles of the hallway floor and a dark wooden table with a green plant on it that he didn't recognise.

'Ah, Titus,' said the governor, coming out from the room with the window that overlooked the ward. 'Come inside,' he said.

It was months since Titus had been in anyone's home, and he didn't think he'd ever been in a home like this before. A carpeted staircase swept up from the hallway and he could hear the sound of a piano being played somewhere on the upper floor. The governor indicated that Titus should go into his office. A huge mahogany desk stood on a Turkish rug. There was a chair behind it with a cushion, still indented from where the governor had been sitting with his back to the fire and a view across to the workshops.

'Now, Titus,' said the governor, sitting down and grasping his hands together in front of him as if he were readying himself for prayer. 'It won't be long before you will be released from this place.'

'Aye, sir.'

'From what I've been told by the chaplain and the schoolmaster, you've used your time wisely whilst you've been with us.'

'Aye. It's true as I've learned to read and write a little.'

'Good. I'm pleased to hear it.' Titus waited for the matter of the pamphlet to be brought up as the governor frowned. 'You were sent here for your association with men who broke into a mill and destroyed machinery,' said the governor.

'Aye. But I broke nowt,' said Titus.

'Even so, you were there. And that made you guilty by association. I believe that you had also been to a Reform meeting before the riot broke out?'

'Aye, that's right.'

'And are you a Reformer?' he asked.

Titus hesitated before replying. 'It interests me,' he said.

The governor shook his head. 'Titus, when you leave this House of Correction I would be unhappy to think of you becoming embroiled in the plots of these misguided men. I would not like to see you back here again.'

'No,' said Titus. He didn't want to be brought back here either, but he wasn't sure that the governor was right to tell him to avoid the Reformers. Did the man not know that his own schoolmaster attended Reform meetings?

'These so-called Reformers are dangerous characters. They strive to undermine the very fabric of our society with their actions and their unreasonable demands. The issue of every man having the vote, for example, will merely mean that the ignorant will make the laws. That cannot be for the best, can it, Titus?'

Titus stared at him for a moment before answering, trying to make out whether the man was serious or jesting. The earnest expression on the governor's face convinced him that the man really believed what he was saying. Titus felt an indignant anger growing within him. He wanted to challenge the governor and ask him if he thought the working man so ignorant that he would make such ridiculous laws as the Corn Bill, which had resulted in starvation all across the country.

'Can it, Titus?' prompted the governor. 'It can only end in mayhem. Look what happened in France.'

'Aye,' said Titus, thinking back to the Reform meeting on the moor and what was said in the speeches. The gentry feared for their heads if folk revolted same as the French had. But that wasn't what Titus wanted. He didn't want the horror of men and women having their heads struck from their shoulders, of course he didn't. But he did want a revolution, a peaceable one where every man could vote freely, rather than having to put up with a government that held its position simply because the members could afford to bribe those who did have the vote to elect them.

'You've done well here,' said the governor. 'You've been a model prisoner. I'm especially impressed by the way you've brought on young Samuel. He was a wayward ruffian, but I have hopes that he will keep out of trouble now that he has a trade.'

257

Titus didn't point out that it was highly unlikely the lad would get paid work when he left prison because there was no work to be had. He worried that Sam would return to thieving on the streets to feed himself and it saddened him to think that the governor believed he had done enough.

'I hope the chaplain has convinced you that a good, Christian way of life will stand you in good stead in the times to come,' went on the governor. 'Will you promise me that you will continue to attend services when you go home?'

'Aye,' replied Titus, who had no intention of doing so. Jennet enjoyed the singing and that was fine, but it wasn't for him. He'd already been counting down how many more times he would be obliged to sit on a hard bench and listen to the Reverend Clay wittering on about the rich man in his castle and the poor man at his gate. It didn't have to be so, thought Titus, even though the rich man was content with the way things were.

'Then all that remains is for me to wish you all the best,' said the governor, standing up and holding out his hand. Titus shook it, feeling the warmth of the other man's grip, relieved that his secret was still safe. He liked the governor, who had treated him well, but he knew that he could never agree with his stance on Reform. He felt a little guilty that he'd misled him, but he wasn't about to give up the fight so easily. Let the gentry quake in their shoes and finger their collars, he thought. Times would change so long as the working man kept fighting for his rights.

He walked back to the workshop and watched Sam for a moment before the lad looked up with a grin.

'In trouble?' he asked. The idea that Titus might have transgressed seemed to delight him.

'No, tha cheeky monkey,' he said, giving the lad a playful clip across the head. 'It were to talk about me gettin' out of here.'

Sam's grin faded and his feet stalled on the treadles. 'I don't want thee to go.'

'I know,' said Titus, longing to hug the boy. 'But tha's a good little weaver now. Tha doesn't need me.'

Sam pulled the lever to set the shuttle in motion again as his feet worked the heald frame. The noise filled the workshop and Titus sat down at his own loom. He didn't want to leave Sam either. He was worried about him.

'I'll write down my address and tha can put it in thy pocket!' he called across.

'How will I know what it says?'

'Tha can ask Mr Wright to teach thee to read.'

*

They came for Titus early in the morning and unlocked the door of his cell. He felt as if he'd hardly slept because of his excitement. He emptied his pot one last time. Then he put on his own coat and cap and walked with the turnkey to the front gate. He was handed his few belongings and a small purse that contained his earnings from the weaving work he'd done. The small door was unlocked and he stepped through. He was a free man.

He looked inside the purse and counted the coins. Five shillings. His first thought was for some breakfast and he walked down towards the centre of the town, wondering if any of the inns would be open at this hour.

The church clock struck six. It was still dark, but there was a glimmer of light in the sky to the east and, although cold, it was fine and Titus hoped the day to come would be a good one. He reached the Old Dog just as the doors were being opened for the arrival of the first coach. He went into the deserted parlour and waited a while until a girl came to ask him what he wanted.

'Eggs and bacon, with bread and butter,' said Titus. She eyed him suspiciously. He put a shilling down on the clean white cloth. 'I can pay,' he told her. 'And I'd like a pot of tea, with plenty of milk and sugar.'

Without a word, she disappeared through a door to the kitchens and he sat back in the comfortable chair and enjoyed the warmth from the fire. It was decadent, he knew, and he felt guilty at the expense. He ought to have gone straight home and saved every penny to give to Jennet, but he'd dreamed of this day for months and just this once he felt the overwhelming need to taste a little of the good life.

The girl returned with a pot of tea and a cup and saucer. Titus lifted the lid and stirred it, but even so, it seemed a weak and insipid brew, not the strong drink he'd been looking forward to. Still, it was an improvement on prison fare and the eggs and bacon were tasty and plentiful when they came. He savoured every mouthful and mopped up the last of the fat and egg yolk with a slice of white bread. How long was it since he'd had a meal like this? He couldn't recall.

When the coach arrived, the peace of the parlour was shattered by a group of shrill, chattering women and their accompanying husbands. They glared at Titus until he grew so uncomfortable that he relinquished his seat by the fire, settled his bill and stepped out on to Church Street. The sun had risen, but had no heat at that time of the year and the north wind was biting. He settled his cap lower on his head and wished he had a muffler. Instead, he turned up his collar and, eschewing the temptation of the coach, he turned his face towards the Blackburn road and began to walk.

It was strange to be at liberty, to be able to look into the distance without being hemmed in by a high wall. It felt good, though, and he settled into a steady pace, growing warmer with the exercise and enjoying the feel of working his muscles once more. By mid-morning he had reached the old hall at Samlesbury and he pressed on, wondering if he would reach home in time for dinner and whether Jennet would have something good to eat. There had been no way to send word to her that he'd been released, but he was looking forward to surprising her and seeing the delight on her face when he walked in the door.

The thought of her smile sustained him as he walked the last few miles. He'd grown tired as he reached the outskirts of the town where the mill owners and gentry were building grand houses for themselves. He passed Spring Mount, the home of Dr Barlow. It could have housed a dozen families or more, he thought as he glanced up at the tall red-brick building, filled with wide windows and topped with fancy finials. The doctor kept a peacock too and he could hear its raucous cries as he turned the corner, glad that it was downhill now all the way to Paradise Lane.

Once there, he hurried along to the door of number ten. He lifted the latch and pushed, but found it shut against him. Titus fumbled in his trouser pocket for the door key that had been returned to him on his release from the prison. He put it into the lock, turned the mechanism and pushed the door.

The house was empty and silent. In the grate, a fire had been banked up with coal and was smouldering, ready to be poked into life. He was pleased to see a full scuttle by the side. At least it seemed Jennet had been warm during the winter. Wondering where she and Peggy were, he went into the back kitchen and saw that there was water from the well in the buckets under the slop-stone and some blue milk in a jug by the sink. He opened the cupboard door and saw half a sack of oatmeal, an almost empty bag of sugar, a tin of treacle, and some tea. Perhaps she'd gone shopping, he thought as he filled the kettle and encouraged the fire into a blaze before putting it on the hob. He spooned plenty of tea into the brown pot and as the room began to warm he took off his cap and coat and hung them behind the door, then pulled his chair close to the fire and waited for the water to boil. It would be so good to have a proper cup of tea at last, to say nothing of sleeping in his own bed.

Jennet had grown used to the sewing room, and because it was only part-time she was able to shop, clean and have tea on the table by the time Hannah got in. Of course the money she earned was considerably less than when she was at the mill, and although Hannah was now earning a weaver's wage, she didn't like to ask her to pay it all towards the household expenses.

'Mary's mother only asks her for two and sixpence,' she'd said when Jennet had broached the subject. 'If I give thee everything I earn, I've nowt left for going out.'

Jennet had wanted to point out that next door had more than one wage coming in, and that she didn't like the way Mary was always suggesting some outing to Hannah – the gallery at the Theatre Royal to see a play performed, a trip to the Wax Figures being exhibited in the Assembly Rooms, or a coach party to the seaside. And Hannah was always in competition with Mary about clothes, insisting that her bonnet was out of fashion or her skirt looked shabby. It wasn't that Jennet wanted to spoil her sister's fun. She knew that she worked hard at the mill and deserved her leisure time. But she found it hard when she needed new clothes for Peggy or a few extra pennies to put a decent meal on the table.

As darkness began to fall, they packed up their sewing for the day and put on their shawls to go home. Jennet finished the hem of the linsey petti-coat she was working on, then folded the garment and added it to the pile of finished items that would be taken for distribution to those in need. She'd been given one to wear herself because her own had split and frayed at the seams as her advancing pregnancy swelled her body. It was utilitarian and not in the least pretty and the wool in the cloth made her itch, but at least it was loose and after the baby was born she would be able to take it in. She longed for the warmer weather to come for many reasons. She would be able to stop feeling so cold all the time, the baby would be born and the constant aching in her back and down her left leg would hopefully improve. And Titus would be home. Jennet hoped that things would get better when he found work and brought in a man's wages.

She climbed the stairs slowly to fetch Peggy from the schoolroom. The other children had gone and her daughter was helping Mrs Haworth to tidy away the chalks and slates. The woman smiled at her sympathetically.

'How long to go?' she asked.

'Another couple of months or so.' Jennet sighed, trying to remember if it had been this hard last time. 'Come on, Peggy.' She dressed the child in her coat and bonnet and they went out on to the street. It was quiet, apart from the constant background noise of the mills. It wasn't market day and those without work were either at home or keeping warm inside a public house. It was too cold to linger on the streets. The gaslights were being lit as she walked home with Peggy's hand in hers. The smell pervaded the streets and made her feel nauseous. Peggy was chattering about her day, but Jennet was only half listening, her mind on what she could make for tea that would be a change from the constant rounds of oatcakes. They turned the corner into Paradise Lane and Jennet stopped in her tracks as she saw the flickering light of a candle in her window. Why had Hannah come home so early? Had she been laid off? Was she ill? Why had she not pulled the curtains?

She tugged Peggy along the last few steps, glancing through the window as she approached the door. There was a man asleep in the chair beside her fire! Her heart beat wildly as she considered running for a constable. Then she realised that it was Titus.

'Thy father's home!' she told Peggy as she pushed open the stubborn door and lifted the child inside. 'Titus!' she called as she shut it behind her.

He opened his eyes and looked confused for a moment, as if he couldn't recollect where he was.

'Jennet!' He got up from the chair and held out his arms.

She fell against him, breathing in the smell of him as his arms enveloped her. She touched his face with her fingers and gazed up at him before hugging him again. 'I didn't expect thee today! I've nowt for thy tea, only oatcakes. If I'd known I'd have got summat special.'

'I thought tha were out shopping.'

'Nay. I've work at the Ladies' Charity Sewing Room on Chapel Street. It's thy daddy,' she told the bewildered child as Titus picked up his daughter, not sure if Peggy even remembered him.

She unwrapped herself from her shawl and hung it on the peg, then turned to find Titus staring at her. His smile had gone and a look of disbelief had taken its place.

'Tha's with child,' he said.

'Aye.' They stared at one another over Peggy's head. In her joy at finding him home, Jennet had forgotten for a moment that he knew nothing of her condition.

'How?' he asked. She could see that he was calculating the months in his head and failing to make sense of it.

'I can explain,' she told him.

Sensing the tension, Peggy began to cry and reached out for Jennet. She took the child from Titus and busied herself unbuttoning her daughter's coat.

'She's tired,' she said. 'Let's have our tea and put her to bed, and then we'll talk. I don't want her upset.'

'Jennet, I don't understand. I've been gone since last April ...' He looked bemused and she wondered how she was going to tell him what had happened. Perhaps it was best to be honest.

'Tha's not the father,' she said as she picked Peggy up again, making a barrier between them as his face twitched and she saw his hands form into fists.

'Then whose brat is it? Did someone force thee?'

'No. No. Not that,' she said. She could have blamed George, she supposed. He wasn't here to defend himself, but her conscience wouldn't allow her to brand the man a rapist when she knew that the fault had been hers. She could have claimed it was Hargreaves'. He had forced her, after all, but if she did, she knew Titus would go across the road and have it out with him, and it wouldn't help any of them if he was sent back to prison.

'Then what?' he asked.

'I'll tell thee later.'

'Tha'll tell me now!' His hand slapped down on the table and both she and Peggy jumped. Peggy began to howl.

'Tha's frightening her. Stop it.'

'I want to know the truth, Jennet!'

She shushed Peggy in her arms, stroking the child's hair and telling her that it was all right, that there was nothing to be afraid of. She hoped her words were true.

'It were when we came to Lancaster for the Assizes. George had come into some money and he were generous to me. He paid my coach fare and when we had to wait overnight for the sentencing, he paid for a room. But there were only one room left. I thought tha were going to be transported ...'

'So tha slept with him?' He sounded astonished.

'It wasn't like that,' she explained. 'I was upset. He comforted me. Somehow one thing led to another. I'm not right sure how it happened. It wasn't as if it were planned—'

'He took advantage of thee!'

'Where's tha going?' she asked as he headed for the door.

'I'm going to sort him out, that's where I'm going!'

'No! He's not there. He's gone to America.'

'So he takes advantage of another man's wife then runs halfway across the world to avoid the consequences!'

'He didn't know about the baby. I didn't know 'til after he were long gone. Sit down, Titus,' she pleaded. 'Sit down and let's talk properly. Tha's only upsetting Peggy with all thy shouting.'

'Tha wants me to sit and discuss it, like it were of no more consequence than what we're to have for us tea?'

'No. No, of course not.' She felt the tears on her cheeks. 'But what's done is done.' She was about to say that if she could have undone it, she would have. But it wasn't true. She'd had the chance and chosen not to.

He pulled the chair out from under the table and sat on it, his elbows on his knees and his head in his hands.

'This isn't the homecoming I were expecting,' he said.

She heard the door scrape open and Hannah came in. She stopped in surprise at the sight of them then looked from one to the other. 'I see tha's told him,' she said.

'What's she doing here?' asked Titus.

'I'm living here.'

He looked at Jennet for confirmation.

'Hannah has work as a weaver,' she said. 'It's her wage as has kept us going these months whilst tha's been away. I couldn't have afforded to pay the rent and feed us otherwise.' She handed her daughter to Hannah. 'Take Peggy,' she said. 'Go and put her in bed. I'll come up in a minute.'

Hannah looked as if she was going to object, but a glance at Titus's face seemed to convince her that it wasn't a good idea. She stomped up the stairs and left them to it.

'If tha hadn't gone to that Reform meeting none of this would have happened!' Jennet threw at him, feeling less afraid now that Hannah was in the house.

'Right, so it's my fault now, is it?'

'Well, tha's partly to blame. I would never have been in Lancaster with George if it hadn't been for thee.'

'I did nowt wrong,' he said. 'And it's not my fault if justice is corrupt. Tha can't offload the fault on to me, Jennet. I've thought about thee every day, counting down the hours until I could see thee again. I were so happy when they let me go this morning. And I were so looking forward to seeing thee. But now ...' He shook his head and looked at her as if she disgusted him.

She sat down on the opposite side of the table. She'd known that it would be hard, but she had convinced herself that he would understand, that he would forgive her.

'I'm sorry,' she said. She could feel the baby squirming inside her, upset at the noise and the anger, suffering for what she'd done even before it was born.

He stood up and reached for his jacket and cap.

'Where's tha going?'

'I don't know.'

'But tha'll come back?'

'I don't know,' he replied. 'I don't rightly know.'

He wrenched open the door and shut it behind him with a slam. She saw him pass the window, head down, hands in pockets, and she was afraid that he would never come back.

Hannah came back downstairs and without a word she brewed fresh tea and set the table. She buttered oatcakes and put a plate in front of Jennet.

'I'm not hungry. Take some up for Peggy.'

'She's asleep.'

'She'll wake later. Save summat for her.'

'Here, drink thy tea.'

Jennet picked up the cup and sipped. It was hot and sweet.

'Is he coming back?' asked Hannah.

'I don't know.'

'Well, I'll bed down in the back room with Peggy anyway.'

'Aye,' said Jennet, and although she wished he would come back, she dreaded the prospect of him sharing her bed whilst he was so angry with her.

After a while she went upstairs and undressed, leaving Hannah to clear away and bank up the fire for the night.

'Shall I lock up?' asked her sister, standing in the doorway with a candle in her hand.

'Best leave it unbarred. In case he comes home,' said Jennet.

Hannah went to bed in the back room and Jennet must have dozed a little after the lights went out because she was wakened by the sound of the door being opened. Someone closed it and she heard unsteady footsteps on the stairs. Her hands tightened around the blankets as she waited, wondering what to do.

Titus came in, staggering a little. He stank of drink and she wondered where he'd got the money to pay for it. She didn't speak and neither did he. She heard him take off his boots and his trousers and then he fell on to his side of the bed. Jennet clung to the edge and waited until he began to snore, then she slipped out, pulled a shawl around her and went to the back bedroom where she squeezed into bed with Hannah, needing her warmth, her familiarity – and her protection.

Chapter Fifteen

They both woke to the sound of Titus swearing and cursing when the knocker-up rapped on the window. They crept down the stairs to persuade the fire into a blaze so they could brew tea. Jennet was feeding Peggy and Hannah was getting ready for work when he came down and slumped in the chair by the hearth. Jennet passed him a cup of tea. He took it without a word and sipped a little before getting up to go down the yard.

'Will tha be all right?' asked Hannah.

'Aye. Don't miss work on account of me.'

'I'll be back at dinner time,' Hannah said as she went out, wrapped in her shawl, and headed down the street.

Titus came back in, looking pale and tired, and sat down by the fire again. Jennet offered him porridge but he shook his head and then winced at the pain it caused him. He'd never been much of a drinker and she'd never known him come home the worse for it before. She cleared the table and washed up, taking Peggy with her into the back kitchen. It wasn't a day for the sewing room and she'd planned to go to the market, but now she wondered if she should go to Ramsgreave instead and tell her parents. They would only send her home, though, telling her to sort it out herself. It wasn't as if she could claim he'd been violent. He hadn't laid a finger on her.

She went back into the parlour where Titus was still sitting in the chair, staring at the flames in the hearth. He looked well, apart from his hangover.

'Did they treat thee well at Preston?' she asked.

'Aye. I can't grumble. There were food enough,' he said.

'Good.' She sat down opposite him. 'I've missed thee,' she said. 'It's not been easy.'

He looked up and met her eyes for a moment. 'I've thought about thee every day, worried about thee too,' he said.

They sat on in silence for a while.

'I have to go to the market,' she said. 'Dost tha want to come?'

'Nay. I'll sit here a while.'

'Come on, Peggy,' she said. 'Let's go and see if Toffee Jem is there.'

With the promise of a treat, Peggy took her hand eagerly and they went out. There'd been a frost earlier and the streets still sparkled in patches. Toffee Jem was standing at the top of Church Street with his tray of confectionery, stamping his feet and rubbing his hands against the cold. Peggy stood on tiptoe to see what was on offer and when she pointed to a twist of barley sugar Jennet handed over a ha'penny without a murmur and allowed her to suck at it noisily as they went around the stalls. She bought some potatoes and a bit of scrag end to make a pie for dinner. Then they got the oatmeal, the milk, a small piece of cheese, and some sugar and treacle. It was extravagant, but it wasn't every day that her husband came home and she hoped that if she could show him that she still cared about him, he might find it in his heart to forgive her.

When they got back, Titus was still sitting in front of the fire.

'I'll have to go to the well,' she said as she put things away.

'I'll go. A breath o' fresh air'll do me good.' He came into the back kitchen with his jacket and cap on and picked up the two empty buckets.

'I'll make a potato pie.'

'That'll be nice.'

He went out and she breathed more easily as the tension dissipated. Their marriage was broken and she had no idea if it could be fixed.

Titus walked up to the well with the buckets clanging on their handles. There was a queue, as usual, and it reminded him of the queue he had joined every morning in the prison to empty his chamber pot. They would all be there now, getting on with their work. Young Sam would be doing his weaving. He would be alone in the workshop unless they'd put a new prisoner in. Titus hadn't realised how much he would miss the boy. He'd been his companion almost every day for months and they'd grown close. He'd managed to hug the lad before they packed up on his last day and he'd slipped his address into his pocket. Sam had promised that he would learn to read, that he would stay out of trouble, and that he would let Titus know how he was getting on. He doubted that the lad would remember once he got out of the prison. He wished that he could be there to guide him. He needed a steadying hand.

The queue shuffled forwards and Titus allowed himself to think about Jennet. He'd been trying to shut it out of his mind, as if it wouldn't be true if he didn't acknowledge it. He'd spent all the previous evening trying not to acknowledge it as he'd bought drink after drink for himself and his companions in the Old Bull. He'd been their best friend although he had no idea who they were and he doubted that they would recognise him this morning. He'd bought ale until all his money was gone and then he'd staggered home, but Jennet had still been pregnant. Now he had a throbbing head, a queasy tummy and an empty pocket. He'd been a fool. He should have stayed at home and faced up to what had happened.

They moved forwards again and when it was his turn he filled the buckets to the brim and walked back to Paradise Lane with them, going slowly so that the water didn't slop over on to his clogs. There were men outside the pubs already, waiting for the doors to open. Some were smoking pipes. Most were looking miserable. He trudged past them.

What had Jennet been thinking of? He'd never even considered that she might go with another man. It was so out of character. Although that George had been a charmer. He had a knack for persuading folk around to his way of thinking. He'd liked him, but when he considered it, the man had abandoned him the night of the riot to save his own skin and that rankled. He remembered how relieved he'd been when he saw him with Jennet at the trial. How pleased he'd been that someone was looking after her. He ought to have realised then what George was up to. And what about his wife? What about Lizzie?

He put down one bucket to push open the door. As he did, the adjoining door opened and a man came out together with a boy with a malformed hand.

'How do,' he greeted them. The new neighbour stared at him for a moment. Then he turned on his heel and strode off without a word. There were nowt so queer as folk, thought Titus as he picked up the buckets and went in.

The pie was cooking and it smelled good. Peggy looked up from where she was playing on the rug and he smiled at her. She returned the smile, but he wasn't sure that she remembered him. He took the water into the kitchen.

'Thanks,' said Jennet without looking at him.

'Lizzie from next door?' he asked. 'What happened to her? Did she go to America an' all?'

'No. She died. She had the fever.'

'Right. So he went alone?'

'He asked me to go with him. Wanted to take our Peggy too. He said he'd take good care of us.'

Titus found it hard to believe her. He thought that maybe she was just saying it to spite him. What would a man like George want with a woman and a small child trailing behind him?

No. The death of Lizzie had given him the freedom to go off to make his fortune. He would never have asked Jennet to go with him.

'So why didn't tha go?' he challenged, trying to force her to admit her lie.

'Because I couldn't bear to think of thee coming home and finding us gone.'

He said nothing for a moment, hoping that she might add that it was because she loved him. But she didn't. She wouldn't even look at him and he realised that she didn't love him any more. Maybe she'd loved George. Maybe she still did.

'It might have been for the best if tha had gone,' he muttered.

'Aye. It might,' she snapped back. 'But it's too late now.'

'When's it due?' he asked.

'In a couple of months.'

'And what then?'

'What dost tha mean *what then*?' She wiped her hands and pushed her sleeves further up her arms.

'Well, I just thought ...' He wasn't sure how to explain what he'd thought. Would she send it to the workhouse so that they could get back to normal? Surely she'd thought about it. 'I just wondered what tha planned to do with it.'

'What dost tha mean *do with it*? What would I do with it?'

'Well, I wondered who would care for it.'

'I'll care for it!' Her eyes shone at him defiantly. 'It's my child!'

'Aye, but it's not mine,' he reminded her. She stared at him as if she'd never considered it before. 'Or didst tha expect as I'd put my hand in my pocket and raise it like my own?'

She picked up the rolling pin and then threw it back down on to the table.

'Tha hasn't put thy hand in thy pocket these past months!' she shouted. 'Who dost tha think has fed and clothed our Peggy? Aye, and I'll feed and clothe this baby too, without any help from thee if needs be. Look at thee!' she raged. 'Tha's not put a penny on the table, but tha had money from somewhere to squander on drink last night!'

Guilt seeped into every part of him. He had intended to give her the money that he'd earned. If he hadn't been confronted by the sight of her swollen belly, he would have done. If anyone was to blame for last night, she was.

'Well, I'll not pay a farthing to bring up another man's child,' he told her. 'Best if it goes to the workhouse as soon as it's born.'

He went back out on to the street and began to walk with no clear idea of where he was going. He wandered amongst the market stalls. The potato cart smelled appetising, but his pockets were empty. He saw a farthing on the cobbles and bent to pick it up. It bought him a couple of oatcakes from a stall and he stood and ate them as the cold wind tugged at his jacket. He needed a job.

He didn't want to go back to the Dandy Mill. There were too many bad memories there, so he set off towards Hornby's Brookhouse Mill to ask if there was work there. As he passed the Assembly Rooms, he saw that a piece of paper had been pinned up on the door. Before, he would have simply glanced and walked by, but now that he could read he stopped to see what it said. The title was clear enough: *Reform Meeting*. With a mounting sense of excitement he read on. There was to be a meeting that evening at seven o'clock. The speaker was to be George Dewhurst, the same man who had spoken at the meeting on the moor nearly a year ago. Titus decided that he would attend.

Jennet cried as she dished up the potato pie. Hannah and Peggy were sitting at the table, but the place she'd set for Titus was empty and she had no idea where he'd gone.

'He told me as I should take it to the work-house,' she sobbed. 'My own flesh and blood.'

'Would Mam and Dad not take it in?' suggested Hannah.

'I suppose they might. It is their grandchild.'

'Ask 'em,' said Hannah as she tucked into the pie. 'It could be a solution.'

'I'll walk up this afternoon. I'll leave this to keep warm,' she said, putting Titus's plate inside the oven, 'in case he comes home.'

After Hannah had gone back to work, Jennet got ready to go to Ramsgreave. She hesitated on the doorstep after she'd closed the door, then decided to risk not locking it. She didn't know if Titus had his key and she didn't want him to come home and not be able to get in. It wasn't as if they had anything worth stealing now, she thought.

Peggy insisted on walking all the way and Jennet was glad not to have to carry her, but it took them a long time to get there and the steep hill seemed steeper than ever.

'Only me!' Jennet called when they arrived at last. Her parents looked up and smiled as Peggy ran across to her grandmother to climb up on her knee.

'What brings thee in the middle of the week?' asked her father.

'Titus is home,' she said.

'Thank goodness!' Her mother glanced behind her, looking for him. 'Has he not come? Is he all right?' she asked.

'He's fine.' Jennet hung up her shawl and came across to sit down near the fire. 'He were a bit shocked – about the baby.'

'Well, tha knew he would be.'

'Aye. But I didn't expect him to be so angry.'

'Tha can hardly blame him, our Jennet. He'll come around.'

'Dost tha think so? He were talking about sending it to the workhouse.

'That were harsh,' replied her mother as she settled Peggy more comfortably on her knee. 'He won't though, will he?' Concern etched her face.

'I'll not let him. But if he refuses to bring it up … I wondered if I might bring it here.'

Her mother didn't reply immediately and Jennet's hopes faded. 'I don't know,' said her mother. 'It were hard work caring for Peggy, and a baby isn't easy. I'm not as young as I used to be …'

'Tha's not sickly, is tha?'

'No, not that.' Her mother waved her worries aside. 'If there's no other way then I suppose we'll have to take it in. It's just that I hadn't thought to begin all that again at my age.'

'Perhaps he'll come around,' said Jennet. She had to cling to that hope, although she couldn't imagine it ever happening.

She stayed a while at Ramsgreave, not wanting to go back to Paradise Lane, but as the dusk began to draw in, her father suggested she'd better get home before dark and she hurried back down the lane, urging Peggy to keep up.

There was a candle burning in the window, and when she went in, Hannah was back from the mill and making tea.

'Mam and Dad all right?'

'Aye.'

'Will they take the child?'

'I think so. If it comes to it.' Jennet sat down and allowed her sister to wait on her for a change. 'Has Titus been back?'

'I haven't seen him. Pie's still here. Shall we eat it?'

'Nay. Leave it for him,' said Jennet. 'He'll be hungry when he comes in.'

'Will tha be all right if I go out for a bit?' asked Hannah as they ate their tea.

'Aye,' said Jennet. 'Where's tha off to tonight?'

'Assembly Rooms.'

'What's on there then? I hope it isn't the laughing gas again.'

'No.' Hannah poured more tea and Jennet could see that she didn't want to tell her.

'Hannah? What's tha going to? I don't want thee getting into any bother. I've enough on my plate as it is.'

Her sister hesitated. 'It's a Reform meeting,' she admitted.

'Oh, Hannah! No! Don't get involved with that. Not thee an' all,' pleaded Jennet.

'But it's all official,' she argued. 'It's just a talk. There won't be any trouble. And if folk don't support it then how will it ever come about?'

'I suppose Mary's at the back of all this?'

'Mary thinks it's important.'

'She'll be wanting votes for women next, never mind men.' Jennet sighed. 'She's a bad influence. I wish tha weren't so close with her.'

Hannah didn't reply. It was an argument they'd had so many times before that everything had already been said and Jennet knew that it was useless to try to convince her sister to give up her friendship.

'Don't be late,' she conceded.

Titus had been kept hanging around at the mill for hours, and then turned away. He would try the others tomorrow, he thought. He was weary and hungry and wanted his tea, but he didn't want to see Jennet with her body rounded with another man's child. If he could lay hands on that

George he'd knock him to kingdom come for messing with his wife. He'd probably only accompanied her to the Assizes so that he could take advantage of her. How he hated the man. He hoped his ship had sunk and that he was fish food at the bottom of the ocean.

In the end his anger overcame his hunger and he hung about the town centre until it was time for the meeting. He followed the excited crowd down to the Assembly Rooms, hoping that tonight wouldn't end badly. But his reading and his discussions with Mr Wright had convinced him that Parliamentary Reform was the only way to resolve the starvation and chaos that beset the working classes. And it was up to men like him to fight for it.

He crowded in with the rest of the workers. Most were men but there were a few women too – the young unmarried girls who didn't have children to care for. A few chairs had been provided around the edge for those who couldn't stand for long, but most folk stood up. The voices rose in a crescendo, then fell as they thought things were about to begin, and then rose again. At length, Dewhurst climbed up on to a hastily constructed platform and quiet rippled across the gathering.

'Good to see so many of thee come out after a long day,' he said. 'Sixteen hours of work, from dawn to dusk and beyond, is more than enough for any man, or woman. And for that amount of toil he deserves a wage as he can live on. I don't need to tell thee that an able-bodied man can earn no more than five shillings a week. And even with two workers to a household, there's only ten shillings for food, clothing, fuel and rent. It's not enough for the moderate needs of a man. Folk are perishing from want of food. Hundreds of weavers and their wives and children have already died, and it's time as Parliament took us seriously!'

'Hear! Hear!'

'And what are the causes of this starvation? I'll tell thee. At the heart of it is the want of a reform of the Parliament! Here in this town, we return not one member to Parliament, whilst there are rotten boroughs with just a handful of constituents who return one or even two members! If we had a representative, chosen by a secret ballot, and by the whole of the population, then we would be granted the relief we so badly need and richly deserve! We don't ask for charity. We ask for a fair, living wage for a hard day's work!'

'Hear! Hear!' roared the crowd, Titus shouting along with them.

'And the first thing that a Reformed Parliament must do is repeal the Corn Bill!'

'Hear! Hear!'

'I propose', went on Dewhurst when he could be heard again, 'to ask all of thee to sign this petition that I will send on behalf of everyone here to the House. We will be heard!'

After the speeches were finished, reams of paper were laid out on tables for signatures. Titus waited until it was his turn and picked up one of the pens with a new-found confidence. He wrote his name and drew a line under it: Titus Eastwood. It would be read in London. They would know that he could read and write. They would have to take him seriously, him and every other person here who had waited patiently to add their name or their mark to the petition.

People began to make their way home, talking animatedly. He saw a few constables hanging about because there were always bound to be a few stupid folk who had drunk too much and who thought it was fun to chuck a brick at a window, but on the whole it was a peaceful meeting with an air of purpose.

As Titus wandered back to Paradise Lane, he saw two girls walking in front of him with their arms linked together. From the back he recognised Hannah. She must have been to the meeting too. He hung back, not wanting to get into conversation. At the corner of King Street, the girls said their goodnights and separated. One walked towards Paradise Lane, but Hannah set off up France Street. Curious about where she was going and what she was up to, Titus followed at a distance. She was young to be out on her own and he hoped that she wasn't carrying on with some lad. It was bad enough Jennet being with another man's child without her sister following suit. At the top of Prince's Street, Hannah turned and as Titus followed her he saw that she was only walking around the block and approaching Paradise Lane from the other direction. He saw her friend go into the house next door and, moments later, Hannah went into number ten. He thought it was odd, until he remembered the man who had refused to speak to him earlier. It seemed that there was trouble with the neighbours to add to his problems. He would ask Jennet about it when he got in.

But when he opened the door he saw that only Hannah was in the parlour and she was lighting a candle to go up to bed.

'There's some potato pie,' she told him. 'Jennet kept it warm for ages but it's probably gone cold by now.'

Without so much as a goodnight, she went up the stairs and left him alone. The fire had been banked up and the room was chilly. He hung up his cap but kept his coat on to sit by the smoky coals and eat the cold meal. It tasted good. Jennet knew how much he loved a good tattie pie and she must have made it especially. There was even meat in it. He felt a little guilty at having stayed out all day. He knew that she would think him ungrateful, but surely she must have realised that she couldn't drop a surprise like that on him without him being a bit put out. Still, as she had said, what was done was done. It had to be faced.

He put his plate in the sink, barred the doors and took his candle upstairs. He went quietly into the bedroom in case she was sleeping, but the bed was empty. She must have gone to sleep with her sister. He couldn't rightly blame her. He knew he'd spoken harshly, but the shock had made him so angry that he couldn't think straight.

What was to be done? he wondered as he lay down. One thing was for sure and that was that he had to find work. The talk of folk dying for want of food had brought home to him how dire the situation was. He'd been shielded from it whilst he was in the prison. Even though the food had been plain, there had been enough. He hadn't gone hungry. And the money he'd earned. He groaned as he thought of it. All spent and wasted. What a fool he'd been.

*

Titus was up before her and had the fire going and the kettle on when Jennet came down the stairs with Peggy.

'I've to go to work today,' she told him.

'Aye. Who looks after our Peggy?'

'She comes with me and goes to school, up-stairs at the sewing room. A Mrs Haworth looks to the children. She's teaching them to count and say rhymes and such. Tha doesn't object, dost tha?'

'Nay. It's a good thing for her to get an education.' He picked up a cloth to grasp the hot kettle. 'I've learned to read and write myself,' he told her. 'I signed my name on a petition last night, for a reform of the Parliament.'

Jennet wasn't surprised that he'd gone to the meeting. 'Tha'll end up in prison again if tha's not careful,' she grumbled.

'I suppose tha'd be glad to see the back of me.'

'Of course I wouldn't. It's been hard and I've been counting the days until tha could come home. I were looking forward to it,' she told him. 'I knew it would be a shock for thee, but I hoped tha would find it in thee to try to understand. It were the work of a moment,' she said. 'It meant nowt.'

'Well, it's had a lasting consequence,' he said, glancing at her belly.

Jennet drained her cup and began to get Peggy ready. She would usually have washed everything up and put it away, but she was late and she left it for Titus.

'Tidy up before tha goes out,' she told him before she pulled the door shut behind her.

She was stitching diligently in the little room on Chapel Street when Mrs Hornby, another of the mill owners' wives who ran the Ladies' Charity, called in to see them. She looked lovely, her cheeks pink with cold and a light dusting of late snow on her fur collar. She greeted them all warmly and spoke a word to each woman as she made her way around the table to admire their work.

'Mrs Eastwood,' she said when she reached Jennet. 'I believe that your husband has come home?'

'Aye. That's right.' Jennet wondered why she was asking. She hoped she wasn't about to have her job taken away. Maybe she didn't qualify now that she had a man to support her. She put her work down and looked up at Mrs Hornby, trying to discern her meaning.

'My husband said that he called at the mill yesterday asking for a job, but he had to turn him away.'

'Aye,' said Jennet. Titus hadn't told her that.

'He was wondering if he'd had better luck else-where.'

'Not yet. I think he was going to look for work again this morning.' She was sure now that she would lose this job if Titus got work.

'Well, if he doesn't get anything my husband says to ask him to call again,' Mrs Hornby was saying. 'He may be able to help. It won't be in the mill, but he's setting up a scheme of work to build a new road up at Revedge. He has that man Macadam coming to see what needs to be done. He'll need labourers and if your husband is interested he'll add his name to the list.'

'Thank you,' said Jennet, relieved.

She hurried home that evening to tell Titus about the job offer only to find the house empty and the breakfast pots still on the table where she'd left them. She felt an unaccountable anger overwhelm her. It wouldn't have taken him more than five or ten minutes to clear things away and wash them as she'd asked him to, but no, he'd gone off and just left them there as if it was nothing to do with him. She settled Peggy on a chair at the table whilst she stoked the fire and put the kettle on. She'd hoped that there might be a cup of tea waiting for her. She would have loved to sit down and rest for a while, but it seemed the days when he had cared for her with such thoughtful tenderness were long gone. She just hoped that he wasn't in the pub.

Titus had spent the day visiting every weaving shed and spinning mill in the town and at every place he'd received the same reply. *Sorry, no work at the moment.* He'd begun to wonder if it was his reputation as a loom breaker that meant that there was scant hope of his being taken on anywhere.

In the end he'd drifted into the Lion even though he had no money. He'd sat down on a stool near some other men and tried to look as if he was one of the crowd, hoping that the landlord wouldn't notice that he hadn't bought anything.

The men were discussing the Reform meeting and Titus listened for a while, nodding as they repeated that every man should have a vote. One of them greeted him as if he knew him and asked him if he'd found a job. When he said no, the man bought him half a pint. Titus felt awkward accepting it, but then realised that perhaps the man had been one of the people he'd bought drinks for in the Old Bull the other night.

They talked on for a while, until Titus realised that it had grown dark.

'What time is it?' he asked. Someone brought out a pocket watch and announced that it was gone seven. 'I'd best be on my way. Thanks for the drink,' he said as he pulled up his collar against the sleet and stepped out into the cold.

He'd intended to get home earlier. He'd hurried out that morning, eager to look for work and had neglected to clear the table. It had slipped his mind and it was only when he'd been halfway down the street that he'd remembered. Rather than turn back, he'd decided that he could do it later. As long as it was done by the time Jennet got home she'd never know. And he'd intended to have the kettle on and the tea ready so that she could put her feet up. He'd always done that for her when she'd been pregnant with Peggy, and when she'd been expecting the boy that they'd lost. The thought threatened to overwhelm him with sorrow. His son. He'd asked to see him before he was buried and he had been so tiny. He could have held him in the palm of his hand and yet he'd looked so perfect, with all his fingers and toes, like a child in miniature, except that he was cold and had no breath in him. He'd hoped that Jennet would fall pregnant again, although he hadn't wanted to rush her. He'd intended to give her time to get over the loss, to settle into their new house – and more importantly he'd wanted to wait until he was bringing home a good wage, so that he could give his family everything they needed. That was why he was so keen to give his support to the Reformers. He wanted a fair wage for a day's work and a say in who made the decisions that affected them all. It was why it had been such a shock when he'd seen her, pregnant again, but with a child that wasn't his. He had been so angry. He'd almost wanted to strike her.

Perhaps this baby would die, he thought as he turned the corner into Paradise Lane. That would be the best solution. He'd seen the horror in Jennet's eyes when he'd mentioned the workhouse. She would never agree to that, but if it died, she would be sad for a while, and then they could try again, and she could have another child that was his and they could pretend that this baby had never happened.

The lamp was burning and the curtains were drawn. Titus cursed himself for staying out so long. She must have come home to find the breakfast pots still on the table and hated him for his slovenliness. He must find a way of making it up to her, although he didn't know how. He couldn't even tell her that he'd found employment.

He pushed open the door and went in, shook the wet from his cap and hung it up. Jennet and Hannah were eating their tea.

'Where's our Peggy?'

'In bed.'

'Sorry I'm late.'

'Thy tea's keepin' warm.' He fetched the plate from the oven and sat down. 'Did tha find a job?' Jennet asked him.

'No.' He saw the hope fade from her face and knew the only reason she hadn't been angry was because she'd thought that he'd been working.

'Tha's been drinking,' she accused him as she smelled the beer on his breath when she passed him a cup of tea.

'Only half a pint. A friend bought it for me.'

They ate in silence for a while.

'I've been to every mill,' he said at last, 'and it's the same tale everywhere. No work.'

'Mrs Hornby came to the sewing room today. She said as Mr Hornby is taking on labourers for a new road at Revedge and tha's to go and see him if tha's no other job.'

'Labouring?' he said.

'What's wrong with labour? It's honest work. And it's better than nowt!' she snapped at him.

'But I'm a skilled artisan!' he said. 'I'm a weaver! I don't want work breaking up rocks and digging holes.'

'Tha'd rather live off my wages, would tha?' she asked. 'Tha forgets as I'll not be bringing them in for much longer!'

'Trade'll pick up soon,' he said. 'Everyone says so. Mills'll be crying out for skilled workers before too long. And I'll be no good to them if my hands are all spoiled with rough work.'

Jennet sighed and began to gather the plates to wash them as if she was making the point that she had to do everything. Titus heard her crashing them about in the back kitchen and felt guilty, but it was unreasonable of her to expect him to become a labourer, he thought. If he went road building he wouldn't be able to keep looking for work in the mills and in the end they'd be worse off.

Chapter Sixteen

'I'm thinking of packing in being a weaver,' said
Hannah when she came in one night. Jennet put
the lid back on the pot of soup she'd been stirring
and looked at her sister as she hung up her shawl
and sat down at the table.

'What's brought this on?' she asked.

'Mary says we can do better than the mill.'

'Doing what?' asked Jennet, wondering what
Mary had suggested now.

'We've been thinking about going into service
instead.'

'Into service?'

'Aye. Working at one of the big houses,' said
Hannah. 'It were Mary's idea. She said the Sudells
are looking for people. There are jobs as maids
and we'd get a room at the big house to sleep in.
Mary's really fed up at home,' she said, 'and it's
not been the same here since Titus came back.'

Jennet sat down beside her sister. She could see Hannah's point of view. It had been all right when there'd been just the two of them and Peggy, but she knew that Hannah was tired of all the arguing. Perhaps it would be better if she went and made a fresh start, she thought. She'd had a racking cough ever since she began work in the mill and at least the air would be fresh out at the Sudells' new mansion.

'I'll miss thee if tha goes,' she said.

'Tha'll miss my wages,' said Hannah with a touch of bitterness. 'There'll only be what tha's bringing in, unless he shapes himself and gets a job.'

'Aye,' said Jennet. Titus's inability to get work at any of the mills and his refusal to take the offer of work on the road-building scheme was the main cause of their arguments. He was convinced that he would be offered work as a weaver soon, but Jennet wasn't so sure. She'd tried to explain that the mills wanted women for weaving because they were cheaper and whilst men were being taken on as spinners Titus had no experience and wasn't willing to learn. All he seemed concerned about was Reform. He went out to meetings every night, asking her for money so he could buy his round of drinks, and then came home all fired up and talking about votes for every man. It would never happen, thought Jennet. The gentry weren't going to allow their workers to have a say in how things were run. It would take away their power and they would never agree to that.

'I suppose tha has to think about what's right for thee,' she told her sister. 'If tha's unhappy at the mill and thinks tha'd be better off working for the Sudells then I'll not stand in thy way.'

'I'm glad,' said Hannah. 'We're going to stop off work tomorrow and walk up to Mellor to ask.'

'Then put on thy best bonnet and make a good impression,' said Jennet. 'They'll be lucky to have such a bonny lass as thee in their fancy new house.'

The morning that Hannah left, with her meagre belongings packed into a little cloth bag, it was as much as Jennet could do to keep the smile on her face and wish her well. At the door, she hugged her hard.

'Tha'll come back to visit?' she asked.

'When I can,' said Hannah, 'but it's only one full day a month and I'll have to go to see Mam and Dad as well.'

'But tha'll come and see me when the baby's born?'

'Of course I will,' said Hannah. She turned with a smile as Mary came out and slammed the door of her house with finality. They no longer cared that Titus knew they were friends and they linked arms and set off up Paradise Lane at a cracking pace, not even looking back to wave before they turned the corner. It was for the best, Jennet told herself as she went back inside.

'Come on,' she said to Peggy, taking her daughter's coat down from behind the door. 'Time for school.' Peggy held out her arms eagerly. She enjoyed her days in the schoolroom with Mrs Haworth; she could count from one to ten now, and say her letters. Jennet was proud of her and Titus was talking about teaching her to read. He wanted her to have an education and it was one subject they agreed on. Jennet wanted a better life for Peggy than the drudgery of the mill. The new baby too, she thought, as they set off for Chapel Street. The new life that writhed inside her also deserved a chance, and Titus saying that the child would learn to read and write in the workhouse was not excuse enough for it to go there. She would fight for her baby, even if it meant destroying her marriage.

On the following Sunday morning, Titus looked up from the pamphlet he was reading by the fire when a tentative knock sounded on the door.

'Who's that?'

'How should I know?' said Jennet, who was ironing his shirts on the table. 'Go and see.'

She watched as he pulled the door open a little and then the morose expression he'd been wearing ever since he'd come home was suddenly replaced by the familiar smile that made her heart ache. He'd smiled at her like that once, she thought, before wondering who on earth it could be.

'Come in, lad! Come in!' said Titus, forcing the door wide. Jennet watched a skinny boy of about twelve or thirteen years step over the threshold and give her a wary look.

'Mornin',' he said, pulling his cap from his head and leaving his fair hair standing up in badly cut tufts.

'This is Sam. I told thee about him.'

'Aye,' said Jennet. Titus had talked a lot about the lad he'd taught to weave at the prison. It was clear that he'd been very taken with him and she'd allowed him to chunner on and on about it, thinking that the affection he clearly had for the boy would fade with time. To be truthful she hadn't listened that carefully, and she'd never even considered that Sam might show up on their doorstep.

'Put the kettle on, Jennet!' said Titus. 'Tha'll have a drink of tea with us, won't tha?' he said to the lad. 'Sit thee down.'

Jennet moved the ironing aside and went to fill the kettle as her husband and the boy sat at the table.

'How long has tha been out?' asked Titus.

'A few days. I hope tha doesn't mind me showin' up like this, but I didn't know where else to go – and tha did leave the address with me.'

'Aye, tha's welcome. Did tha manage to read it?'

'I had Mr Wright read it to me,' said Sam. 'But I did have some lessons with him. I can read a bit now.'

'Good lad!' Titus patted his shoulder and Jennet thought he would have hugged the boy if she hadn't been there. 'Has tha had owt to eat?'

'Not since yesterday.'

'Tha must be famished. Jennet, fetch some oatcakes for the lad. Is there any treacle left to go with 'em?'

Jennet went into the back kitchen to look. They were hard pushed now that Hannah was no longer bringing in a wage. Titus was still refusing to take work on the road-building project and all they had to live on was her wage from the sewing room. It was hard enough to keep themselves without giving away food, but she put oatcakes on a plate and scraped the last of the treacle from the jar. Titus would be asking for it again come teatime, she thought. He seemed to think that the money she earned was boundless and she was worried that they would starve when the baby came and she could no longer work. Perhaps they'd all end up in the workhouse, she thought. It was likely, if something wasn't done. But Titus wouldn't listen. He just kept saying that things would look up soon and he would get work and that she wasn't to worry. One of them had to worry though.

She put the plate on the table and added a dash of milk to the cups whilst the tea brewed. Titus had put his pamphlet in front of the lad and was testing him to see what words he could read. He didn't seem to know many and it sounded like he was guessing them, but Titus looked pleased with him and encouraged him to eat as much as he liked – and he'd soon scoffed the lot.

'Has tha no more?' Titus asked Jennet when the plate was empty.

'No. That was thy tea,' she told him, taking pleasure in the idea that he would have to go hungry for the rest of the day.

'So, what's tha going to do?' Titus asked Sam as Jennet went to the chair by the fire with her tea and sipped at it.

'I don't rightly know. Mr Liddell told me as I should get a proper job, but I don't know how to set about it. I was hoping as tha might put in a good word for me.'

Titus scratched his head. 'Truth is, Sam, there's not much call for hand weaving any more. I haven't even been able to get work myself.'

'Tha's been offered work but tha's too stubborn to take it!' Jennet told him, unable to hold her tongue.

'Only labouring work,' he said. 'That's not for a skilled worker like me.'

'It'd put food on the table!'

The lad looked uncomfortable as he glanced between them. 'I shouldn't have come,' he said, getting up from the chair.

'Nay. Sit thee down,' said Titus before glaring at Jennet. 'I told thee as tha'd be welcome here and tha is welcome. Hast tha got anywhere to stay?'

'No. I've slept rough for the last few nights.'

'That's no good. Tha can stay here if tha likes, until tha gets sorted out.'

'But, Titus …'

'There's room now that Hannah's gone,' he said. 'And when the lad gets work he'll be able to pay a bit of rent.'

'I will!' said Sam. 'I'll gladly pay my way, Mrs Eastwood. And I'll help out with the chores and such, and I'll be no trouble.'

Jennet met his eager blue eyes and had to admit that he seemed a willing sort. 'Well, maybe just for a day or two,' she conceded – against her better judgement, knowing that once the lad got his feet under the table it would be very unlikely that he would move on.

Titus moved Peggy's bed into the front bedroom, squeezing it in across the foot of their bed. It was a tight fit and Jennet was worried that there would be no space for the crib when the new baby came, but perhaps Sam would be gone by then, she hoped. She made up Hannah's bed with fresh sheets and told the lad he could keep his belongings in the small chest of drawers beside it. He shrugged his skinny shoulders.

'I have nowt,' he told her.

'Nothing at all?'

'Only what I has on.' He grinned. She looked at the too short trousers, the worn clogs, frayed shirt and a jacket that would never keep him warm in the biting winds.

'And tha has no family at all?'

'Me mam's in the workhouse at Preston, and my two little sisters. I don't want to end up there,' he said. 'I've heard it's no better than prison. I want to get a job and earn proper money. Not the few pennies they gave me at the prison, but real money so as I can pay my way. I'll not be a burden on thee, I promise,' he told her.

'Well, we'll see,' she said. 'Mind tha keeps this room neat and tidy. I'm not cleaning up after thee.'

Jennet was convinced that young Sam would be an added burden. He seemed eager enough, but all he knew was handloom weaving and if Titus couldn't get work, what chance did he have? But a few days later, she came home from the sewing room to find the table piled high with food and Sam with a huge grin on his face.

Jennet stared in amazement. There was a shoulder of mutton, a bag of potatoes, onions and a sack of oatmeal. There was even a loaf of fresh bread and the smell of it made her want to tear off the crust and eat it there and then.

'Where has all this come from?' she asked.

'I bought it,' he grinned, delighted at her incredulity.

'What with?'

'Money, of course!' He laughed and pulled off his cap to smooth down his hair.

'But, where from?'

'I've been earnin' a bit. Casual work, tha knows.'

'Tha never said.' Jennet thought the lad had been hanging about with Titus all day, either outside the mill or in the beerhouse talking about Reform. Titus had never said that he'd got work.

But she wasn't going to look a gift horse in the mouth, she thought as she surveyed the food on the table.

'I promised as I'd pay my way,' he reminded her.

'Aye, tha did. And I'm grateful,' she told him, picking up the meat to take it through to the back kitchen. She could roast it over the fire and they'd have some for their tea, with the potatoes. Then they could eat the rest cold tomorrow. It would be a rare treat. 'But tha shouldn't have spent all thy money on us,' she said, glancing at his bony ankles poking out of the legs of his trousers. 'Tha could do with some new clothes and a warm coat.'

'I'll buy summat next time,' he told her. 'I don't feel cold, and the warmer weather's coming soon. I just wanted to say a thank you for takin' me in.'

'See, I told thee he were a good lad,' said Titus later after they'd eaten until they were full and Sam had gone off out with John from next door, to treat him to a half-pint at the beer shop.

'Aye,' said Jennet. 'It helps that he's earnin' a bit now and again, but we need a regular wage comin' in,' she reminded him. 'We'll have nowt to live on when the baby comes and we can't rely on a child's generosity.'

The next day wasn't a sewing room day so when she'd done her chores, Jennet got Peggy ready and they walked down King Street to the vicarage. Much as she hated the idea, she needed to speak to Mrs Whittaker about what would happen when the baby was born. As she waited to cross the road near to the Hotel, with Peggy's hand clutched tightly in her own, she saw John from next door lingering on the edge of a group of gentlemen waiting for the Manchester coach. She watched as he approached one of the men and appeared to ask him the time, prompting the man to take out his pocket watch and consult it. Although she didn't speak to her neighbours any more she saw their comings and goings and heard their voices through the walls. She knew that John had been out of work since his accident and that he'd been in the habit of hanging around the house all day. It was good to see him out and about, she thought.

She heard the coachman's bugle and drew Peggy closer against her as the horses raced in. Then she saw Sam out of the corner of her eye. He was talking to John as the gentlemen got on to the coach and she watched as Sam touched John's elbow and they hurried away together. It seemed there was no work for them today.

'Gee-gee?' asked Peggy as they approached the vicarage door.

'Not today, love,' said Jennet as she knocked, doubting that Peggy would be taken up to the nursery again.

The maid opened the door and Jennet wondered if Hannah looked so prim and important in her black dress up at the Sudells' house. She hadn't seen or heard from her since she'd left, but she thought about her every day.

'Yes?' said the maid with her disdainful expression.

'Is Mrs Whittaker in, please? I'd like a word with her.'

'I'll see if she's at home. Wait there,' said the maid before shutting the door on them. Jennet stood and watched the comings and goings down the street. A wagon passed with bales of cotton to be delivered to one of the mills and she wondered if Titus was right when he said that things were looking up. She hoped they were because she hated having to come and beg for help like this.

The maid opened the door again. 'Mrs Whittaker says to step inside. Wait here,' she instructed, leaving Jennet standing in the black and white hallway. 'She'll be out in a moment,' she added and without offering to take their coats she picked up a duster and began to flick it over the bannister rail whilst watching them out of the corner of her eye as if they were untrustworthy.

'Mrs Eastwood.' Mrs Whittaker came out of the parlour. She looked lovely in a pale grey dress, but her smile was not reassuring. 'What can I do for you?' she asked.

Jennet felt awkward. It seemed she wasn't going to be asked in and offered hot chocolate today – even Peggy seemed unsure and began to suck her thumb.

'I'll have to be away from the sewing room for a few weeks when the baby comes,' she said, 'and my husband hasn't got work yet, so I was wondering if we might get some help ...'

'I'm sorry, Mrs Eastwood, but I don't think there's anything more I can do for you. I have tried,' Mrs Whittaker told her, 'but the Ladies' Charity doesn't have an infinite amount of money to give away and it can only go to the most deserving cases.'

Jennet felt her cheeks burn. She'd thought that Mrs Whittaker was her friend, but it seemed that she was out of favour.

'Your husband has been offered work,' said Mrs Whittaker, 'and he's refused it. So that makes you ineligible for relief.'

'And what about my job – after the baby?'

'Well, I can't promise it will still be there,' said Mrs Whittaker. 'I'll do my best,' she went on, softening slightly, 'but you must see that you've put me in a very difficult position. I pleaded your case with the committee. Jobs are hard to come by and men don't normally turn them down.'

'I'm sorry,' said Jennet. 'My husband can be stubborn.'

'I know it's not all your fault,' said Mrs Whittaker, 'but you haven't helped yourself, have you? This baby. It isn't your husband's, is it?'

'No,' whispered Jennet.

'Was it Hargreaves? At the mill?'

Jennet wondered whether to blame him. It could have been his, after all. But she decided to be truthful.

'No. It was a neighbour – the one who paid for me to go to the Assizes. He was kind. I was going to go to America with him if Titus was transported ...' Her explanations trailed off, seeming inadequate even to her own ears.

'I see.' Mrs Whittaker's face had taken on a look of disappointment and Jennet felt that she'd let her down, and after she'd shown her such friendship as well. The maid ushered them back out on to the street and Jennet walked home, wondering how on earth they would feed themselves with no money at all coming in.

Chapter Seventeen

Jennet was making neat little stitches with her head bent over the work. It was her turn for a seat on the side of the table next to the fire and her back was nicely warmed although her feet still felt cold in her damp clogs. The springtime occasionally taunted them with false promises, but the continuing flurries of snow and a bone-chilling east wind reminded them that winter was not quite done with them yet.

She finished a seam, knotted and fastened off the thread and then shifted on the chair to try to ease her pain. It seemed to be coming in waves and she remembered that the same thing had happened as she was approaching her time with Peggy. The false contractions had gone on for weeks before she finally gave birth.

She reached for more thread and was holding up the needle to the light when a particularly sharp pain made her draw a breath.

'What's to do?' asked Alice.

'Just a bit of backache,' she told her. She shifted restlessly on the chair again, wishing that it was dinner time so that she could get up and walk around to ease her discomfort.

'Tha looks peaky,' said Alice. 'When's tha due?'

'Not for another month.'

The woman studied her. 'Nay, lass,' she said after a moment. 'Tha looks as if thy time's a lot nearer than that.'

Another wave of pain burned through Jennet's back and she closed her eyes until it passed.

'Tha's in labour, mark my words,' said Alice. 'Mrs Aspinall!' She called to the matron who had gone to supervise a group of new workers in the back bedroom. 'Jennet Eastwood's baby's comin',' she said when the matron appeared in the doorway. 'She'd best get home.'

'No. It's nowt but early pains,' protested Jennet as another one coursed through her and she bent over the stitching until she could catch her breath.

'What arrangements hast tha made?' asked the matron.

'Arrangements?' Jennet was reluctant to admit that she'd made none. She'd thought that she had weeks to go. She'd supposed that her mother would come. Titus had made it very clear that it was nothing to do with him and he wanted no part in it. 'My mother lives at Ramsgreave,' she said. 'I can take Peggy there.'

'Tha can't walk all the way to Ramsgreave now,' said Alice.

'Dost tha have any family in Blackburn?' asked Matron.

'Only my husband. But I don't rightly know where to find him.'

'Men are no use anyway. Alice here will take thee home and then go for thy mother. I'll make sure tha doesn't lose any wages,' she told Alice. 'Stay to help if needs be. Peggy can stay here for the time being.'

They set off for Paradise Lane through a driving flurry of snow carried on the wind. It stung Jennet's face and she had to keep pausing to clutch at windowsills as each wave of pain came.

When they arrived, Alice got her settled on the chair with a blanket round her and put more coal on the fire. Then she went to fetch Jennet's mother, telling her she'd be as quick as she could. Jennet closed her eyes and gripped the arms of the chair, trying to count until the pain subsided. She was in no doubt now that the baby was on its way and all she could do was pray that Alice would get back with her mother in time.

After a while she heard the mill hooter sound for dinner, followed by the clattering of clogs and the sound of voices as the workers made their way home. She heard her neighbours' front door slam and their voices drifted through the wall and the enveloping fog of pain. They were arguing as usual, although she had no idea what it was about today. The fire burned low, but she couldn't get up to put more coal on and she hoped it wouldn't go out. She was so cold.

The workers went back to the mill and it was peaceful again. It seemed an age before she heard footsteps and the sound of her own door being opened.

'Help me get her up to bed!' came her mother's voice. 'She's no use there.'

Arms lifted her and she staggered up the twisting stairs a few at a time, stopping to bend over with the agony. She allowed her mother to undress her as if she were a child again and she lay down on the bed.

'It won't be long now,' said her mother. 'Not long at all.'

But her mother was wrong. Jennet's pain went on and on for hours. Wave after wave of agony and no sign of a child. She began to sense that her mother was concerned and she could hear her whispering to Alice.

'I'm going to die,' she said. It seemed the only thing left to do. 'Look after Peggy. Tell Titus I'm sorry.'

'Don't talk nonsense,' said her mother. 'Alice has gone to knock at the Dispensary and ask Dr Scaife to come. He might have summat as'll help it along.'

Jennet groaned as another contraction ripped through her and she wondered whether death might be the better option. Then she heard voices again and she saw the doctor bending over her.

'I'm not an expert in these matters,' she heard him say, 'but I think the baby is stuck the wrong way round. I could try to turn it but it might do more harm than good. Dr Barlow is the best man to get. He's made a study of such matters.'

'But he'll want payin',' said her mother.

'Even so. It's your daughter's life and the life of your grandchild, Mrs Chadwick. I think we should ask him to come.'

Their conversation faded in and out of Jennet's consciousness. She had thought that she might lose the baby sooner and that it would be her punishment for what she'd done, but no, this was more fitting. She would lose her own life and the child would perish with her because it refused to be born and face the shame that awaited it. Then Titus would be free to find another wife, one who was faithful to him. She just hoped that whoever he chose would be kind to Peggy.

Jennet drifted on through the pain, although it didn't seem to grow any worse and she was becoming used to it now. Besides, she knew that it wouldn't go on for ever. It had to end soon. It must be late, she thought, because someone had lit lamps. She could smell them. Her bedroom seemed to be full of people, strangers. There was a warm hand on her belly. She didn't know whose it was. She thought she could hear her mother sobbing and she tried to stretch out a hand to comfort her. It would be all right, she thought.

Someone was saying something to her.

'Mrs Eastwood? Jennet?' Was it an angel? St Peter? Had she reached the gates?

'Let me in,' she pleaded, eager to leave her suffering behind.

'Jennet? Can you hear me?'

The fog cleared a little and she saw someone leaning over her. He was holding her hand and peering at her anxiously. He didn't look like an angel. Surely they were all white, with wings. This man wore a dark blue coat and a white shirt. His iron-grey hair was receding at the temples.

'Jennet. I'm Dr Barlow. Your baby is struggling to be born. But I can help you, if you agree. I can operate. I can make an incision and take the baby out.'

'No!' cried her mother. 'Tha'll kill her!'

'I can assure you that that will not be the case, Mrs Chadwick. I have performed this operation before and the mother survived.'

'And the baby?'

'Sadly stillborn. But the mother delayed in making a decision. Your daughter's baby is alive and Jennet is young and healthy. I see no reason that both can't be saved. Jennet. Jennet?' he repeated her name with more urgency. 'Do you agree to the operation?'

Jennet stared at him through a haze of pain and confusion. She wasn't sure what was happening, but he seemed earnest and kindly as he took her hand again. 'I promise that I will do my very best to save your child and you as well. It is possible. But if you wait the chances will diminish.'

'Do it,' she said. She didn't really care if she lived or died. It was all in God's hands now. God, and this man standing in her bedroom.

'We'll need to get her downstairs,' said Dr Barlow briskly. 'Dr Scaife, will you assist me? You're not afraid of a little blood, are you?'

'No. I'm interested to see the procedure.'

'Good man. Start to get the bandages ready. Mrs Chadwick, can you and your daughter's friend get Jennet downstairs? We need to lay her on the table. Bring some pillows to support her head. And a little wine will help, if anyone can procure it.'

Floating on pain, Jennet was half carried across the bedroom and down the stairs, one by one. The table had been cleared and Dr Scaife was putting a sheet on it. They helped her up on to its hard surface and a pillow was tucked under her neck and shoulders. The surgeon had taken off his coat and was removing shiny and frightening instruments from his bag.

'Lie back and try to relax,' he told her as he wielded a small sharp scalpel. 'Someone give her wine or gin, or anything you have.'

Jennet felt a cup pushed against her lips. Someone was holding her shoulders down so that she couldn't move. She wasn't sure what was going on. Then a fierce agony ripped through her as if someone had cut her body open. She heard herself scream. She could smell blood and she felt warmth and wetness flow over her.

Jennet didn't know how she managed to bear it, but it seemed only moments before she saw something wet and wizened lifted from her. The cord was cut and the baby was wrapped in a towel. She heard a cry and realised it was alive.

'A little girl!' said her mother as the baby was handed to her. 'She looks healthy too.'

So the child would live, thought Jennet. 'Take care of her,' she whispered. 'I'm going ...'

'Jennet! You are not going to die,' said the surgeon. 'I'm about to place some sutures into the uterus. Then everything will be returned to its normal position. Dr Scaife, if you could just place your hands here ... and here. That's excellent.'

Jennet felt the surgeon tugging at her stomach. Alice had turned deathly white and had to sit down.

'There,' said Dr Barlow at last, 'if you'll apply the lint and adhesive strips, Dr Scaife, and then we'll bandage the abdomen tightly. We'll put you back in bed after that, Jennet. I'll give you a tincture to help you sleep. Your mother can care for your baby for now.'

'Don't let Titus take her!' pleaded Jennet, remembering her husband's threat to take the baby to the workhouse.

Titus and Sam turned into Paradise Lane. They'd been to a Reform meeting at the Assembly Rooms and Sam was all fired up about the injustice of the gentry having everything, leaving the working man in poverty.

'It ain't right!' he kept saying. 'Why should some have everything and the rest of us starve?

I know what I'd vote for if I were given the chance.'

As they approached the house Titus could see a bright light falling on to the pavement. There must be more than one candle lit, he thought, and the curtains weren't properly shut. As he reached for the door, it was pulled back and a woman he didn't know came out shaking her head and flapping her hands at him.

'Tha can't come in!'

'What dost tha mean *tha can't come in*? This is where I lives!' He tried to push past, but she closed the door behind her and grabbed hold of his arm.

'Surgeon's in there with Dr Scaife. Jennet's took bad. They're gettin' the baby out.'

'Surgeon?' he repeated, gazing at her anxious face by the light of the gas lamp. He tried to look in through the gap in the curtains but she pulled at him again.

'Come away! They're operatin'!'

Titus stared at her, taking a moment to comprehend her meaning.

'Operating? Cuttin' her open, tha means?'

'Aye. Dr Barlow says he can save 'em both.'

Titus stared at the window again. Voices were drifting out on to the street. He heard a woman cry out and realised that it was Jennet.

'No!' he said, not knowing that he had even spoken. A dozen thoughts crowded his mind. Would the baby die? Would that be a good thing? Would Jennet die as well? What would he do if she did? Why had he remained so angry with her? What if he never saw her again?

'Dr Barlow is the best surgeon there is,' the woman was telling him, shaking his arm to get his attention. 'We're lucky he came. He's done this afore and the mother lived. Jennet'll be all right. I'm sure she'll be all right. Come back in a while,' she said, before going back in and firmly shutting him out of his own home.

'What'll we do now?' asked Sam.

'I don't know.' Titus was cold and hungry and had been looking forward to his tea. He continued to stand on the street where he could see glimpses of people in their parlour, gathered around the table. Then the woman pulled the curtains. But he still stood, watching the shadows flitting to and fro.

'We can't stand here all night,' said Sam. 'We're gettin' wet through. Let's go to the Lion. My treat.'

'All right,' Titus agreed reluctantly. Even though he'd spent all day hanging around the mills, hoping for at least some temporary or part-time work, there'd been nothing. Sam, on the other hand, had been luckier. He'd done some work and had money in his pocket. 'But make a note of what tha spends,' he told him, 'and I'll pay thee back when I get a job.'

They ordered pot luck, which was a tasty stew, and a half-pint each. The seats near the fire had been taken long since and they were forced to sit near the chill of the wall. Titus could feel his wet trousers clinging to his legs, and the damp of his jacket seeping through to the shirt underneath.

'Were they really cuttin' her open?' asked Sam, wide-eyed at the thought.

'So yon woman said. I don't even know who she was. Must have been a midwife,' said Titus. He had no idea what plans Jennet had made for the birth and he'd never asked. It was easier to pretend that it wouldn't happen, that this pregnancy of hers would somehow disappear so that he wouldn't be forced to think about it. But now he was afraid that she might die. He'd been a fool, he thought as he nursed his beer. He still loved her, but he'd been so angry that he'd wanted to punish her by pretending that he didn't care for her any more. He'd wanted her to feel as hurt as he'd felt when he came home and saw her there with her belly swollen with another man's child. But she'd been right to blame him as well. He knew that it was partly his own fault. If he hadn't got himself arrested that night, it would never have happened. And that had been George's fault too. The man had abandoned him. Maybe he'd had it all planned from the start. Maybe that's why he'd asked him to the Reform meeting. George were a wily beggar and it wouldn't surprise him. He'd probably asked him so as he could get him arrested – get rid of him to clear the way for him to make advances to Jennet. He couldn't believe his neighbour had even tried to take her away with him to America. And as for Lizzie? Well, who knew what she'd died from? It was all very convenient.

'Another drink?' asked Sam, pulling coins from his pocket.

'Nay, lad. Put thy money away. They'll be closing in a minute or two anyroad, so we'd best be making tracks.'

Outside the sky had cleared and a frost was sparkling on the cobbles. The lamps were still burning on Paradise Lane and Titus saw that the horse that had been tied to the mill gates had gone. It must have been the surgeon's. He tapped on his own front door and waited.

His mother-in-law opened it and he tried to judge from her face what had happened, whether he had returned home a widower. She put a finger to her lips and beckoned him in. There was just a single candle burning inside now. The table was empty, the wood glowing as the firelight reflected on it. Jennet always kept things well polished.

Mrs Chadwick picked something up from the crib by the fire.

'A little girl,' she said, moving the blanket aside for him to look. He glanced at it. Its face was red and wrinkled and it had a thatch of dark hair.

'Jennet?' He hardly dared to ask. He could feel his heart thumping as he prepared himself for the news.

'Upstairs, in bed.'

'Dead?' He breathed the word.

'No!' Mrs Chadwick reassured him. 'No. Dr Barlow says she'll recover well, so long as no infection sets in. He's promised to come back tomorrow. He's an amazing man,' she said as Titus slumped down at the table. 'I were that frightened when he talked about cutting our Jennet open, but I've never seen such skill. He knew where to cut, and knew every organ that were inside her. He had the baby out in no time and put her all back together again with sewing, neat as tha likes. I'd never have believed it if I hadn't seen it with my own eyes.'

The baby in her arms cried a little, like a mewling kitten, and she jogged and shushed it. 'She's hungry,' she said, 'but I don't want to disturb Jennet. I've given her a bit o' sugar water to put her on, but she needs her mother's milk. Hast tha eaten?' she asked him.

'Aye. We had a bite at the Lion. Sam here's had work and he paid for it. He's a good lad.' Titus smiled at his young friend. He didn't know what he would have done without him tonight and he was thankful that Jennet had agreed he could stay with them.

'Get to bed, then,' she told them. 'I'll stay down here and nurse the baby.'

Titus and Sam crept up the stairs. When Titus peeped into his own room he saw that Jennet was asleep, breathing deeply. They must have given her something, he thought. Peggy was there, sleeping too, her hair loose across the pillow and her eyelashes casting shadows on her cheeks in the candlelight. She snuffled a little and shifted. Titus moved away so as not to wake her and went into the back bedroom to strip off his damp clothes before getting into the bed with Sam. He blew out the candle and lay awake for a while, listening to the baby cry every now and then. What was to be done with it? he wondered. They couldn't afford to feed one child, never mind two.

Jennet woke from a dream that someone had sliced her open. She tried to sit up and gasped at

330

the soreness all across her stomach. Then the events of yesterday came back to her. Well, she thought, she was still alive.

'Mam!' she called, wondering where the baby was.

'Shush, Jennet.' Her mother came in carrying the child. 'I've just managed to get her to sleep for a bit.' But as if to disprove her words, the baby began to cry.

'Give her here.' Jennet stretched out her arms and her mother placed the baby into them. She was tiny, with a crumpled face and dark hair. Jennet felt a rush of love as the child grasped tight hold of her finger, but there was a likeness to George that made Jennet sorry because she knew it would make it even harder for Titus to accept her.

'She needs a feed,' said her mother. 'Can tha manage?'

She helped Jennet to ease herself up a bit, propping her on pillows so that she could put the child to her breast.

'There. She's latchin' on like a good 'un,' said her mother as the child snuffled and searched for the milk. 'How's tha feelin'?'

'Sore.'

'No fever?' Her mother pressed the back of her hand to Jennet's forehead. 'That Dr Barlow's a miracle worker,' she said. 'I'd heard of such things, but never thought I'd see it done. I thought I were sure to lose thee, and the child.'

'Did Titus come home?' asked Jennet.

'Aye. He slept in the back room with that young lad. He's eager to see thee. I'll send him up.'

Jennet didn't want to see him, but after her mother had gone down he came and stood just inside the doorway watching her nurse the baby.

'Did tha get some sleep?' she asked, to break the silence.

'Aye, a bit.'

'Did tha get some tea?'

'Aye. We went to the Lion. They wouldn't let us in here.'

'Dr Barlow had to cut the baby out. He had me on the table.'

'Aye, so they said.'

'It's a little girl.'

'Aye,' he said. 'I've seen her. Dost tha feel all right?'

'I'm tired, and sore where I was cut.'

'Aye. I suppose tha would be.' He stood for a moment longer. 'Well, I'd best get off,' he said, without elaborating on where he might be going. 'I'll see thee later. Maybe we can talk when thy mother's gone home.'

Jennet closed her arms around the child. She would ask her mother to stay as long as she could. She was afraid that if she was left alone with him he might snatch the baby from her and take it to the workhouse.

Chapter Eighteen

Dr Barlow called again around dinner time. He examined the cut to her stomach, then looked at her tongue and took her pulse before announcing that everything seemed to be progressing well.

'What do we owe thee, doctor?' asked Jennet when he was done, wondering if they had anything they could take to the pawnshop that would raise enough money to pay his bill. She supposed they might manage without the table and chairs, although she'd be sorry to see them go.

'Don't worry about that,' he told her, squeezing her hand. 'Pay me when you can.'

Jennet found herself crying with relief. 'I'm that grateful,' she told him. 'More than I can say.'

'Dr Scaife will call in a day or two to check all's well, but I don't foresee any problems. Take care of yourself, Mrs Eastwood, and the child.'

'I will,' she said and he nodded his head and went back down the stairs. She worried that her thanks had been inadequate. He'd saved her daughter's life and probably hers as well. And although she'd once thought that it might be better if they both died, now that she had her baby in her arms she knew that both their lives were precious.

In a day or two she felt stronger and her mother helped her down the stairs to sit by the fire for a while.

'Tha'll not go home just yet, will tha?' she asked her.

'I'll stay and look after thee and the childer a while longer,' she agreed. 'But I can't stay for ever, tha knows.'

'I know, but I'm afraid of what he might do,' said Jennet, meaning Titus. Although he'd said no more about the workhouse since the baby had come, she was still worried that he was just awaiting his opportunity and would take the child when he saw his chance.

'He'll do nowt, Jennet,' said her mother. 'He thinks the world of thee and he'd never do owt to hurt thee. But tha needs to get things sorted out. I'll tell thee what. I'll take Peggy up to Ramsgreave tomorrow, and that Sam can come an' all, for his dinner. It'll give thee some time alone to talk things through.'

Titus saw Jennet shiver after her mother closed the door behind her the next morning. 'Tha looks chilly,' he said. 'Shall I go up and find thee a shawl to put on?'

'Aye. If tha doesn't mind,' she said. She seemed wary of him and he felt ashamed that he'd made her afraid.

He needed to get this right, he thought as he climbed the stairs. He might never get another chance to make peace with her. He wished that he could put things back to how they'd once been, but he knew it was too late for that. He wanted to set things right, but he also needed her to acknowledge his suffering before he could begin to forgive her for what she'd done.

In the bedroom, he pulled open the drawers of the tallboy, looking for Jennet's indoor shawl. When he opened the bottom one and reached in, he felt something rustle. There was paper hidden inside a stocking. Glancing over his shoulder to check he was alone, he pulled it out to see what it was. It was an envelope and he recognised Jennet's name on it. Curiosity got the better of him and, as it was already unsealed, he opened it to see what was inside. He found a short letter and a bank note for ten pounds. He stared at it. Where on earth had that come from?

He unfolded the letter and saw that it was from George. All his anger welled up again as he began to read.

Dearest Jennet,

I am sorry for what happened that night in Lancaster. You were upset and I took advantage of you. It was unforgivable.

I am not surprised that you do not want to come with me to America. You must think that I am a despicable person. I also know that you love your husband very much because you would not consider leaving him, even for a moment, and are determined to stand by him. He is a good man and you are probably far better off with him than you would ever be with me. Be reassured that you have made the right decision.

I have never thanked you enough for all the help you gave me when Lizzie was ill and when she died. You cared for her, and then you cared for me during my time of need, and I let you down. I know that I can never truly repay your kindness, but I hope that the enclosed will be of some use to you until Titus comes home.

I wish you both the very best for the future.
Your affectionate friend,
George

Titus looked at the bank note again. Was it even genuine? He held it up to the light. He was no expert but it seemed real enough to him.

'Titus!' called up Jennet. 'Have you found the shawl?'

'I've found summat,' he replied, sitting back on his heels and wondering how she would react if he told her that he'd been reading her private letter. Should he just put it back and say nothing? Maybe she hadn't been planning to tell him about the money. He recalled her threat to leave him if he continued to insist that the baby be sent to the workhouse. He'd laughed at her. Laughed, thinking that she could never do anything of the sort. But with ten pounds in her purse she could go anywhere. He frowned and folded up the bank note ready to hide it away again.

'Titus?' He hadn't heard her soft tread on the stairs and he turned to see her in the doorway, with the baby in her arms, staring at him. The letter was still in his hand.

'I didn't mean to pry.'

'It's a letter from George,' she said, coming in and sitting down on the edge of the bed. 'Can tha read it?'

'Aye.' A thought occurred to him. 'Dost tha not know what it is?' he asked.

'It's a letter. But I don't know what it says.'

'And the other?'

She shook her head and for a moment he considered not telling her that it was money, but sense got the better of him. 'It's a ten-pound note,' he said.

'Ten pounds?' She stared at the note in disbelief when he handed it to her.

'Where would George get that much money?' asked Titus.

'He were paid. It came from Mr Eccles for some gadget he'd invented at the mill. But I thought it were his money to go to America,' said Jennet, shaking her head. 'Why would he give it to me?'

'Guilt?' suggested Titus.

'We'll have to give it back,' said Jennet. 'We can't accept this.'

'And how are we supposed to do that?' he asked. 'Dost tha know where he's gone?'

'Only that he said he were takin' a ship to America.'

'So there's not much chance of returning the money then?'

'No. But it isn't ours,' she said.

'It would stop us having to worry about buying food for a good while if we had that much in our pockets,' he pointed out.

'No.' She shook her head. 'We should pay Dr Barlow and then keep the rest for Bessie.'

'Bessie?' he asked, not knowing who she meant.

'The baby!'

He stared at the tiny child in her arms. She was fast asleep now that she'd been fed, a little frown etched on her forehead and her hands in tightly balled fists as if she was ready for a fight.

'I didn't know tha'd named her,' he said.

'I named her for Lizzie. She would have liked it,' said Jennet. 'And if that money's spent on owt, it'll be spent on her. It'll pay for her keep. I'll hear no more talk of the workhouse now, because George left it for me, not for thee. So it's up to me what it's spent on. If tha wants to eat tha can work instead of spending all day talking about Reform and not bringing a penny home!'

She had a point, thought Titus. Besides, he didn't want to live on George's money. It was shameful to be a kept man. Perhaps it was time to admit that he would never get taken back on at the mill and accept the work on the road building.

'Aye. Tha's right,' he told her as he folded up the note and put it back in the envelope. 'Use it as tha sees fit.'

'And no more talk of the workhouse?'

'No. She can stop,' he said, glancing at the baby. She wasn't his daughter. Never would be. But with the money there was nothing to stop Jennet going away, and if she did, she would take Peggy with her, and he wouldn't risk that.

'Cup of tea?' he asked to acknowledge their fragile truce.

'Aye. That'd be nice,' she said.

But before they could move there was a hammering on their front door that shattered the Sunday silence. They both jumped and the baby woke and began to cry.

'Who on earth can that be?' asked Titus, going to look out of the window. He could see a man peering in and his heart began to race as he recognised John Kay, the constable, and one of his runners. His first thought was that they'd come to haul him back off to the prison and he considered not answering the door, wondering whether he could slip out of the back without being seen. Then the banging came again, echoed by knocking on their neighbour's door as well.

'Who is it?' asked Jennet, looking alarmed and clutching the screaming baby as close as she could.

He saw that she was frightened too. But they'd done nothing wrong, he reasoned. It must be a mistake. Although it had been a mistake last time and nobody had listened.

'Tha'd best answer it,' said Jennet. 'They're not going to go away.'

Titus went down the stairs. The door was being thumped again and he was sure it would fly off its hinges at any moment. He lifted the latch and pulled it open a fraction. The constable added his weight to it and flung it wide.

'Where's the lad who's staying here? Samuel Proctor,' he demanded, peering into the room. 'It's no use tryin' to hide him!'

'He's not here.'

'He'll not get away down yon yard. I've men round the back an' all.'

'He's not here,' said Jennet, coming down with the baby.

'Where is he then?'

'I don't know. Out somewhere,' said Titus with a glance at Jennet. 'What dost tha want with him?' he asked, although his heart was already sinking with the realisation that the money Sam had spent so freely might not have come from honest employment after all. Titus cursed himself. He'd been so wrapped up in his own affairs that he'd neglected to ensure the lad was keeping on the straight and narrow. He knew that he'd failed him and it would break his heart to see Sam go back to the prison – or worse, depending on what he'd done.

The woman next door was screaming and cursing with words that made Titus want to cover Jennet's ears. She had the constable's runner by the arm and he was trying to shake her off like a rabid dog whilst his other hand was clamped around the neck of the collarless shirt worn by the young lad with the damaged hand.

'Let him go! Let him go! He's done nowt wrong!' she was shrieking.

Titus looked at Jennet and saw that her face was white and she'd had to sit down. The baby had stopped crying but was giving distressed little gulps as Jennet jogged and shushed her. Thank goodness Peggy wasn't here to be upset by it all, he thought as he watched next door's lad being dragged down the street.

'I'll be back!' warned Kay. 'He'll not get away with it!'

Titus wanted to ask what he wouldn't get away with, but the constable had marched off and he was left staring at his screaming neighbour who was being restrained by her husband. He pointed a finger at Titus with his free hand.

'Tha'll pay for this! Thee and that slut of a wife of thine! My lad never put a foot wrong until tha brought that thievin' gobshite home from the prison with thee! Tha'll pay!' he warned again before ushering his sobbing wife into the house. 'Mark my words! Tha'll live to rue the day!'

The door slammed and Titus turned to look at Jennet. They stared at one another for a moment, half listening to the wailing and shouting coming through the wall.

'I saw them,' said Jennet. 'Sam and their John. I saw them near the coach stop when I went to visit Mrs Whittaker. I thought nothing of it at the time …'

'Pickpocketing,' said Titus, feeling his anger rise. How could the lad have been so stupid? How could Sam have let him down like this when he'd persuaded Jennet to take him in and give him a chance? He'd kill him when he got his hands on him.

'Aye,' said Jennet. 'He's not coming back here.'

Titus didn't blame her. Sam couldn't come back anyway. As soon as the neighbours saw him they would run for the constable. He would have to walk up to Ramsgreave and warn him. He reached for his jacket.

'Where's tha going?'

'To Ramsgreave.'

344

'No! Tha's not to bring trouble on my mam and dad. Just wait until he comes back and then send him on his way.'

Titus hesitated. Jennet had a point. He didn't want the Chadwicks to be accused of harbouring a criminal, but he couldn't just let the lad be taken by the constable.

He sat down at the table. 'He's not a bad lad. Not really,' he told her. 'And I'm partly to blame. I knew he had money, but I believed him when he said he'd had work. I should have known.'

'Aye. He's given me money for his keep,' said Jennet. 'Though I'd never have spent it if I'd known it were stolen.'

'We could all be in trouble,' said Titus, suddenly seeing the seriousness of their situation. 'If it goes to the court and he says as we spent stolen money we could be accused as well.'

'What are we going to do?' The fear was stark on Jennet's face. 'I can't go to prison!' She began to sob and the baby started to cry again.

'Shush, shush.' He went across and knelt by the chair and put his arms around her and the child. 'Don't fret,' he told her. 'I'll think of summat.'

He had to find a way of getting the lad away, far away, he thought. Somewhere the constable would never find him, somewhere he couldn't make a confession that would involve them. But how?

Then the solution dawned on him. Jennet wouldn't like it. But it seemed to be the only way out.

'As soon as he comes back we'll send him on his way,' he told Jennet. 'We won't have long, but he might be able to get away if he's quick enough.' He hesitated, but he knew he had to get her agreement if there was to be any chance of them having a future together. 'He'll not get far without money,' he said.

'No!' Jennet was adamant. 'That's Bessie's money!'

'Jennet.' He sat down opposite her and twisted his fingers together as he searched for the right words. 'If they catch him he'll not just get sent to prison again. He's older now. He'll be treated as an adult and it's not the first time he's been in trouble. I've heard of lads being hanged. Tha doesn't want a life on thy conscience, dost tha?'

Jennet looked down at the red and crumpled face of the baby in her arms. When she'd got up that morning she hadn't even known that the money existed. If she'd known about it sooner it would all have been spent long since. She thought of all the times she'd gone hungry to make sure that Peggy had enough to eat, not caring about herself or the baby because it belonged to George and would have to thrive or not as best it could. And all the time the money had been there. Money she could have used for food – and maybe if she'd been better fed the baby would have been born more easily. She rocked the little scrap in her arms and was overcome with guilt. She ought to have taken better care of herself. If she'd died, this little girl would have gone to the workhouse for sure and goodness knows what sort of a miserable life she would have had there. But now there was money to feed and clothe her, so she'd never know what it was to go hungry or have no boots to wear, and Titus wanted to give it away to some thieving lad he'd befriended in the prison. It wasn't right. And yet a part of her could see that it was.

One of the things that Dr Barlow had said to her was that he was sorry, but she wouldn't be able to have any more children. And Jennet knew how much Titus wanted a son. He'd been heart-broken when she'd lost the little lad. He'd not said owt, and he'd not shed tears, but she'd seen the sadness in his eyes and she'd imagined how happy he would be if she could give him another son one day. Now she never would, and young Sam was the nearest he would ever come to being a father to a boy. She could see that he loved him, and she'd taken hope from it, hope that one day he could love little Bessie too.

She liked Sam as well. Even though she'd tried not to be charmed by him, she'd found him hard to resist. She'd laughed at his jokes. She'd taken his money, and willingly put food on the table without ever checking where it had come from. She should have known when he came in with clean hands and without an ounce of fluff on him that he hadn't spent the day in a mill.

'I know it's a lot to ask,' said Titus.

'Couldn't we just give him some of it? We ought to pay the surgeon at least.'

'Go to the bank with a ten-pound note the day after we've had the constable hammering on our door?'

She could see that it would point suspicion at them. They'd all end up in prison.

'Where would he go?' she asked.

'There's enough for a ship to America, and to keep him fed for the crossing,' said Titus. 'If he can get himself to Liverpool he can buy a ticket. They'll take the note and give him change. He doesn't need to use his own name.'

'Will he agree?' she asked.

'He doesn't have much choice, does he?'

Chapter Nineteen

Jennet's mother brought Peggy back as it was getting on towards teatime. She frowned when she saw Jennet's pale and tear-streaked face.

'Hast tha not sorted out thy differences?' she asked as Peggy leaned over the little crib to watch her baby sister sleep.

'We've come to some agreement,' said Jennet, reaching to tidy her hair. They'd decided to say nothing to her parents about the constable coming. 'Where's Sam?' she asked.

'Sam? He didn't stay long after his dinner. Said he was meeting a friend.'

'Right.' She glanced at Titus.

'What's to do?' asked Mrs Chadwick. 'Don't tell me he's in bother.'

'What makes tha say that?'

'I'm not stupid, our Jennet. I've seen his sort afore,' she replied. 'He'll charm the birds from the trees but I'd not trust him to fetch water without getting into trouble. He's a nice enough young lad, but ...' She looked from one to the other of them. 'He is in trouble, isn't he?' she said and in the end they told her what had happened.

'Tha must send him away,' she told them. 'Don't bring any more trouble down on thyselves.'

It had gone dark and Peggy had been put to bed before there was a tapping at the back door. Titus jumped up and dragged Sam into the house.

'Stupid lad!' he railed at him. 'What were tha thinking of? We've had yon constable here looking for thee!'

Jennet felt a stab of sympathy for the shame-faced boy who stared up at Titus like a dog that had been soundly kicked but had no idea why.

'I've done nowt wrong ...' he began to protest but Titus silenced him with a cuff around the head.

'Tha's been thievin' again!'

'Shhh!' Jennet warned him to be quiet with a glance towards the wall that divided them from their neighbours. 'They'll hear if tha doesn't keep thy voice down,' she warned.

'Dost tha want to go back to prison?' demanded Titus in a threatening whisper. 'Because that's what'll happen. If not worse!' The boy turned pale and his bottom lip began to tremble. 'Tha should have thought on that afore tha went helpin' thyself to gentlemen's pockets!' Titus told him.

'But ... but they has more than they needs. They said so at the Reform meeting. They said it wasn't fair that the gentry has everything and we have nowt. I was only tryin' to help,' he said, turning to Jennet with a pleading look on his face. 'I only wanted to put food on the table.'

'I believed thee when tha said tha'd worked hard for that stuff tha fetched for us,' she told him. 'I'd never have taken it if I'd thought it had come from stolen money. Tha's involved us with it too.'

'And John from next door!' Titus told him.

'John? He were supposed to be meetin' me at the beer shop, but he didn't show up.'

'That's because he were hauled off by the constable this afternoon. He's in the lock-up and will be brought afore the magistrates tomorrow. He'll go to prison for certain.' Sam looked shamefaced as Titus berated him. 'And they'll come back for thee an' all,' he said. 'But tha knows that. Or tha wouldn't have climbed over the yard wall.'

'I saw a man hanging about on t' street corner,' admitted Sam. 'I thought it were best to avoid him.'

'Tha'll have to go,' Titus told him.

'Tha's throwin' me out?'

Jennet could see that he was very near to tears. He was only a child, really, she thought, and he'd never stood a chance. Nobody had ever taught him the difference between right and wrong and it seemed that going to the Reform meetings with Titus had only served to convince him that the gentry were fair game.

'Tha needs to get away,' said Titus, his anger fading and his tone gentler as he pulled Sam towards a chair at the table and pushed him down on to it. 'Pour the lad a cup o' tea,' he said to Jennet.

She gave him the last of the oatcakes that she'd saved from teatime and spooned four sugars into his cup. He'd need his strength, she thought, if he was to evade the constable.

'Tha needs to get away,' repeated Titus. 'Constable'll come knockin' here again and again until he finds thee. Tha'll have to go tonight, and tha'll need to move fast.'

'Where to?'

Sam had taken off his cap and Jennet ached to smooth down his rumpled hair.

'Hast tha any money left?' asked Titus. Sam felt in his pocket and took out a sixpence and three pennies. 'That'll not get thee far.' Titus glanced at Jennet with a pleading look. She knew that he was leaving the decision up to her. But what else could she do? The love that her husband had for this lad was clear on his face.

'I'll fetch it,' she said and took a candle to go up the stairs.

Peggy was asleep in the front room and little Bessie lay in her cot on her back with her hands on either side of her head. Jennet felt such a surge of love for her daughters. And ten pounds would buy so much food to keep them happy and healthy. She opened the drawer quietly and found the bank note. It was hers. George had given it to her, and it was her choice what she did with it. She stared at it in the candlelight. If she sent Sam away with nothing he would surely be caught and hanged. She knew that she couldn't have his death on her conscience. He wasn't a bad lad at heart, and she had grown fond of him.

She went back down the stairs and put the note on the table. 'That's for thee,' she told Sam. 'On condition that tha promises me tha'll give up thieving and tha'll live a good and honest life, and that tha'll make summat of thyself.'

Sam stared at the sheet of fragile paper. 'What is it?' he asked.

'Ten pounds,' said Titus. 'So minds tha keeps it safe. Get thyself to Liverpool and when tha gets there take it to a broker and ask for a steerage ticket to New York. They'll give thee change too – enough to pay for food on the ship. And when tha gets there, tha needs to get work, proper work, not thievin' work.'

'Where did it come from?' Sam asked, picking it up and fingering it.

'It's not stolen!' Jennet told him. 'It were a gift.'

'I can't take thy money,' said Sam, pushing the note away from him.

'Aye, tha can,' said Jennet, pushing it back again. 'Tha can take it because I want thee to have it. But tha has to promise me that tha'll never steal owt ever again.'

Sam looked up at her with tears brimming in his eyes. 'Nobody ever cared about me afore.'

'I care about thee,' said Titus, putting his arm around the boy's shoulders. 'Jennet cares an' all. Just promise that tha won't let us down.'

'I won't,' he said, wiping his face on the back of his hand.

'Best get on thy way, then,' said Titus. 'Fold that up and keep it safe. And remember, don't touch it until tha gets to Liverpool. And when tha gets there get the first ship tha can.'

The boy nodded. He drained the last of his tea and stood up. 'I'm that grateful,' he said again.

Titus hugged him close and Jennet thought that he was never going to let him go. Then he opened

354

the back door, gave him a leg-up over the wall and he was gone. They went back inside and barred the doors back and front before banking up the fire and going to bed.

'I'll make it up to thee,' said Titus, staring down at Bessie as she slept. 'I'll go and ask about work on the road building first thing tomorrow morning.'

Jennet watched as he stroked the baby's face with his finger. She hoped that one day he would be able to love the child as much as he loved Peggy, and as much as he loved Sam. But for now she was content that he'd seen reason and that there would be no more talk of the workhouse.

'What about them next door?' she asked as she heard a door slam and Nan began a tirade of shouting and wailing again. 'Can we do owt to help their John? Because he's a good lad and it weren't his fault he were injured and couldn't work. Sam led him astray and whose fault will it be if they hang him?'

'John's younger. He's never been in trouble afore. They'll be lenient.'

'But he'll still go to prison.'

'Aye,' agreed Titus. 'He'll go to prison. And I don't rightly know how I can prevent it. I'll speak up for him, if they let me, but I doubt it'll make a difference.'

'They'll hate us even more,' said Jennet, glancing towards the dividing wall. 'How can we go on living next door to them? I'm afraid of what they might do,' she said, remembering Joe's threats.

'We'd best try to get away,' agreed Titus. 'We'll see what other houses there are that we can rent.'

Jennet nodded. She'd be glad to leave. Paradise Lane had brought them nothing but trouble and she hoped that if they could start again, in a different place, they might rediscover the happiness that this house had taken from them.

Welcome to

Penny Street

where your favourite authors and stories live.

Meet casts of characters you'll never forget,
create memories you'll treasure forever,
and discover places that will stay with
you long after the last page.

Turn the page to step into the home of

Libby Ashworth

and discover more about

THE

COTTON
Spinner

Dear Reader,

I hope you've enjoyed meeting Jennet and her family in this first book of The Mill Town Lasses series. Jennet and Titus were my great, great, great, great grandparents and although I don't know what their lives were really like, I wanted to share my vision of the hardships they faced as they were forced to move away from their home in the countryside to find work in the burgeoning mill town of Blackburn.

Their lives must always have been hard, but progress, in the form of the Industrial Revolution, was about to make them much harder. They had to adjust to a new life where they were ruled by the factory hooter and expected to work for up to sixteen hours a day when they had been used to being their own bosses. And the conditions in the town were horrible. There was no running water – just a pump at the All Hallows Well, and no sewer to take away the filth except for the river Blakewater.

When I was a child one of my grandmothers lived in a house like the one I've described in the book. Two up, two down, with a steep, twisty staircase and the facilities 'down the yard'. My other grandmother and many of my great aunts all worked in the mills as weavers, beginning as half-timers at twelve years old – going to school in the morning and then working a shift in the mills. They didn't finish at half past three in the afternoon either! Even a half shift was six hours' work.

It was the mill owners who benefitted most from the new factories. It was a Preston man, Sir Richard Arkwright, who is credited with being the founder of the factory system, and funnily enough there may be another family link there. My great grandmother was an Arkwright and according to my grandma she claimed to have been a descendant of Richard, from a branch of the family who was disinherited for marrying into the 'wrong' religion. I've been unable to verify it, but I like to think it may be true even if I don't entirely admire the man!

But this story isn't just about my family. It's about all the millworkers in all the northern towns, and especially the women who were so hardworking and resilient and brought up families and supported one another through shocking and appalling times. In the end they triumphed and I admire them for that.

I do hope you will join me for the next two books in the series as I explore the challenges that Jennet and her family face in the future.

Libby x

Cotton Spinners

From medieval times, and even earlier, spinning was women's work. They spun flax and wool, and when the cotton arrived at the docks in Liverpool and Lancaster, women began to work with that as well.

The earliest spinning was done on a distaff or a spindle. No Lancashire cottage was complete without a loom for the man of the house and a spinning wheel or two for his wife and daughters to supply him with warp and weft.

Then clever men began to invent ways to make the work easier, although their inventions were not always popular. James Hargreaves, who lived up at Stanhill, near Blackburn, invented the Spinning Jenny in 1764. In 1767, Sir Richard Arkwright said this about him - *he constructed an engine that would at once spin twenty or thirty threads of cotton into yarn for the fustian manufacture, but because it was likely to answer in some measure the end proposed, his engines were burnt and destroyed by a mob . . .*

But the inventions were unstoppable and in 1779, Samuel Crompton, at Bolton, invented the Spinning Mule, and gradually the mules evolved into huge machines that could spin dozens of threads at a time. The difference that this made to women was profound. These new machines were very heavy and, before they were powered by steam engines, they had to be pulled and pushed by hand. Women didn't have the physical strength for that. So spinning became a man's job and the male spinners quickly became the elite of the cotton industry whilst weaving became women's work.

Then entrepreneurs decided that it would be beneficial to get all the workers together in one place. For home workers it meant that time wouldn't be wasted walking into town to collect raw cotton from the putter-out and then having to walk back with the finished cloth at the end of the week. At first the weavers and spinners retained their self-employed status, but it was only a matter of time before they became employees and were forced to bend to the rule of the mill owners who began to demand that they work long hours for low wages. No wonder resentment grew and radical men and women began to demand a fair day's pay for their work.

Luddites

I think most people have heard the term 'Luddite' and know that it's used to refer to someone who is reluctant to accept the changes that come with new technology. Its origin was in the cotton towns of the Industrial Revolution and the popular image of the movement is gangs of men descending on the mills to trash and break the machinery that they believed was stealing their livelihoods. But why the name 'Luddite'? Well, it comes about because the men were followers of a General Ludd. Just who General Ludd was and if he even existed at all is debatable. Like Robin Hood, he is a mythical folk hero who was determined that the rich shouldn't take all the wealth and leave the poor with nothing.

One theory is the name originated when a weaver named Edward Ludlam from Leicestershire broke two stocking frames in a fit of rage. Later, when machines were broken people would joke that *Ned Ludd did it*.

There is a story that General Ludd was once almost captured by the militia at Stalybridge, but that he retreated to an underground hiding place by shinning down a mineshaft on a rope. A guard of forty soldiers was stationed at the pit mouth to either capture him if he came out or to ensure that he starved to death below. But three nights later, a detachment of General Ludd's own army drove the besiegers away, allowing Ludd to climb up the rope and escape.

It does remind me of the stories of Robin Hood and his Merry Men and I think the stories were spread for the same reason – to give people hope that there was a saviour out there who would bring them justice. But the tide of the Industrial Revolution could never be turned and workers could never go back to the familiar life that they had once known.

Victorian Prisons

I think most people have a mental image of Victorian prisons being grim places, maybe with prisoners chained to walls whilst lying on filthy straw and existing on bread and water. So, I was quite surprised when I went in search of some authentic detail to discover that although the prisons were harsh places, by 1826 they were not as brutal as I'd imagined. Things had changed in the years since Elizabeth Fry began her campaign for improvements to the prison system in 1813 and when Sir Robert Peel, another local man incidentally, was prime minister he passed the 1823 Gaols Act. This introduced regular visits by prison chaplains amongst other things, including the prohibition of leg irons and the payment of gaolers so they had no need to depend on money from their prisoners to provide their wages.

The chaplain of the Preston House of Correction was the Reverend John Clay and each year he wrote a report on the prison. The reports make fascinating reading and it's his descriptions that I've used to create an authentic regime for the time Titus was imprisoned there. Although it wasn't pleasant, he was at least fed and clothed and in some respects was better off than Jennet who was struggling at home without him. That was a contrast that was intentional.

I may have stretched the truth a little by allowing him some interaction with young Sam. The regime favoured separation, silence and plenty of religious education. A reward of extra food on a Sunday was on offer to those who attended the church services. The emphasis was on rehabilitation and it's true that prisoners who were illiterate had the opportunity to learn to read and write to give them skills to better themselves when they were released. Although, sadly, the prison governors and reformers didn't address the fundamental flaw in their regime, which was that although work was provided for everyone in the prison, there was scant employment for the prisoners when they returned to the streets and many took up crime once more simply to feed themselves and their families.

Dr James Barlow

When I was eleven years old I went to a secondary school that was housed in old house on Preston New Road, near its junction with Montague Street, in Blackburn. Local readers may remember the house as Spring Mount. It was the original girls' grammar school and was Blakey Moor Girls' School when I was there.

It was a lovely old building and I used to run my hands over the sturdy wooden bannister rails and wonder about the people who once lived there. It was only when I was researching for this book that I discovered the house had been built for Dr James Barlow. It was his home and the site of his successful medical practice. He is a fascinating man and is credited with performing the first caesarean section in the UK in which the mother survived.

In 1822 he published a book *Essays on Surgery and Midwifery: With Practical Observations and Select Cases*. It is possible to track it down online. It's not for the faint-hearted but I did draw on a few of the details from his writing for my description of the birth of Bessie.

Dr Barlow came to Blackburn after the breakdown of his short marriage to Elizabeth Winstanley. He never remarried and passed his fortune to James Barlow Stewardson Sturdy, who went on to become Mayor of Blackburn. Some sources claim he was his adopted son, but my own research seems to indicate that he simply made him his heir. James Barlow Stewardson Sturdy appears on Vladimir Sherwood's painting *Laying the Foundation Stone to the Cotton Exchange, Blackburn*, which is displayed in Blackburn Museum. A portrait of Dr James Barlow hangs on the stairs in the museum at Bolton.

Dr Barlow died on 20 August 1839 at his home in Blackburn. And yes, he did keep a peacock that used to annoy people with its noise!

If you enjoyed *The Cotton Spinner*, read on for an exclusive extract from Libby Ashworth's next book in The Mill Town Lasses series,

A
LANCASHIRE
Lass

Libby Ashworth

Coming August 2020
Available to pre-order now

Chapter One

'Gone? Gone where?' asked Hannah.

Sally, the scullery maid, shrugged her shoulders. 'I came down to set the fires and get the water on to boil, but Cook never showed up and when I knocked on her door there were nobody there. All the bedrooms are empty. Upstairs and down.'

Mary hurried in, pushing her hair into her cap.

'What's to do?' she asked when she saw their faces.

'Sal says everyone's gone.'

'Don't be daft,' said Mary, glancing at the row of bells, high on the wall, as if she expected them all to start tinkling at any moment. 'We'd best get started on making some tea and toast before Mrs Slater gives us a rollicking. I'll scramble the eggs.' She reached for a dish and the bowl of eggs and began to break them one by one, whisking as she did.

'Sal says the family's all disappeared as well,' said Hannah reaching out to steady her hand as she picked up another egg. Mary hesitated then gave Sally a fierce look.

'Hast tha been to look?'

'Aye. I crept in to lay the fires, but their beds weren't slept in and their drawers were left open and nothing in 'em. And I can't find Mr Cox or any of the footmen. I thought I were all alone until Hannah came down.' A sob caught in her throat and she sat down on Cook's chair and pulled a rag from her sleeve to wipe her nose. 'I didn't know what to do.'

'Let's go to look,' said Mary to Hannah, setting down the whisk. 'There's bound to be an explanation,' she added as they hurried up the corridor past the house-keeper's room and the butler's pantry. Both were deserted. 'Folk don't just disappear in the middle of the night,' said Mary as they walked through the empty breakfast room, and glanced into the dining room where the table had been cleared and reset after last night's supper. They went into the empty drawing room. The blue cushions were all plumped, but the blinds were still pulled down and Sal had neglected to clean out the hearth.

'Where can they be?' asked Hannah, as they crossed the main hall with its cabinet of stuffed, exotic birds and looked into the billiard room where the only sign of life was the score from the last game still chalked up on the board. They went up the main staircase, normally forbidden to them except for the early morning dusting, and tapped on the bedroom doors before opening them. No one was there. It was like Sal had said. Drawers and wardrobes were left open and the beds were untouched with the covers still folded back for bedtime.

'Moonlight flit,' said Mary.

'No.' Hannah knew of people who'd done that. But they were poor people who couldn't afford to pay their rent, who disappeared in the middle of the night with a few belongings piled onto the back of a cart, to avoid their debts. 'People like the Sudells don't do that.'

'What other explanation is there?' asked Mary and Hannah had to admit that she couldn't think of one.

They went down the stairs and back to the kitchen to find Robert, the hall boy, sitting at the table with Sal drinking tea and eating buttered toast.

'They've gone,' he said.

'We can see that,' Mary told him. 'Does tha know why?'

'Aye,' he said. 'I woke in the night with all the kerfuffle from the yard and went to see what were afoot. Harry shoved me back inside and told me to keep my trap shut. He said Mr Sudell has lost all his money and wanted to leave afore he were found out because of the shame of it.'

'Lost his money?' said Hannah. 'How could he lose his money?' It wasn't like a sixpence slipping out of his pocket, she thought. They said that he had a million pounds.

'Bought too much cotton,' said Rob. 'He had it stock-piled, but now that the price has fallen he can't make his money back. He's bankrupt. There's nowt left.'

'But what about all this?' asked Hannah. 'The house alone must be worth a fortune.'

'It'll have to be sold to pay off his debts.'

'What about us?' said Hannah, suddenly realising that this was her problem too.

Rob shrugged. 'They took some of the staff – them as had been with 'em for a long time. But the rest of us are out of a job. I suppose we'll be expected to clear out afore the bailiffs come.'

Hannah sat down at the table and reached for a piece of toast. It was unthinkable. This was her home now. She loved this place. She'd thought that leaving her job in the mill in Blackburn and coming to work here was the best decision she'd ever made. The air was clear, up here on the hill, away from the smog and the smoke and the grime. She'd had no intention of ever going back, but now she wondered what other option there was.

Mary went back to scrambling the eggs.

'We may as well eat these,' she said. 'Who knows when we'll get another meal. There's bacon too. Get it on to fry.'

'How long dost think we have before they throw us out?' Hannah asked her friend. They'd gone to sit in the drawing room to pretend that they were gentry.

'Not long,' said Mary from her cushioned seat at the window. She nodded her head to where a cloud of dust in the distance betrayed the approach of horses up the long winding driveway. Hannah groaned. She was enjoying lying full length on the blue damask couch and she'd hoped that they would have longer before they were forced to leave.

'It's all right for thee,' complained Mary. 'Tha parents or sister will take thee back, but there's no way I'm going back home. I'd rather starve.'

'It won't come to that. Lots of the mill owners are building themselves big houses. They must need staff.'

'I doubt we'd stand much a chance without a character reference. We were lucky here,' Mary reminded her. 'But things have changed. No one gets taken on now without a letter from their former employer. And it doesn't look like we'll be getting one.'

'Or the wages we're owed,' said Hannah as she reluctantly swung her feet to the floor and bent to lace her boots. The horses had arrived outside the main door and men were surveying the front of the house. It seemed that they would barely have time to pack their belongings before the house was secured and they were sent on their way.

Half an hour later Hannah and Mary were walking down the long drive towards the road with their bags in their hands. It was less than a year since they'd walked up it with such high hopes. Hannah had been so happy. She'd been overjoyed when the Sudells had agreed to employ her as a maid at their new country house, and after she'd been promoted from a scullery maid to a parlour maid she and Mary had talked excitedly about the possibility of becoming a lady's maid, with all the excitement and glamour of looking after Mr Sudell's daughters, being responsible for their lovely dresses, doing their hair, hearing their secrets and maybe even meeting someone special. Hannah longed to meet someone special. She'd seen such handsome men arriving at the Sudells' door in their carriages for visits and parties. Men who wore silk cravats, and whose hands were soft and clean and who looked like they'd never had to weave a length of cloth in their lives. How she'd wished that one of them would notice her as she crept about the house with her dustpan and brush. She knew that it was silly and that she ought to resent those who didn't have to do a turn to earn their living. She knew she should set her cap at some hardworking lad, but it didn't hurt to dream she told herself. After a long day wasn't she allowed at least a few minutes of imagining what her life could be like before she fell into an exhausted sleep?

Now a very different future beckoned. There was no point going home to her parents at Ramsgreave. There was no work for her there and she needed to earn her keep. So, if there was no chance of another position as a maid, she supposed that she would have to go to her sister, Jennet, and her brother-in-law, Titus, and ask if they would take her back as a boarder. Then she would have to go to the mill and try to get her job back. It wasn't what she wanted, and she silently damned Henry Sudell for having ruined her life.

When they reached the end of the drive, the bailiff pulled the tall iron gates closed behind them and began to secure them with heavy chains.

'That's it then,' said Mary. 'I suppose we'd better start walking.'

'Where will tha go?' asked Hannah as they took the lane that led down the hill towards the Preston to Blackburn road. 'I could ask our Jennet and Titus if they'd take thee in. They don't live on Paradise Lane any more,' said Hannah, knowing that Mary wouldn't want to live next door to her own family. 'They moved on soon after I left.'

'I don't blame them,' said Mary. 'I wouldn't want to live next door to my father either after what happened. Where are they now?'

'On Water Street, next to the river. Come home with me for today at least,' said Hannah. 'I'm sure tha'll be welcome to stay for a night or two until tha finds summat else.'

She tried to sound hopeful and positive, but the truth was that she wasn't entirely sure of her own welcome. Things had been difficult before she left. When Titus was in prison and it had been just her and Jennet and little Peggy, things had been all right. They'd struggled of course, but they'd managed. But when Titus had come home and found Jennet pregnant with another man's child, he'd been upset and difficult and they'd done nothing but argue. In a way she couldn't blame him. It must have been hard for him and it hadn't been entirely his own fault that he'd been sent to the House of Correction in Preston – or so he said. His story was that he'd been to a Reform meeting on the moor and got caught up with some loom breakers afterwards and been arrested. He'd been lucky not to be transported and it was when Jennet thought she would never see him again that she'd slept with George. She was going to go to America with him, but when Titus got the prison sentence instead of being shipped off to Australia she'd decided to wait for him and George went on his own. It was only after he'd gone that she found out she was having his child. She'd expected Titus to understand and forgive her, and he had in the end, but even Hannah could see that the love they'd once had for one another had taken a harsh blow. And so she'd left them to themselves, to try to mend their marriage, and now she had no idea what sort of reception she'd receive when she turned up unannounced on their doorstep.

Hear more from

Libby Ashworth